BLACK FEATHERS

A Dystopian Urban Fantasy Novel

Angels of the Apocalypse

CINDY CARROLL

Black Feathers
Angels of the Apocalypse Book 1

by Cindy Carroll
All rights reserved

ePub ISBN: 978-1-7770055-2-8

Print ISBN: 978-1-7770055-4-2

For my husband, always

S tranded almost magicless in the downtown core, Rachel Malak's gun jostled on her hip as she ran up Toronto's University Avenue toward the scream. Urgent footsteps followed her, but she pushed the noise out of the way, waiting, listening for the next scream. Without her powers, she had to rely on the woman in danger to guide her. At least, she assumed it was a woman based on the octave of the shriek. Another scream broke the night. She veered left and stopped short in an alley between a sushi house and an investment firm.

Dusk gave way to night, and weak fingers of light from University Avenue streetlights illuminated the shadows of the alley. The decay of rotting fish from a dumpster assaulted her nose. If this were a cartoon, she would expect to see squiggly lines rising from the garbage. She huffed out a breath and avoided inhaling deeply, despite the run she'd taken to get here.

Huddled on the ground, a petite blond woman cowered beneath a hulking man who stood over her. Large, red marks on the woman's face would soon blossom into angry bruises. Heat rushed through Rachel's body, and she tensed. Pulse in overdrive, she crossed her arms over her chest and focused on the man with his back to her.

"Bitch! The additional cost of protection is a blow job. You can't walk away before I'm finished."

Great. Another man taking advantage of a vulnerable woman. Not that she saw anything wrong with them. A woman had to make a living. It was the oldest profession for a reason. But the sex workers in the city needed her help a lot. How could she redeem herself if nothing changed, no matter how many times she stepped in to help?

"Lay another hand on her and you'll be tending to a heap of bruises of your own." Heart pounding at the possibility this rescue might be different, Rachel planted her feet equidistant apart, prepared to use all the police combat training magically granted to her.

The hulk spun to look at her. Straightening to his full height, biceps the size of hams flexed while he sized her up. A tree-trunk-sized neck sat atop a barrel of a chest. Muscled legs that could probably squeeze the life out of a giant angled toward her. Under different circumstances, she wouldn't have been surprised if he turned green and went on a rampage of destruction.

A leer crossed his face. His gaze traveled up and down her body in a slow perusal that made her want to have a long, hot shower. He clenched his fists. Anger sizzled under the surface of his glare, and now, it had a new outlet. He wouldn't find her as much fun to play with.

"You want to finish the job she started?" He thrust his chest out and tilted his head.

She perused him just as thoroughly, stopping at his cock. It peeked out of his jeans, half limp, but hardening with his anger and hatred.

She flicked a black lock of hair over her shoulder. "I don't think you'd want that. I bite."

He barreled forward, a gleam flashing in his eyes. Rachel took a deep, cleansing breath, then stepped aside. Behind her now, he stopped and turned around. This time, he raised his fists and barreled toward her. Blind with fury or testosterone, he didn't see her foot. She stuck it out, and he fell hard on the filthy ground.

"Bitch. You'll pay for that." Lips flattened, his face flushed red.

Rachel turned her attention to the silently sobbing woman, huddled a few steps away, but she watched the attacker out of the corner of her eye. She pulled out a business card and placed it in the woman's hand.

"If you want to press charges, let me know."

With a swiftness that surprised Rachel, he was on his feet and grabbed her from behind, wrapping his arm around her neck. A step to the side and a thrust of her hip was all it took for her to throw him over her shoulder. Following him down, she delivered several hard shots to his body, and when he lifted his head, she used her elbow to knock him out.

Winded, she arched her back to work out kinks she didn't know she had there. For the thousandth time since arriving on Earth, practically powerless, she missed her angelic magic.

Footsteps drowned out the prostitute's soft whimpers. Rachel turned to the entrance of the alley. Sarah and Becky, her sisters, stood there smiling. Blond tendrils, pulled away from Sarah's efficient bun during her jog to catch up, framed her delicate face. Despite the physical exertion, Becky's pale skin was still perfectly made up, and her red hair hadn't moved a millimeter. How much hair spray did they use at the TV station?

Rachel nodded at her sisters. "It's about time. What took you so long?"

The woman Rachel had saved jumped to her feet and scrambled out of the alley past them. Her whimpers faded until the only sounds left were the rumble of the traffic in the crowded street and the shuffling gait of pedestrians out on a Thursday night.

Rachel shrugged off her blazer, unfurled her wings, and tried to examine them.

"Any change?" She held her breath, waiting for the affirmative response she'd been longing for.

Sarah and Becky came closer, one on each side, examining her extended limbs. "Sorry, sweetie," Sarah said. "Still black as night."

"Fuck. What does an angel have to do to get some white back in the wings?"

Sarah and Becky gasped in unison. "You can start by cutting back on the swearing," Becky suggested.

"Please. You think He cares? Man decided what words are good and which ones are bad. They're just words. As long as I'm not taking His name in vain, I'll say whatever I want." Rachel flattened her wings against her back again and put on her blazer. "And right now, 'fuck' just about sums it up."

Five saves—six if you counted the teacher they saved together when they first got here—since she'd been exiled from Heaven and she was still no closer to earning her powers back.

"Fine, whatever, swear all you want," Sarah said. "You still have to figure out why He exiled you."

"But you guys haven't figured out why you were exiled and you're getting the color back in your wings."

She eyed a small, almost minuscule spot on Becky's wing. The angel had saved a cat. How was that fair?

A moan from the ground grabbed her attention. She'd completely forgotten about the bullying hulk. Something about the guy's face looked familiar, but she'd seen hundreds of criminals since arriving in the city. The faces were starting to blur together.

"I thought we were getting a drink," Sarah said.

Rachel leaned down to whisper in the guy's ear. "If I hear you've been beating up sex workers again, I'll destroy your favorite body part."

Though he glared at her, the man covered the family jewels with both hands. Blood trickled down his square-jawed face from a cut over his eye. It would have been better if the prostitute had stayed to press charges. Rachel's gaze fell on a tattoo that peeked out from under his blue T-shirt. A niggling feeling in the back of her head recognized it, but her stomach grumbled, pulling her attention to their next mission. There would be food with that drink.

As they came out of the alley onto University Avenue again, Rachel spotted a homeless man sitting on the side-walk. Layers of dirty clothes swallowed his slight frame. If the other two saw him, they said nothing. Rachel approached him and tensed, anger at her lack of magic to help souring her mouth. She hated this part of the city. Every poor soul huddled on the hard concrete, newspapers for blankets, broke her heart. And it seemed to get worse every week. They'd only been here three weeks. If they didn't earn their wings back and return home soon, how much more awful would this place get?

With a speed that shocked her, the homeless man reached out a grime-encrusted hand before they could pass and grabbed her wrist.

"The end is nigh!" Watery blue eyes pleaded with her. A scar along his chin stretched taut.

Rachel jerked her arm, but his grasp held firm. "Dude, the end is nigh? Who fucking talks like that?"

"Rachel!" Becky crossed her arms over her chest, her green eyes reproachful.

"What? I'm serious. No one talks like that anymore."

The homeless guy let go of her, and his eyes grew wide when he looked at Becky. "You're that woman on TV."

A deep blush tinged Becky's cheeks. She beamed at him, her smile showing all her pearly whites. Rachel still didn't understand her sister's humbleness when confronted by people who recognized her. She picked a job that put her in the spotlight when they got here. She could have picked anything, as long as it kept her in the city, and she chose TV reporter for the local network station.

"I am. How nice of you to notice." Becky squatted to look the man in the eyes. "Tell us about this end is nigh prediction you have."

From where she stood, Rachel smelled the rotting food in the man's teeth. She didn't know how Becky could stand to be so close to him.

"Not my prediction." He looked over his shoulder like someone might be spying on them. "I heard people talking. Yeah, that's it. People talking about it."

"What people? Do you know them?" Becky prompted.

He nodded. "The priest. He went that way." He pointed up the street to a major intersection.

Didn't tell them much. From there, people could go pretty much anywhere in the city. Not that she bought this end is nigh bullshit anyway. They shouldn't believe it, either.

Rachel sighed. "Beck, you *know* the end is not nigh. What are we still doing here? I thought we were going to have a few drinks and let off some steam."

"It wouldn't hurt to hear him out," Sarah said.

Rachel shot her a look. "Seriously? We know it's not possible. We know when it's going to happen, remember?"

Becky stood and glared at her. "It wouldn't hurt you to be more compassionate. We should help people."

Jaw clenched, Rachel narrowed her eyes at them. "Fine. Chat all you want. Meet me at the bar."

She marched off in the vague direction of his pointed finger. Their usual bar wasn't too far away. One thing she did like about this mortal thing was the effects of alcohol. Who knew it could be so much fun? When she got her angelic power back, would she still be able to get drunk? She doubted it, so she might as well enjoy it while she could.

Less than a minute later, the *tap, tap, tap* of heels followed her. She turned to see Becky and Sarah running to catch up. She stopped to let them.

Baron's was the best blues and jazz bar in the city, with live music every night of the week, if you liked that sort of thing. Rachel held open the door for Becky and Sarah, then followed them inside. A group of six tables occupied the floor near a small stage at the front of the place. The rest of the bar held four booths on the right side and tables dotted throughout with enough room between them for wait staff to get through. The bar stood on the right, after the booths. Five stools, all of them occupied, allowed for some elbow room for each patron. The shelves of liquor behind the bar ranged from the cheapest vodka to the most expensive scotch. Despite it being a weeknight, the place was already packed, but thankfully, Steve, the owner, had taken a liking to them and always held a table at the back. They wove their way through the throng of people, squeezing between forty-something stockbrokers, thirty-something artists, and twenty-something university students. Soulful blues poured from Steve's playlist, forcing patrons to lean in close and shout at each other to talk.

Before they finished settling into their seats, drinks appeared on the polished wood table. Their usuals. One of these days, Rachel would pick something different to keep the bartender on his toes. They smiled their thanks at the waiter, who hurried away to take a food order from a young couple a few tables over.

Sarah took a sip of her drink and sighed. "I needed that."

"Hospital too busy for you?" Rachel asked.

Sarah gave her hands a disgusted look. "It's hard not being able to just heal everyone who comes in."

"Where would the lesson be in that? If He'd wanted us to perform miracles, He wouldn't have sent us here with no angelic power," Becky noted.

The longer they were here, the more Rachel realized the world expected miracles in order to reinforce their faith. But if they didn't have faith, the miracles wouldn't happen. Biblical catch-22. Based on the increased crime in the city, Toronto needed a miracle, PFS—pretty fucking soon.

"Miracles happen every day, but the humans are too wrapped up in themselves to notice," Rachel pointed out.

"Not so loud. You don't like them very much, do you?" Becky grabbed her pint of beer and took a long swallow.

Rachel glared at Becky. "No one's paying any attention to us." She looked around the room at the oblivious customers, all too absorbed in loud conversations of their own to care what the three of them said. "I wouldn't be trying to rid the streets of criminals if I didn't like them."

Sarah shot her a skeptical look. "We know why you

chose detective when you got here. And it wasn't because you like people."

Rachel took a sip of her White Russian. "Whatever. I'm doing good here and have nothing to show for it." She fought the urge to unfurl her wings to check for patches of white. Disappointment was a bitch.

"You saved that prostitute. But wasn't that a Grange member assaulting her?" Becky asked.

Like any other big city, Toronto had its fair share of gang activity. A few rival gangs worked the streets of The Six, the affectionate name locals called the city. Mostly, they provided the gang task force with twenty-four seven work in the form of weapons offenses and drug-related incidents. A confrontation between gangs had been brewing for months now—gang activity of every kind on the rise, making each group more visible. Becky had done two pieces on the escalating violence already.

"It looked like one of the Grange crew." She thought about the hulk out cold in the alley. "Pretty sure it was the Grange leader's enforcer, Tony. I'll make a report to the gang task force, and they'll follow up. Since she's not likely to press charges, there wasn't much I could do. I have bigger fish to fry in the city."

Becky rolled her eyes. "We're all doing important work."

It took every ounce of tact Rachel had not to comment on Becky's choice of profession. How was a reporter's work more important than fighting crime? Becky leaned closer, waiting for Rachel to say something. So far, they hadn't fought, but if they were stuck here much longer, petty fights would erupt. It wouldn't annoy her so much if they knew why they'd been exiled. How could she do things to earn her powers back if she didn't know why she was here?

"Sure, we do." Rachel took another sip of her drink.

Becky scowled. "You could teach the hookers…"

"Sex workers," Rachel corrected.

"Fine, sex workers. You could teach them some self-defense moves so they can protect themselves."

Sarah took a sip of her white wine. "Becky has a point. We could work on it together. Maybe start a YouTube channel that Becky could run."

Rachel rolled her eyes. "Bigger fish to fry, remember."

The TV above the bar flashed an image of a priest. Below his picture was a headline: *The end is nigh. Again.*

"Isn't that the priest who 'predicted' the end of the world would happen last year?" Rachel asked.

Becky nodded. "Father Ianetti. That's him."

"He was wrong then, and he's wrong now," Rachel said.

"Isn't his church in the direction the homeless guy was pointing?" Becky took another long gulp of her amber lager.

"Wouldn't surprise me if Father Ianetti was working the streets, trying to rile people up." Sarah took another sip of her drink.

Surprised by Sarah's cynicism, Rachel put her hand to her sister's forehead. "Are you okay?"

Sarah swatted away her hand, stifling a yawn. "I hate that now I have to sleep. How do humans deal with getting tired?"

Rachel snorted. "With irritability. Welcome to being human. It sucks."

Father Ianetti waved goodbye to the last of his parishioners, then shut the church door and, for the first time in twenty years, locked it. Our Lady of Amity prided itself as being one of the few churches in the city to never lock its doors. But tonight, he needed no interruptions. It had taken every ounce of his willpower not to rush the sermon. After delighting his flock with The Word, they lingered longer than usual, chatting in the entryway to the old church. Most nights, he joined them, happy to get to know them outside of the confessional. Tonight was different. Tonight, an important mission required his undivided attention. And it had to be done now. The work of God could not fail. He checked to make sure the door was secure, then made his way to the rectory at the back of the church. He had sent the office staff, the choir, and the associate reverend home early. The signs were there; he needed to act. This time, he would not be wrong. He would make sure of it.

He carefully took off his cassock and hung it in the wardrobe. Chilled air circled him, prickling his skin. He walked to the trunk at the foot of his bed and moved aside his few personal effects. At the bottom, nestled under the sweater his mother gave him when he joined the clergy, a plain brown box held the first item he needed. He slipped off the lid of the box. The black robe he had purchased from a cosplay store on Queen Street sat still folded, waiting to fulfill its purpose. He pulled out the robe from its home and laid it on the bed. Before donning the garment, he needed to purify himself.

Taking a deep breath, he stepped into his en suite bathroom. He stripped off the rest of his clothes, then stepped into the heavily salted bath of now cool water and submerged himself as part of the purifying ritual. Holding his breath, he slowly counted to calm his racing mind, the grit of the salt under his back keeping him in the present moment. When he could no longer hold his breath, he pulled the stopper from the tub with his toes and stood, enjoying the caress of the water as it sluiced from his body. After walking into the bedroom again, he toweled off, then wrapped his ceremonial cloak around his shoulders. The rough, raw linen did nothing to warm him.

Leaving his rooms, he padded barefoot past the back entrance to the church. A full moon streaming through the stained-glass windows splayed colors across the tiled floor in the hallway. He needed no other sign from God, but over the past months, he'd seen plenty. Love for the community spurred him on, drove him to do what was just and righteous. Others would come to his way of thinking, eventually.

A cleansing of the evil in the world was the only way to make it a better place for those yet to come. Saddened by the need to perform the summoning ritual, he nevertheless scurried to the dark wood cabinet near the rectory's back door to gather the ritual tools he had secured there—solid, pure black pillar candles, the herbs, and the sigil he required. He'd drawn all the sigils he needed months ago on parchment paper. They were the easiest items to obtain for the ritual. The candles, though, had been harder to find than he'd expected.

With the items in his arms, he slipped out the back door to the small grassy backyard. The high brick fence would afford him the privacy he needed. With his circle already marked, he placed a flat stone in the middle to act as an altar. The church yard hadn't been used in several months, so that was another thing he had been able to do in advance. Anything he could do to save time helped his cause.

He arranged the candles in a circle, and in front of these, he placed the ritual knife—the athame he'd procured from an occult shop on College Street. In the middle, he placed a pewter bowl. For months, he'd gone over the words he would recite, making sure he had the pronunciations correct. If anything went wrong, he would fail the mission, and the world could not afford that.

He removed the robe, inhaled deeply, and raised his arms over his head, calling on the four corners and the four elements. Satisfied his circle was sealed, he lit the candles and started the incantation. He repeated it over and over again, the Latin spilling from his lips so fast the words were barely discernible. After the seventh incantation, he lifted the athame over his head and then brought it down to slice the tip of his finger. He held it over the small bowl in the middle of the circle of candles, squeezing to get five drops of blood. He tossed in the herbs required for the summoning. As a final step, he set the sigil alight and dropped it in the bowl. The ashes mixed with the herbs and his blood.

With the spell complete, he waited. Instead of praying to the God he served as he had so many times before, he pleaded with the Devil to grant his wish. It was for the best. It had to be done. As a man of the cloth, how could he ignore the signs? The end was coming—he'd predicted it, done the math. He knew exactly when it would be here. This would make sure of it.

Minutes passed and nothing happened. He couldn't have forgotten something. He'd practiced this spell for months to ensure he would get it right when it mattered.

Suddenly, the air around him stilled. Hairs rose on the back of his neck. Images of fires, sinners burning, the devout being lifted, filled his mind. A suffocating heat overwhelmed him, robbed him of breath. He fell to the ground, gasping for air. The sound of a horse's hoofs rang in his ears. A wisp of white smoke, in the shape of a horse, formed in front of him. It galloped past him, thundering hoof beats almost deafening as the ethereal beast rushed by.

A man appeared out of thin air. Tall, at least six-five, with the darkest hair Father Ianetti had ever seen, the man surveyed the yard and building, surprise lighting his crystal blue eyes. Naked, as all others first coming into the world, the man took in the darkness and the robe puddled at Father Ianetti's feet.

"When is this?" The man's deep voice boomed in the quiet of the yard.

"November. First quarter of the twenty-first century."

Instantly, jeans formed around the man's muscled legs. A black T-shirt covered his large chest, the left sleeve touching the top of a crossbow tattoo on his bicep. A worn leather jacket completed the man's outfit.

The man smiled, and a chill went through Father Ianetti. "Thanks for the invitation, Father."

Before the reverend could say anything, the man strode from the yard. The metal gate of the church crashed open and banged shut. Step one of Father Ianetti's mission was now complete. There were more to summon, but he would need his strength.

Chapter Two

Outside the church, Conquest closed his eyes and inhaled deeply, sampling the air. The soulless had a distinct scent, and he focused on finding that aroma in the bustling city. Power hummed through his body. The vibrancy of the metropolis would charge his powers. Powers he needed to manipulate the meek. While the soulless were easy to convince to do his bidding, the humans with souls would be a greater challenge. And when had he not liked a challenge? For now, he needed power, he needed minions, he needed to put the first part of the plan into motion. The priest hadn't summoned him for shits and giggles. There was work to be done.

This was going to be fun.

He tasted the air again to pinpoint which direction had the highest concentration of the soulless. He turned right, sauntering slowly along the sidewalk. Bright neon signs proclaimed everything from fresh food to girls, girls, girls. A low moan coming from an alleyway drew his attention. He focused on the sound, moving as fast as he could without drawing attention. No reason to alert the humans to other-worldly activity before everything was in place.

When he reached the alley, he spotted a man pushing himself up from the ground. Fresh bruises were forming on his face almost like time-lapse to his perception. Conquest peered deeper into the man to make sure he had the right target. A sweet, decaying scent wafted lightly from the man's being. Soulless.

"Fucking bitches." The man growled as he stood. He shook his head.

"I see no female dogs here," Conquest said.

The man glared at him. Muscles bunched under the man's shirt, obviously still eager for a fight after losing the one that caused the bruises. From his comment, Conquest guessed the perpetrator was a woman.

"You need to back the fuck up, man. I'm in no mood for outsiders. This is your only warning."

Conquest stepped deeper into the alley, squaring his shoulders. A light on the building to the right flickered. Another light on the other side of the alley popped, plunging that side into total darkness.

"I think I'll stay," Conquest said.

He sampled the air again, a fresh wave of sweet decay reaching his nostrils. Heavy, urgent footfalls approached. He moved into the center of the alley, past the man, to make room for the soon-to-be new arrivals, and turned to witness their appearance.

"I warned you," the man said.

Before the soulless man could charge at Conquest, a group of five equally large thugs entered the alleyway behind him. One stood out from the rest. He took off a leather jacket sporting six stripes on the shoulders and handed it to a thug on his right side. Tattoo sleeves on both arms depicted judgment day. He wore dark jeans and a black T-shirt. The others stood in front of him as if in protection. Conquest perused the rest of them and noticed the same stripes, though in varying degrees of numbers. One person had half a stripe. Others had two, three. Only the man at the back had six.

They ignored him for the moment, and the leader directed his attention to the hulk in front of Conquest.

"What the fuck happened, Tony?"

"Bitch got away."

"Payment?" the leader asked.

The man rubbed his jaw. "She had help. Got away before I could collect."

"Help? From him?" The leader turned his attention to Conquest. Any other person would find the man's look intimidating.

Conquest stared at Tony, daring him to lie.

"Nah, man. Some cop."

The leader continued to stare at Conquest. "You don't belong here." He nodded to the hulking guy. "Tony, take care of him."

Eager to redeem himself for losing a fight against a woman, Tony charged at Conquest as if in slow motion. Conquest held up a hand just as the man entered his personal space. A hard thwack filled the air. Tony stopped abruptly and fell backward onto the ground.

"Sending someone else to fight your battles? What kind of leader are you?"

"Man, you must be new here. Bruno is the leader of the Grange gang," half-stripe said. "The most badass leader of the most feared gang in The Six."

The leader puffed out his chest and stood a little taller. Conquest laughed.

"Why don't you do your own dirty work instead of sending others to defend you?" Conquest glanced at the hulking guy, still out cold on the ground. "It makes you look weak."

The men surrounding Bruno gasped. Each one of them backed up slightly and looked at their leader for a response. Muscles flexed. Some leaned closer, ready to sprint forward like a racing horse as soon as they were given the okay.

The one with a patch over his left eye jerked closer, but Bruno put up a hand to stop them from barreling into the fray.

The leader stepped forward and eyed Conquest, sizing him up. He turned to his men. "I'll take care of this." He cracked his knuckles and rolled his head from side to side. "You won't live long enough to regret crossing me."

Conquest inhaled, the mildly sickly-sweet scent of the man's soulless body reminding him of his purpose. To lead, he had to vanquish their leader. The soulless were easily manipulated. Being in charge of one of the largest gangs in the city would help him conquer the entire province.

He stood his ground, patience his greatest virtue. The pettiness of the man's life, filled with meaningless criminal acts that nevertheless made him feel important, provided everything Conquest needed to set the plan in motion. Bruno's breathing quickened the longer Conquest waited. The gang leader's eyes narrowed, his jaw tightened, hands fisted at his sides.

The leader's minions stifled their agitated movements even though they itched to jump into the fight that hadn't started yet. Conquest eyed Bruno and the second the man moved, Conquest tensed, ready for him.

Bruno barreled forward, fists raised. Conquest blocked the first punch but allowed a right hook to land on his jaw. Give them what they want, and they'll come back for more. Bruno smirked, the arrogance dripping off the man bolstered by the gang members' cheers. When Bruno threw the next punch, Conquest side-stepped him easily. The gang leader lurched forward with the momentum.

"Fuck. Tricky bastard, aren't ya?"

Conquest stood his ground and waited for the next charge. Fueled by anger, Bruno punched aimlessly, left and right. Conquest blocked them all, then landed a right hook to the guy's jaw. Without letting him recover, Conquest delivered an uppercut that snapped Bruno's head back.

Silence from the gang members pulled his attention away momentarily. Though mute, they flexed muscles, shuffled their feet, leaned forward as if held back by an invisible force. Bruno held up a hand to them, shaking his head.

"This bitch is mine." He swayed, then straightened. Blood dripped from a cut above his right eye.

Grinning, power hummed through Conquest's body at the whiff of a soul walking past the alleyway. Before he could corrupt the souled, he needed to take care of this piece of shit. Having drawn out the fight longer than necessary, he summoned every ounce of power he had. The punch he landed shot Bruno across the alley into the back door of a restaurant. While the gang leader shook his head and put out an arm to push himself up, Conquest marched over and pummeled him in the face. He doubled over, and Conquest kicked him a few times in the ribs. Groans of pain drifted across the alleyway. The gang members shuffled. Conquest felt their desire to leap to Bruno's defense.

With a final blow to the gang leader's face, the man's head jerked backward, hitting the pavement. As Bruno huffed out his last breath, Conquest discarded the jacket he was wearing and turned to Bruno's men. The thug holding the former gang leader's jacket stumbled forward, slapping the garment into Conquest's hand. He shrugged into the leather jacket and surveyed his new minions.

At the loft, Rachel sat at the kitchen island, too awake to go to bed yet. Sarah plopped a cup of steaming hot chocolate in front of her. A smile with two dots above it for eyes—drawn using chocolate syrup on top of the whipped cream—made her grin. With the familiar padding of footsteps in the kitchen and the tapping of a keyboard in the living room where Becky worked on another news story, the loft was beginning to feel like home. The cozy beverage was the icing on the proverbial cake. And Rachel didn't like it. Not one bit. Earth would not tempt her to stay longer than she had to.

"The sugar will just keep me up longer." Rachel grabbed the mug and took a tentative sip. "Ohhh, that's nice." She sighed. The hot liquid burned her lips, but she sipped again. Chocolate soothed her. Warmth spread through her body. She still couldn't get used to having to sleep and eat. But she did like food.

A crash from above had them racing out the door, down the hallway to the fire door, and up the stairs to the rooftop garden.

They barreled through, and the door banged open all the way. Becky wedged a rock in the frame so they wouldn't be locked up there again. It had taken hours last time to get the door opened.

At first, the only thing Rachel saw was the perfect view they had of the city, then a groan from behind the plants drew their attention to the edge of the roof.

They rushed over. Crumpled among the now crushed autumn flowers, a fallen angel moved. She turned her face to them, rich brown eyes bloodshot and rimmed with tears. Her brown hair almost blended into her now black wings.

She stood on shaky legs, chin trembling as she looked up. Rachel's heart broke for her. She remembered that unexpected fall from Heaven, the path she couldn't return on until she earned the privilege back. The arrival of another angel made her stomach churn. It could mean only one thing.

"Shit," Rachel said.

The new angel gasped. Becky helped her out of the flowers, shaking her head with a soft *tsk*.

"Rachel!" Sarah gave her a stern look.

"Hi. I'm Leah." The new angel shuffled forward, extending her hand.

Rachel clasped the angel's palm in a quick shake. "Nice to meet you, Leah. But shit." At the look of horror on Becky's face, Rachel sighed. "Don't you realize what this means?"

"She was just exiled, Rach. Have some sympathy. Don't you remember what it was like? It hasn't been that long for us," Becky chided.

"I remember vividly. I have tons of sympathy for her. But you do realize what it means?"

Leah stood straighter and brought a wing forward; her face contorted in pain when she saw the darkened limb. "He didn't even tell me why."

"Welcome to the club, honey," Sarah said.

"Angels! Focus! We can help her through this in a minute. Think about what this means."

After more than a minute of three blank and puzzled expressions, Rachel sighed again. "Four angels, four horsemen."

"No!" Becky shook her head.

A chill that had nothing to do with the cold, late

November air washed over Rachel. "What else could it mean?"

Sarah's eyes widened. "But the apocalypse isn't supposed to happen for centuries."

Leah gasped. "Do you think we're supposed to stop an apocalypse?"

Rachel didn't know how the end of days could be coming so early, but she was more certain now than ever. Their fall from grace had a purpose. She briefly wondered if they had actually done anything to get exiled or whether it was merely a preventative measure. But her wings with large swaths of black convinced her they *had* done something to earn their fall. He wouldn't take away their powers unless they'd done something *wrong*. If she was right and an apocalypse was coming, they needed to get their angelic powers back, fast.

"I think that's exactly what we're supposed to do." Adrenaline shot through Rachel's body at the thought of defeating the horsemen without their powers.

"How are we supposed to do that?" Leah asked.

"We need to figure out who ordered an apocalypse to begin with," Sarah said.

Becky's brow furrowed. "Can someone do that? Summon an apocalypse?"

Rachel nodded. "It's rare, but I heard rumors when I first became an angel that in the beginning, He formed a process for man to summon one, only to be used if He so decreed it to be done. But then He decided He didn't want to give mankind that kind of power. Since the word of God can't be destroyed, he had the steps hidden across the planet.

Becky's eyes lit up. "Research mode!"

Rachel rolled her eyes at Becky's enthusiasm for losing herself in data and headed back to the rooftop door. They couldn't do anything up here. They needed information. For that, they needed to go back to the loft.

———

The gang members straightened, standing at attention while Conquest scrutinized them. Despite the ease with which he'd dispatched their leader, the men glared at him, nostrils flaring, cracking knuckles. Eye patch guy's lips pressed into a hard line. Their desire to take him down like he'd done to their leader proved their loyalty. A fight response was good, but he needed to get them under control now.

"Gang rules mean I am leader," he said. "You will do as I say. Thoughts of revenge will only get you killed." He pierced each member with a hard stare. "Allegiance can be very rewarding. I will need my best men to help me with an important task."

Eye patch guy stepped forward, gaze down. "Paul here. I live to serve. What do you need?"

"Numbers have been dwindling," Conquest said.

A member with three stripes stepped up. "It's getting harder and harder to collect protection money."

Conquest laughed. The naïveté of youth. "Gang members..."

The man snapped to attention. "Chris."

"We need to recruit, Chris. I want to see the books. Now."

Another member nodded. "Of course. We will go right to headquarters." He hesitated and shied away. "What do we call you?"

His real identity would be revealed soon enough. For now, they needed to think of him as human. "Victor."

Victor looked at the body of their former leader, the

decay already starting, going infinitesimally faster than a normal corpse because he lacked a soul. No one would be able to determine the variance, but he could see it.

"Get rid of that thing." He waved his hand in the direction of the body.

Two of his new minions jumped into action.

"Where?" Chris asked.

"Do you not have minds of your own?" He eyed the group critically. Muscle, testosterone, rage they had in spades, but he needed them to start thinking differently. It was no wonder the police were making a dent in the crime in the city.

Paul bristled. "Yes. Since you're the new leader, we thought you had a place you wanted to use."

Nice save, but he doubted the man's statement. At least he had the intelligence to be offended by the comment. There might be hope for them yet.

"I don't care. Someplace where it will take a few days to a week to be found."

They looked at each other. "You want him found?"

Victor laughed. "Where's the fun if no one else knows he's dead?"

"Okay." They picked up the dead former leader.

"When you're done with that, meet us back at HQ."

Victor left the alley, the rest of the minions scrambling after him. He grinned at their eagerness to please. Once on the sidewalk, one of his minions gently nudged him to the left. Victor walked in that direction, sweeping his gaze along the path. People milled about even though the hour was growing late. The lights from the city chased shadows away from the sidewalks and streets, but they failed to illuminate alleyways. Those little nooks of the city were where the criminal element tended to gather.

As he walked toward wherever the gang headquarters

was, Victor inhaled the night air. A hint of the lake reached his nose. The scent of hot dogs and French fries from the various food trucks wafted around him. Now that he'd taken human form, his stomach grumbled.

Of all the smells the city had to offer, the best was the scent of the soulless. He walked faster, urged on by the promise of a large group of candidates. At the corner of Richmond and Duncan, he paused.

The minions were almost out of breath behind him. That would change, too. You couldn't conquer if you couldn't keep up.

Two men lounged against the wall beside the door of a bar. Though they looked scruffy and nonchalant, their eyes darted around, taking in everything going on in the vicinity. Someone stepped out of the establishment, allowing loud music to spill out. The taller man looked up, a grin on his face. He pushed away from the wall and nodded at his companion, a short, stocky man with the start of a lumberjack's beard.

The two men trailed the man who had left the bar. Victor watched them for a moment before following. Before they could catch their prey, he overtook them and stopped in front of them. The man who had just left the bar continued on his way, oblivious to what was going on. Victor's new minions stood behind the two men, their eyes questioning.

Tonight, the bar patron got lucky, not because Victor wanted to save him but because he wanted so much more damage in the long run.

"Gentlemen! I have a proposition for you," Victor said.

"What the fuck, man? You can turn over your money then, since you decided to stick your nose where it don't belong." The taller man bunched his fists at his sides.

Victor grinned. The desire for violence made his job so

much easier. "I would like to discuss with you a new opportunity to shape the city. Earn money instead of having to rob random people out for a good time. Be feared and admired."

The minions gave him a questioning look and shrugged their shoulders almost as one. They'd been together too long, become too complacent. Their former leader hadn't been much of a leader.

"It's all how you sell it," he said over the short man's shoulder. He turned his attention back to the men. The tall one's fists had loosened. The stocky one nodded.

"We might be interested in that," the tall one said.

"Good, follow us to our headquarters, and we'll talk business."

"This is legit, right?" the stocky one asked. "You're not going to rob us or anything."

Victor laughed. Two hoodlums worried about being robbed. Or worse. He looked into their eyes, peered down into the soulless belly of them. They would do nicely for now, but he needed to recruit people with souls. That's where the heavenly currency was.

"It's legit." He nodded at Paul. "Lead the way so we can get these two situated properly."

The new guys didn't look like gang members yet, but they would when he was done with them. The minions led the way through the streets of Toronto to a building in a neglected part of the warehouse district. A few houses were interspersed among the large buildings.

When they stopped at an old, dilapidated house with rotting stairs, Victor paused. "This is where you meet?"

Paul nodded. "We take what we can get. No one bothers us here. We can run the drugs and weapons without interference."

Victor took the stairs two at a time, holding the

handrail as he went. At the top of the stairs, he almost ripped the railing off, the rotting wood barely holding it together.

"That's going to change. Appearances matter, fellas. Don't forget that. We need something bigger, too. Something we can easily defend."

He pushed his way through the door. It creaked loudly in the almost complete quiet. Not much happened in this area of the city. Tourists didn't venture this far. Who wanted to look at old warehouses? The location was acceptable, but the building needed too much work. He had other jobs to do.

Inside, the entryway was dark. No lights chased the shadows away until halfway down the hall. A bright light from a room at the end of the corridor flickered in a rhythm he didn't recognize. He walked farther into the building and found a few gang members in the back room playing video games on an old TV. A glance around the room told him they'd tapped into the power of a nearby warehouse that still had electricity. How long that would last was anyone's guess. With the money they brought in from their various activities, why were they living like this?

The members in the back stood as soon as he came into the room, sending video game controllers crashing to the floor. Electronic death knell music heralded the demise of first one player, then the other.

"Victor, welcome to your new headquarters," the one on the left said. Back straight, thickly muscled arms at his sides, intelligence sparkled in the man's brown eyes. Darkly tanned skin belied a seemingly sedentary lifestyle indoors. "I'm Deacon. This is Ernie." He jerked his head in the direction of his video game opponent.

Victor looked at Paul, who glanced at the phone in his

hand. So, they had been warned a new leader was approaching.

"Pull out all the receipts, cash, inventory of the drugs we're selling, weapons we're supplying. I want to see it all. We're turning this into a profitable 'venture,' and the first order of business is to get our house in order. To do that, we'll need a new location."

Minions jumped to do his bidding. Once he had an inventory of what they had and how they laundered the money, he could set up a legitimate warehouse rental. It might take him a good part of the day tomorrow to find the right real estate agent, but he didn't doubt there was one who would get them what they needed. The new recruits stood in the center of it all, looking lost. Victor motioned for them to sit. "I'll let you in on my plans for you in a minute."

Chapter Three

Leah stood in the middle of the loft, eyes wide, her gaze darting in every direction so fast, Rachel's head began to swim. The angel turned around so she could see everything. Facing the door again, she shook her head. She hurried off to the left, toward the bedrooms.

"There are only three bedrooms." She rushed back to the kitchen and plopped onto a stool at the island.

Becky, sitting at the island, smiled. "That's okay. You'll see."

"Before we get into the apocalypse stuff, we need to get Leah set up." Rachel pulled her laptop closer.

Sarah bustled around the kitchen, pulling milk out of the fridge, popping five tea bags into the teapot on the stove, and finally opening the cupboard above the sink.

"We need to do dishes," Sarah said, placing the last four clean cups on the counter. "I can't cook like this. We really should cook more."

Leah lifted an arm and pointed to the kitchen.

"Stop!" Rachel, Becky, and Sarah yelled in unison.

Leah snapped back her hand as if the fires of Hell singed her fingertips. "I was going to clean the dishes."

Rachel got off her stool and stood behind Leah. "Unfurl."

Leah sat straighter and stretched her wings out behind her.

Rachel scrutinized the dark expanse of feathers. Amid the black, a small, golf-ball-sized patch of white was nestled close to Leah's shoulder.

"No damage done," Rachel said.

"What do you mean?" Leah blinked, big brown eyes threatening tears.

Rachel sat again. Becky sitting and Sarah standing bracketed Leah for moral support.

"You guys are scaring me." Leah clasped her hands in her lap.

"He left you with just enough power to set up an identity. A new life. Once you set that up, all of your angelic power will be gone." Rachel touched Leah's shoulder gently.

The newest angel nodded dully. Stooped over, she stared at her hands. Any moment, Rachel expected to see shaking shoulders, wails of despair. It's how they all felt when they first arrived.

"Until you gain it back. You *can* get it back," Becky added hastily. She unfurled her wings and pointed to the small grey dot in the center of the black. "That wasn't there when I got here. And it stayed even after setting up my identity."

Hope blossomed in Leah's eyes. "Why did it come back?"

Rachel scoffed. "We don't know why saving a cat gave her back some powers, but it did."

The kettle boiled, and the switch clicked off. Sarah poured the water into the teapot and set the burner to low.

Leah sat up straighter and smiled. "What do I choose?"

"The second-guessing was the hardest part for some of us. Sarah went back and forth between a few different jobs before settling on doctor," Rachel explained.

"Did you second-guess your decision?" Leah pinned Rachel with an inquisitive stare.

Rachel leaned closer to Leah and stared the new angel in the eyes. "No. I was confident my choice was the right one. Still am."

"Once you decide on a profession, a history, an identity, use your power to set it up. From that moment on, everyone who needs to know you will know you." Sarah returned to the kitchen to pour their teas.

"And we'll have another sister," Becky said.

Sarah put their drinks in front of them and took a seat on the other side of the island. "Now that we think we know part of the reason why we were sent here, you can pick something that can help us stop the apocalypse."

Leah's face drained of all color. The weight of a world slumped her shoulders. Her wings pulled in to lie flat against her back. When the three of them arrived, blissful ignorance allowed them to pick whatever job they fancied. With the truth of their exile apparent, Leah didn't have that luxury. If she'd fallen with them, they would have known, or at least deduced, right away what their new purpose was. They would have picked professions to properly arm themselves to stop the end of the world. How could a cop, a reporter, and a doctor stop an apocalypse? It sounded like the start of a bad joke.

Becky pulled her laptop closer and logged into the TV station's system to look for any signs of an impending apocalypse. The tapping of keys filled the room. The speed of the clicking increased.

A few minutes later, Becky lifted her hands off the keyboard and leaned back in her barstool. "Wow. How did we miss these?"

"Miss what? Have there been a lot of signs?" Sarah asked.

Becky turned the laptop so they could all see the screen. A list, more than twenty events long, showed happenings worldwide that could indicate the end of the world. Or they could just be weather phenomena.

"The street prophet! We need to find him. Ask him what he knows," Becky suggested.

"Why?" Rachel didn't think he could help them now.

"Because he told us this earlier. We blew it off as rantings from a man who likely had mental illness, but now, we have to consider another possibility. He might actually know something."

Rachel nodded. "I'd like to look into the priest, too. It can't be a coincidence that he's raving about the end of the world at the same time an apocalypse is brewing."

Becky went back to flipping through web pages detailing the weather phenomena. "Is it even possible to stop it once it's begun? Based on the 'signs' I found, the countdown to the apocalypse started decades ago, before we even got here."

"Why did He wait so long? If it started decades ago, how is it possible for us to stop it now?" Leah asked.

"Logic would dictate that it is possible. Why would He send us here if the apocalypse couldn't be stopped?" Sarah said.

"We'll give you some time." Rachel shoved a laptop in front of Leah. "Search the internet, job postings, anything that might help you decide."

Leah straightened again, took a deep breath, and started typing.

While they waited for their new arrival to decide what she wanted to be, Sarah returned to the kitchen and emptied the dishwasher. Everyone's tea sat on the island getting cold. Rachel clasped her cup and took a large gulp. It would have been more soothing if it had been hot, but the lukewarm liquid still calmed her. Downing the last of her drink, she put the cup in the sink, balanced precariously on a pile of randomly stacked dishes and cutlery.

Sarah gave her a dirty look.

"Fine." Rachel picked it up and put it in the top of the now empty dishwasher.

"The pressure is on now to find out why we were exiled," Becky said, tapping away at her laptop.

She pulled up a jumble of websites that focused on the end of the world and maximized a browser window. Various artists' depictions of the four horsemen, from medieval woodcuts to modern realism, splashed across the screen.

Rachel walked back to the living room side of the open concept floor and paced behind Leah while Sarah continued to tidy the kitchen. Rhythmic tapping sounds stirred Rachel into a pace that matched the speed of Becky's typing. Leah entered something sporadically, hitting the enter key with more force than necessary to start the search.

Typing sounds from the island and the clattering of dishes in the kitchen stretched every nerve Rachel had. The cop in her wanted to do something. Now. All this waiting around drove her nuts. It wasn't until after she'd picked her profession that she realized how much police work required no action. At all. That knowledge had flooded into her mind after she'd used all the power she had left to establish herself as one of Toronto's finest.

Mid-step, images flashed into Rachel's mind. Knowledge of years of growing up with Leah, meeting Leah's coworkers, saving Leah when she fell through the ice at their cottage. The images arrived out of order and out of context, then coalesced into a coherent life story that now included Leah as their youngest sister.

Rachel whirled around to study Leah. "Teacher? That's what you chose? How is that going to help us stop the end of the world?"

Leah sat up straighter, confidence shining in her eyes. "I don't know how yet, but it will."

The next morning, Rachel entered the kitchen to find Sarah, Leah, and Becky already at the island. The sink was empty. The green light on the dishwasher was on. Sarah pulled out plates and placed them on the counter.

Rachel took a seat beside Leah. Becky sat on the other side of the island, already looking more perky than anyone had a right to be at six in the morning.

The smell of pancakes made Rachel's stomach grumble. She raised an eyebrow at Becky.

"Thanks to Leah's power. Not only did she add another bedroom for herself to the place, but she stocked the fridge and pantry. I guess healthy eating was part of her identity."

Leah shrugged. "Sarah mentioned wanting to cook more."

They had been lax about buying food and keeping the place looking like a real home. But they'd thought they wouldn't be here very long when they first arrived. Turns out, earning your wings back wasn't as easy as the movies made it out to be. And being human was tedious. They earned enough money between the three of them to eat out or order in every night. From the crisp clean smell of the place mingled with delicious aromas, she guessed that was going to change now that Leah was there.

"Thanks for that," Rachel said.

Sarah piled the plates with fluffy pancakes, butter melting across their golden surface. She grabbed maple syrup from the fridge and plunked it down in the center of the island.

When the mugs were full of coffee and the sugar and cream were set out, Sarah took her seat and dug in.

"Wait," Leah said. "Shouldn't we say grace?"

Rachel rolled her eyes. Everyone put their forks down. "Fine, to yourself, quietly."

When they finished grace, they said "amen" in unison.

Rachel poured a generous amount of syrup over her pancakes and cut into them with a fork. "Now that we know we're dealing with an attempted apocalypse, we need information on the horsemen."

"I'm still not convinced it's possible," Leah said.

"There's four of us for a reason." Rachel shoved the forkful of pancake in her mouth before the syrup could drip off.

"How can we do anything to stop them without any angelic power?" Becky asked.

"We have to get it back. We've known that since we got here, but now, it's a lot more urgent. You and Leah should start looking into the horsemen. What's needed to summon them if it's not their time to be here. What's needed to send them back."

Becky paused with her mug halfway to her mouth. "Why us two?"

"Because it's sort of what you do already. She's a teacher and you're a journalist." She tried to keep the contempt out of her voice when she said *journalist*. Becky's chosen profession might actually help them.

"Why can't you and Sarah help?"

"Because we have to do our jobs. If something happens, I need to be at the station. Sarah needs to be at the hospital. You can do the research from work. It will look like you're actually working."

Sarah suddenly grabbed the TV remote from the corner of the counter and turned up the television in the living room. Having the open concept floor plan made it easier for them to watch TV and eat at the same time. It kept the living room relatively clean since they were hardly ever in there. They tended to gravitate to the kitchen for some reason.

A breaking news banner flashed across the local news. Violence across the city spiked overnight again. Fourth night in a row. With an apocalypse now in play, the increased violence didn't surprise Rachel.

"That's not good," Sarah said.

"If the apocalypse has started, it's only going to get worse," Rachel observed.

They finished eating, and everyone shoved away from the counter. Sarah speared them with a dirty look and glared at their empty plates and mugs.

Chastened, they each took their dirty dishes to the sink.

"That will do for now," Sarah said. "But from now on, they go in the dishwasher. I'll empty it later. You know what they say about cleanliness."

Rachel groaned. "I don't think He cares how messy or clean our kitchen is when there are bigger things afoot."

Sarah finished tidying up the counter and did a quick wipe of the surface with a cloth. "Maybe. I'll feel better with the place clean. Is that better? We could be here for a while. Why not keep the place nice while we're here?"

"Fine. Whatever." Rachel ducked into her room to grab her badge and gun.

She opened the loft door but stopped at the gasp behind her. What horrible thing had she done this time? She spun around to see Leah's eyes wide. Sarah frowned.

Becky grinned, holding up a blazer. "Forget something?"

Rachel glanced at herself in the hallway mirror, her black wings unfurled behind her. Shit. If her wings had been cloaked, a soft, silver outline of them would be visible to angels. She snatched the blazer away from Becky, flattening her wings against her back, and shrugged into it. "I get why you two can cloak your wings. But I don't think it's fair that she had enough magic left over to cloak hers, too." She pointed at Leah.

"Get over it," Becky said.

"It doesn't make sense," Rachel insisted.

"There's a reason. We just don't know what it is yet." Sarah turned off the kitchen light.

Rachel let it go, for now. Based on her efforts so far, she wouldn't be getting her angelic power back anytime soon. There would be plenty of time to ponder why the teacher got to keep some of hers. Rachel shifted her shoulders to move her wings into a more comfortable position. No matter what she did, the limbs hated being confined. They needed to be able to breathe.

She pinned Becky and Leah with a stern look. "If you two find out anything, text me."

Victor stood on the sidewalk in front of the gas station with his minions and the two new recruits. The taller one shuffled his feet, while the stocky one darted his eyes back and forth looking as guilty as they would soon be.

So far, there had been slim pickings for new members, but word would get out once they accomplished this coordinated effort across the city. At two other stations in Toronto, Deacon and Ernie waited for his signal to start.

"Try to look casual," Victor said.

Frank, the tall guy, stood a little straighter and pulled out a smartphone. His stocky friend, Gary, still gazed around, unable to shed the guilt. Broad daylight was different than the cover of darkness. Victor shook his head. He had his work cut out for him if he wanted to turn the gang around. How had they survived this long without him?

He pulled out his phone and called Deacon. "Are you ready?"

Deacon sighed. "The two possibles are ready. Eager to prove they have what it takes."

"Wait for my signal."

He called Ernie, who answered on the third ring. Chatter in the background made it hard to hear him. "Are you ready?"

"Ready. The new recruits want to get the party started."

"Good. Wait for my signal." Victor puffed out his chest.

Later, he would put others through the same test. The first test of many to make sure they were worthy of the cause. Of course, they didn't know what he really wanted them for. Didn't know the role they would play in the end of the world. He doubted they would care even if they did know. Lacking a soul did that to you.

He had to organize these small strikes before coordinating bigger operations.

Four other minions confirmed they were ready. When he was satisfied everyone was in place, he took a deep breath. The gas station was busy this early in the morning. At least one out of every three people who pulled up to the pumps had souls. He could smell them even from the curb.

Eager to get started, he forced himself to wait, going through the plan in his mind again. Ending the world took patience. This one little step would go a long way toward the main goal. He wanted the right mixture of victims and bystanders. With six simultaneous targets, he knew the attacks would make the news.

He sent a text to the group chat. Technology was a wonderful thing when coordinating crime. In two minutes, they would all send in the new recruits to prove their worth.

"Countdown has begun," he said to his two fledglings.

"We're ready," Frank replied.

From the sidewalk, Victor could see a few customers inside the station. The cashier was a man in his mid-thirties who smiled at everyone even if the customer wasn't paying attention. Another wave of customers pulled up to the pumps, lulled by the magically lowered prices.

When there were five people inside the station, Victor checked the time on his phone.

"Time to get to work."

Frank and Gary squared their shoulders and marched through the doors. As Victor followed them, he looked up and spotted the cameras pointing at all areas of the station, from the pumps outside to the store inside. With a wave of his hand, he distorted the pictures. When the police pulled the footage, they would see nothing to help them.

Inside the station, Victor and Gary flanked the door.

Frank walked up to the counter. The clerk smiled at him and waited a beat before speaking. "Good morning, sir. What pump are you paying for?"

Without warning, Frank punched the guy in the face. It took three shots before the pain and fear registered on the man's abused face. "The money, now!"

The clerk shook his head. "I can't do that." He leaned away.

"You'd rather die? This place doesn't care about you. Give me the money now and we walk away."

Chest puffed out, Victor beamed. The man had some hidden talent.

Frank grabbed the clerk's shirt to keep him still while he landed a few more blows. Blood poured like a faucet over the cream-colored counter from the guy's broken nose.

Customers at the back of the store screamed. They ran to the front but stopped dead in their tracks when they saw Victor and Gary.

"Give me the money!" Frank demanded again.

Gary stalked to the back of the store and grabbed one of the customers cowering by the chips—a younger guy wearing jeans and a T-shirt who looked like he could be on his way to school instead of a job.

"You want your customers to pay the price, then?" Gary asked.

Before the clerk could answer, Gary punched the guy he was holding in the face. He crumbled to the ground. Gary kicked him in the stomach. The guy writhed on the floor, groans of pain and whimpers for Gary to stop escaping his lips.

Frank slammed another fist into the clerk's face.

Victor grinned. His pocket buzzed, and he fished out

his phone. Deacon's number flashed on the screen. "Report."

"It's going well, I guess. Why can't they use guns? It would go much faster with guns."

Victor took a deep breath and counted to ten before answering. Guns. Always man's go-to response. It made them lazy. "I want them to fear the man, not the weapon. Anyone can hold a weapon and demand something. How will they fare with someone who can fight?"

"Fine. No weapons. But it's gonna take longer."

"It will take as long as it takes. Make sure they get the job done."

He ended the call and watched his new recruits. Customers huddled at the back of the store, unwilling to come into harm's way. How bold would a lack of weapons make them? That was part of the test, too. Would anyone leap to the clerk's defense if they thought the assailants didn't have weapons? Or would they leave their fellow man to fight for himself?

The young guy hadn't been trying to help. He'd wanted to escape. From the looks on the faces at the back of the room, they all wanted the same.

The clerk finally lifted a trembling hand to the cash register and punched a few buttons. A bell sounded, and the drawer zinged open. Hand shaking almost violently, he reached in, grabbed all he could, and plunked it on the counter, smeared with his own blood.

Frank let go of the guy's shirt. The clerk sagged back against the wall. The hope on his face was priceless. He thought they would leave now. But maybe they were just getting started.

Chapter Four

Caleb Bishop froze at the groan coming from the living room, his hand hovering over the knob on his bedroom door. At this time of the morning, Karl should be passed out in bed. Sounded like he didn't even make it past the sofa in his drunken stupor this time. Caleb glanced over his shoulder at the window, contemplating how badly he would injure himself if he fell while trying to scale down the building. The fire escape was in his father's room, on the other side of the living room.

Caleb took a deep breath and turned the knob slowly. He opened the door a crack and listened for more sleep mumbling. A deep snore filled the small apartment. He pulled open the door wider, giving him enough room to slip into the hallway. Another snore reassured him, but his heart beat faster and he froze to gulp a deep breath.

When he reached the living room, his father was splayed on the sofa—one shoe on, one shoe off. One arm draped over the end of the furniture, another hung over the side, his knuckles brushing the floor.

Caleb tiptoed around the sofa. With escape in sight, he

inched toward the door. A snort from behind him caused his stomach to sink. His heart raced. Legs trembling, he crept forward, not daring to watch his father for fear of waking him. The springs on the sofa creaked.

"Where the hell do you think you're going, boy?" Anger dripped from his father's voice.

Fuck. If he'd listened to his friend and stayed at his house, he could have avoided this. But that would have caused just as much wrath or more. His father would have been incensed at his absence. He wouldn't track him down at his job or a friend's, though. He would have stewed all day until Caleb got home. That beating would have been worse than the one he was about to get now.

He turned around to see his father wobbling on legs still impaired by alcohol. The man wouldn't be sober until at least noon judging from the sway and the bloodshot eyes.

"I'm going to work." Caleb kept his gaze down as he spoke.

"Before making me breakfast?" Knuckles cracked.

The threat in his voice sent a familiar chill through Caleb. "I could whip something up before I leave," he offered.

As he walked toward the kitchen, giving his father a wide berth, the man's arm snaked out to slap across Caleb's cheek. Caleb shook his head to clear it. Before he could get around his father, the man struck another blow. This punch hit him in the jaw. He tasted blood from a cut lip. His head throbbed.

In a heartbeat, his father wailed into him, landing punch after punch. Caleb collapsed to the ground and rolled up to protect his stomach and head. Anything left exposed was fair game. His father punched his ear, his thighs, the back of his head.

Blood trickled onto the floor and into his mouth.

"You need a lesson in respect, boy. I raised you. How dare you disrespect me like that?"

Caleb remained silent. Nothing he said would stop the beating. The thing to do was wait it out, hope his father didn't break any bones this time. As his father yelled, the scent of the alcohol lingered in the air. Not for the first time, Caleb thought about lacing the old man's booze with something. It would have to be strong enough to kill him, though. If it wasn't, Karl would figure out what Caleb had done, and he would pay the price.

After an interminable five minutes of blows, his father stopped. Heavy breathing filled the small apartment. His father's upper body swayed, eyes half-closed, and he collapsed on the sofa, exhausted from his effort.

Freedom now or stay and make the man's breakfast? It might appease him temporarily, but something would set him off again. If he escaped now, he could always not come back.

Caleb dashed past his father, grabbed his backpack by the door, and rushed out of the apartment. His father's shouts followed him down the hall. Though the old man was too tired and still too drunk to follow him, footsteps shuffled inside the apartment. Caleb bypassed the elevator and beelined for the stairs. There was no way his father would follow him on those. Too bad. He might lose his balance, fall down the stairs, and break his neck.

Caleb ran down the stairs so fast, he thought he would end up tripping. When he got close enough to a landing, he jumped over the last few steps. Anything to get him out of the building faster.

He reached the main floor slightly out of breath. Before going to work, he needed to clean up. His lip throbbed. What would he tell his boss? Not willing to admit his home life was anything but stellar, he didn't want to tell his boss something that would disappoint him, either. A mugging would illicit sympathy and explain his wounds. Satisfied with his cover story, he exited the building and turned toward one of the only things open this early on a weekday that would have what he needed to wash away the blood. The gas station a few blocks away.

The bell above the door to the gas station jingled. Victor smelled the soul before it entered the building. A man, a boy really—he couldn't be more than eighteen or nineteen —stopped short the second he crossed the threshold. The newcomer's eyes took in the customers huddled at the back and the clerk behind the counter, his face as bloodied and bruised as his own.

The boy hunched his shoulders and turned to leave.

Victor waved his hand, and the door closed. The boy pulled on the handle, but the door didn't budge. Resigned to staying, the boy turned again and walked to the back of the gas station, keeping his gaze trained on the clerk and the customer currently on the receiving end of his minion's beatings.

At the bank of fridges, the boy stopped and looked down at the woman huddled on the floor in front of the sandwiches. She moved over slightly.

Victor nodded to Frank.

Frank laid a few more punches, and the newcomer's gaze widened. After two solid hits, the boy flinched and looked away.

If he could turn the boy, the tainted soul would be worth more to the apocalypse than a hundred of the soulless minions. Though they all had free will, the soulless were easily manipulated, quick to go for the high, the fix, the enjoyment of something without thinking about the consequences. They didn't care much for the consequences. But the souled, they were a different story.

The newcomer opened one of the fridges and pulled out a bottle of orange juice. He placed the bottle against the side of his face, close to his swollen eye.

Every time Frank landed a punch, the new guy flinched.

"That's enough," Victor said.

None of the customers were willing to jump into the fray to help. They remained huddled in their spots, hoping they were invisible. Good. They'd already become so lacking in empathy and so selfish that further violence wouldn't likely spur them into action.

The punching stopped, and both of his potential new recruits released their victims.

Frank pointed to the clerk. "This guy hit an alarm button."

Conquest clenched his fists, shaking his head at the bloodied man.

"Both of you head back to headquarters and stay there until I get back." He waved a hand at the door, magically unlocking it.

They nodded and hurried out of the gas station.

In the distance, the sound of sirens pierced the early morning air. The door swung shut, muffling the sound. He gave it no more than five minutes until law enforcement descended on the scene.

He walked to the back of the station, the fear in the eyes of the customers feeding his determination. The newcomer stood his ground. From the look of him, he'd already had one beating that morning and he wasn't going to put up with another. Victor stood beside him and waited for the cops to burst into the place.

Strobing lights made the inside of the store look like a fun house.

The door swung open, and two detectives walked in. The woman was tall with ebony hair. The blazer she wore matched her outfit, but on the unseasonably warm morning, it seemed out of place. The man towered over her.

One had a soul. Victor inhaled deeply. The other, not souled or soulless, intrigued him. Too close together, he couldn't tell which was the enigma, but he vowed to find out.

They flashed badges. "I'm Detective Malak. This is Detective Williams. Who can tell us what happened here?" the woman asked.

Victor raised an eyebrow. "Detectives responding to a gas station robbery?"

Detective Malak focused her attention on him. "We were on our way back from a homicide when we heard about the robbery. We're here until the major crime unit for robberies arrives."

The clerk behind the counter groaned. The woman hurried over to him. She grabbed a pile of napkins from the counter and touched them to the man's wounds. She pulled out a radio and clicked the button to talk.

"Requesting an ambulance at the gas station at Adelaide and Spadina. We've got two severely wounded individuals."

"ETA five minutes," a voice crackled back.

"Can you tell me what happened, sir?" she asked.

Silence greeted the woman's question. She stood and walked over to the customer at the back of the store, who Gary had left beaten and bloodied. She bent to examine his wounds. "Can you tell me what happened?"

The customer flashed a look at Victor. He shook his head. When the woman on the floor moved, Victor pinned her with a glare. She retreated again, pressing her back more firmly against the fridge doors.

Detective Malak's partner checked the clerk again. Both victims were bruised and bloodied, but they could both speak. Would they? That was the real test here.

He inched closer to the newcomer. Fear and anger oozed off him until it was almost overpowering, exhilarating if you could smell it.

"The ambulance will be here soon," the female detective reassured the customer. "Can you tell me anything about what happened here?"

Her partner glanced up at the blood-smeared counter. He took in the open cash drawer.

"I can't remember," the customer muttered.

She stood. "Did anyone see what happened?" Hope in her eyes dwindled in the silence.

The anticipation was like electricity sizzling over his skin. Would they, or wouldn't they? Humans, unpredictable at times, usually chose self-preservation when the threat still lingered. Head shakes all around made Victor smile on the inside. He couldn't reveal his glee yet. Right now, he looked like another bystander unless the others outed him.

He watched the newcomer out of the corner of his eye. The young man's gaze flitted around the room as if waiting for someone to step up and say something. After all, everyone knew who had robbed the place. Everyone remained silent. The moment the young man realized no one would talk for fear of reprisal, his shoulders straightened. He stood taller. The desire to be feared, and therefore powerful, poured off him in waves.

"Really? No one saw a thing?" Detective Malak asked.

"I heard a commotion, but I didn't see anything," the woman on the floor said.

Others nodded.

Detective Malak marched over to the newcomer at the back. Her gaze took in the wounds on his face. "What's your name?"

The young man looked at Victor, who gave an imperceptible nod. "Caleb Bishop."

"Did you sustain those injuries here, Caleb?"

The newcomer shook his head vehemently, wincing at the force of his denial. "I don't know anything."

"Where did you get the wounds?" Her voice had softened, and her eyes shone with sympathy.

"Not here. It's no big deal."

She moved her attention from the newcomer to Victor. "What about you, sir? You look fairly fit. You didn't think you could stop what was going on?"

"I arrived just after it happened. Had I been here during the altercation, I would have intervened." He glanced around the store, daring anyone to contradict him.

She raised an eyebrow, then turned to the young man again. "He's not with you?"

Caleb shook his head.

A commotion from the door pulled the detective's attention from the newcomer as the crime scene unit arrived. A couple of street cops entered the building and conferred with Detective Malak and Detective Williams. Shortly thereafter, other detectives, likely from robbery, arrived with a CSU team.

Immediately, the CSU set to work putting down ident markers, snapping pictures, taking swabs, and bagging evidence.

"The robbery unit will still need to take statements

from everyone. Anything, no matter how small, might help us find the person who did this," Detective Williams said.

When Detective Malak turned to look at her partner, Victor snagged her attention for a second. Recognition flashed through him, so fleeting he almost thought he'd imagined it. She was the enigma.

An ambulance screeched to a halt outside. More strobing lights filled the building. EMTs rushed in and did quick assessments of the victims. They carefully loaded them onto gurneys and out into the morning sunshine.

Her gaze scanned the room again, resting on Victor. He made eye contact briefly, then averted his eyes, taking on the same attitude as the other customers. Detective Malak frowned.

An hour later, most of the police personnel filed out of the gas station. The ambulances had left with the clerk and customer on board.

The manager of the gas station had arrived shortly after the crime scene unit and turned off the pumps and the sign to discourage more customers. At some point during the day, the station might open again.

With most of the police gone, the remaining customers hurried out of the station. Scrambling like scared rats, they piled out into the mid-morning crowds. The line of curious onlookers had died down with people's need to get to work outweighing their desire to indulge their curiosity.

The newcomer lingered in front of the fridge.

"You could be feared like that," Victor said.

Caleb turned to him. Desperation and hope shone in the boy's eyes. "I want to be feared."

On the way back to the car, Rachel paused and looked over her shoulder. The young man with the bruised face still stood beside the tall, muscular man as if under protection. Something about the whole thing smelled off to her, but she couldn't put her finger on why. He said he wasn't there when the robbery took place, yet his face looked like someone had used it as a punching bag. From witness accounts outside the station, there had been two men, but of course, no one got a good look at either of them.

"I'll meet you at the car," she said to Williams.

"You're going back in there? It's not even our case."

"I have a few more questions. I won't even be ten minutes."

Williams huffed and stomped over to the car, checking his watch as he leaned against the driver's side door.

Rachel stalked back into the station. The jingle of the bell garnered her attention from the two men. Everyone else had left.

Approaching the young man, she scrutinized the bruises on his face. He shifted from one foot to another and glanced up at the larger man. Victor, if she remembered her notes correctly. She didn't know what the exchange between them meant, but she suspected they hadn't told her the entire story. She believed the wounds hadn't happened during the robbery, but that meant someone else had abused Caleb.

"I had a few more questions if that's all right," she said, looking directly at the young man.

He shrugged. The larger man stood his ground.

"You said you didn't get those bruises during the robbery. Was that the truth?"

Maybe he'd lied because he didn't want to go to the hospital. Maybe he didn't want to go to the station to answer more questions. Maybe he was one of the robbers.

She doubted that last thought, but mankind had a habit of surprising her. And not always in a good way.

"Ya, it's the truth. I missed all the commotion here."

"Then how did you get them?"

She'd allowed herself to be distracted earlier when she'd asked about them. This time, she wouldn't be so easy to dismiss. Despite the two men not looking remotely alike, the large man hovered near the younger one like a protective father. Could be adopted.

"Football with the guys. A bunch of us play. It's not flag football. I got tackled a few times."

"Really? Where do you play?"

Caleb looked upward for a split second. "Over on McCaul in the park."

During the time she'd been back on Earth, she'd passed the park a number of times. Often, there were people playing various games there. Though she doubted the man's word, his story was plausible, but she didn't believe him. She had no cause to question him further if he didn't want to tell her the truth. She couldn't force him to reveal what really happened. Maybe it was football. Right now, she could only go on instinct. And her human instinct had been dormant for over a thousand years. It would take time to trust it again.

Caleb stared at her for a moment, then averted his gaze, taking great interest in the top of his shoe. Rachel looked from Caleb to Victor, curious about their relationship. Victor stared her down like a protective parent.

"Are you sure you don't have anything to tell me?"

Caleb nodded. With a thrust of his chin, he crossed his arms over his chest.

Admitting defeat, she sighed, pulled out a business card, and placed it in his hand. "If you want to talk about anything. Like how you really got those bruises."

"He won't. He's fine." Victor clapped him on the back.

She glared at him. Not because she thought the man had caused Caleb's injuries, but because they both knew something they refused to share.

She hadn't seen Victor in the neighborhood before. Based on her encounter, she suspected this wouldn't be her last run-in with him either. She would have to keep an eye out for him.

She fixed Caleb with a gaze she hoped conveyed sympathy. "Anything you need to talk about, call me. Anytime."

She left the gas station and found Williams still leaning against the car. He checked his watch.

"A minute to spare. Get anything new?"

She sighed and rolled her eyes. "What do you think?"

"You had to try."

She nodded. "Maybe the victims at the hospital will be a little more talkative."

Rachel stood by the window in the small hospital room, watching the heart monitor beside the bed while the clerk struggled to sit up. To help the swamped robbery unit, she and Williams were questioning the victims from the gas station. The clerk pressed the button to raise the back of the bed in an effort to help, but every move he made caused him to flinch in pain. The pink and red welts on his face would turn to ugly purple and blue soon enough. She suspected the injuries she couldn't see were the most severe. Based on his cringes of pain with every movement, the robbers had broken at least one of his ribs.

"We know you need your rest, John, so we'll be as quick as we can." Rachel pulled out her notebook.

Detective Williams stood on the other side of the bed, looking at John with genuine concern. "Can you describe either suspect?"

"It happened so fast, I didn't get a good look at no one."

The phone on her belt buzzed. Rachel removed the phone and swiped to answer the call, walking toward the hospital room door as she said, "Malak."

"Get the victim to tell you anything yet?" her boss, Detective Sergeant Diego Reyes, asked.

She slipped into the hallway. "Not yet and I don't hold out much hope that he will."

"Keep trying. Hill and Vargas from the robbery unit are trying at Scarborough General. Six gas stations were targeted. At the same time. Turn your findings over to them when you're done."

Rachel let that sink in for a moment, her mind whirling with possibilities. A coordinated attack across the city on such small targets didn't make sense if it was a terrorist group out for practice.

"Thanks, boss. We'll see what we can find out."

She poked her head into the room. "Williams, can I see you out here for a second?"

When he'd joined her in the hall, she filled him in on the other attacks.

"At least no one got killed," he said.

Had a death occurred during any of the robberies, their unit would take over the case formally. "This time. Does this feel gang related to you?"

He shrugged. "It definitely feels off. The local gangs have never had the discipline to pull off this kind of coordinated attack. And really, why would they?"

"Part of a new recruiting method? None of them used

weapons as far as I can tell, either. Which is also unusual for the gangs around here."

"If it was gang related, the victims would have seen the members around the neighborhood," Williams said.

"That won't matter. The gangs strike fear into most people. They won't talk. But we have to try to convince them." She nodded at the door.

They entered the room again. John still sat up in bed. His left eye was swollen shut. Angry red cuts marred his face. His bottom lip was split in the middle. The damage could have been a lot worse. If it was some sort of new initiation, she didn't want to think about what the next step would be. No weapons this time didn't mean there wouldn't be any in the future. Survivors this time didn't mean that trend would continue, either.

"John, can you tell us if this was gang related?" Rachel asked.

Williams glared at her but being subtle was getting them nowhere.

Terror froze the victim's face in unblinking silence before he finally shook his head. Too adamantly for his wounds judging by the cringe of pain that followed.

"No gangs. I didn't see any colors or any gang members. No. Definitely random. Nothing to do with the Grange."

Rachel flipped her notebook closed. For the time being, they couldn't do much if the victims refused to tell them the truth. Though they had surveillance video, she doubted it would reveal anything. Some businesses in the area used the video cameras as a deterrent to theft with no real technology behind them.

"Thanks for your time, John," Detective Williams said.

They left the room.

"That was helpful," Detective Williams said.

Rachel stopped at the elevator and pressed the call button. "Actually, it was. Despite his protests, we know it had something to do with the Grange gang. The question is why? And did all the attacks across the city have to do with them?"

Back at the police station, Rachel shuffled through paperwork. There was plenty to keep her busy, but the other robberies niggled at something in her brain and wouldn't let go. She called up the case files for them on her computer and skimmed through the robbery detective's notes for each one. Casualties that resulted in hospitalization occurred in all of the robberies. And none of them involved weapons of any kind. Not even a knife. While thankful the injuries hadn't been more severe, the lack of weapons boggled her. Gangs were not known for their restraint when it came to guns. Show off the merchandise and all that. That's why the city had a drug problem and an illegal gun problem. Not to mention the other side "jobs" the gangs were involved in.

Detective Williams approached her from the kitchen. He plunked a steaming cup of coffee on the corner of her desk.

Rachel flashed a smile. "Thanks."

She took a sip gratefully, savoring the hot liquid. Every new food, every new drink, was a culinary adventure, but she loved going back to old favorites. She needed to appreciate it while she still could because she refused to remain on Earth longer than she had to.

After setting the mug back on her desk, she regarded Detective Williams solemnly. "I have a bad feeling about these robberies."

He pulled out his chair and settled into it. A frown crossed his face. "I don't like the sound of that. Your feelings are usually right."

Chapter Five

Later that evening, Rachel sat at the back of Baron's with Sarah, Becky, and Leah. The TV above the bar scrolled the day's news. The bartender pulled drafts of beer and plunked them on trays for the harried waitstaff to bring to thirsty customers. The scent of fried food in the air every time the door to the kitchen swung open caused Rachel's stomach to grumble. Music blared, making conversation difficult until there were lulls in the playlist.

Leah sat, eyes wide, taking in the sights and sounds. The waiter brought over drinks, placing a steaming mug in front of the newest angelic arrival.

Leah cupped the mug with both hands and sniffed deeply. "They had this in the teacher's lounge at school. Have you tried it?"

Rachel smiled. "We all love our coffee. You should have ordered decaf, though. You'll be up all night if you drink that."

Ignoring the warning, Leah took a sip of the hot liquid. She sighed like she'd never tasted anything quite so delicious.

"How was your first day?" Sarah asked.

"Weird. Everyone knew me like I'd always been there. I remembered conversations I never had with people. Leyla was there. I remembered when she went missing even though I wasn't here. And all of us saving her at that old warehouse."

Becky nodded. "You get used to it. Eventually, it all blends together, and you forget that you just got here."

Leah tilted her head to look over her shoulder. "Still no white in my wings. I helped a lot of students today."

When the waiter dropped off their meals, they waited for him to hustle away again before digging in. Everything Leah put in her mouth was a new sensation for her, and they didn't want to draw attention to themselves any more than they already had. The restaurant staff thought they knew them well, but Rachel didn't want to do anything that would mess with the fragile façade. Who knew how long the magic would last? Would they need to keep topping it up so everyone in their new lives would continue to remember them? She sat straighter, her gaze darting around the bar as panic skittered through her. At least Becky had a little magic left. But nothing Rachel had done so far had made a blip on the power scale.

"Have you tried this?" Leah asked, a forkful of fries, gravy, and cheese poised in the air. A drop of gravy dripped onto the table, and the cheese stretched until it was hair-thin.

"Wait until you try pizza," Sarah said.

When they finished their meal, they left the bar through the side entrance so they wouldn't have to force their way through the crush of people in the front. A band was setting up, which meant the music would get even louder. Maybe they should have picked a quieter place to be their local bar.

As they turned onto Queen Street West, Rachel observed the street prophet from the night before, settling into his spot. It had been too late after getting Leah settled to go in search of him. And on their way to Baron's for dinner, his place had been empty save for the telltale box, newspapers, and a variety of personal items. Every time someone passed by him, he reached out a soiled arm, revealing a tattoo of Omega on the inside of his wrist. Frail fingers clutched the material of a sleeve belonging to a businessman.

"The end is nigh!" He shrunk at the withered look the man gave him.

The man shook his arm free and hurried along the sidewalk.

"I hate to admit it, but we really do need to talk to him," Rachel said.

After witnessing the accosting of the businessman, other passersby gave the street prophet a wide berth. A woman with her teenage son went so far as to step off the curb to avoid the man.

Rachel approached him with a smile. His eyes narrowed in suspicion, and he recoiled into himself to get away from her. Leah pushed past Rachel and smiled at the man. Becky and Sarah followed suit.

"I don't know you." He pointed at Leah. "Them, I know. She's mean." He pointed at Rachel.

"She's sorry about that," Leah said, her voice soft and gentle. She bent her knees so she could look into his eyes. "She was having a bad day. We wanted to know more about this prophecy about the end of the world."

His eyes brightened for a second, then darkened again. He shook his head and shuffled backward until his back hit the wall of the building. Eyes wide, he craned his head from side to side, looking for an escape.

"Please," Leah said. "We believe you."

He flicked a finger in Rachel's direction. "She doesn't."

Rachel sighed and bent down as well. Maybe he didn't know anything, and it was a coincidence. These kinds of street prophets popped up all the time in big cities. Most of the time, their predictions were bullshit. But he'd said before that the priest talked about the end of the world. If he was talking about the priest from the news, he had been wrong before, so why was this prophecy different?

Becky stepped in and touched the man's arm. "Remember me?"

He smiled and nodded. "From television."

"That's right. The priest who talked about the end of the world, was it Father Ianetti from the television?"

He paused for a moment, looking at them all in turn. When he got to Rachel, he scowled and continued to look at the others. He nodded. "The teacher knows all. He's educating his flock at Our Lady of Amity."

Leah smiled. "Thank you." She stood, stretching her back. "Ouch. What is this fresh damnation? Pain from squatting down for a few minutes?"

"Welcome to Earth," Sarah said.

"I don't know if he'll be there, but we should go over to the church and see," Rachel said.

"Sermons nightly!" the street prophet yelled.

Gasps and derogatory comments from pedestrians pulled Rachel's lips into a frown. No one had a right to judge except God. She didn't know why the man was on the streets, but she'd been wrong to dismiss him so easily before. Unfortunate circumstances could happen to anyone. Circumstances piled on top of each other could force people into lives they'd never pictured for themselves before. Remembering her earlier treatment of him twisted her stomach. She'd been just as guilty of judgment.

"Thank you," Rachel said. At the man's stunned look, she touched his arm. "Really, thank you. Do you need anything? When was the last time you had a hot meal?"

He looked skyward as if trying to remember. "Last week."

Rachel rummaged around in her purse and pulled out a twenty-dollar bill. She shoved it into the man's gnarled hand.

"Thank you." Light returned to his eyes.

As they walked down the street in the direction of the church, Sarah stuck out a hand toward Rachel's forehead.

Rachel slapped it away. "I'm not a horrible angel."

Darkness had fallen hours ago, and the light pollution of the downtown core lent an ethereal glow to the evening. Once at the church, they stopped. The huge stone structure occupied three lots. Its parapet reached high into the sky. Two large wood doors at the top of the stone steps invited a steady stream of worshipers to enter. Leah frowned.

"I see the glow from the streetlights, but where is the golden glow surrounding the church?"

"Haven't seen one since we got here," Becky said. "Not enough angel power, I guess. Ironic really, when the glow shows us where we can get safe harbor."

"Even without angel power, we should still see the glow," Rachel said. "Fallen angels are still welcomed in the true houses of God so they can repent and return to the fold. This priest doesn't have God's ear."

"The building looks old," Sarah said.

Leah pulled out her smartphone and typed a few things onto the screen. She held the device aloft triumphantly. "It is one of the oldest churches in the city!"

Latecomers for the evening sermon hurried by them, running up the steps to the church. They followed suit.

Rachel held open the ancient, heavy wood door until everyone was inside.

Parishioners scurried, quiet like church mice, into polished wooden pews. High stained-glass windows let in some of the moonlight. An organist at the front of the church, behind the altar, played a hymn as people took their seats. Silence descended on the building when Father Ianetti took the pulpit.

The angels slipped into a pew at the back for a quick escape.

"*It is* the guy from TV," Leah whispered.

A woman with her daughter turned to glare at them. "Shhhh."

They shrank back into the pews and waited for the priest to begin.

When he raised his hands in welcome, a chorus of applause echoed in the church. He adjusted his robes, then put notes onto the altar.

"Welcome, my children. The word is good, and God is happy you have blessed us today. He wants you to know that the pure, the righteous, will survive the coming apocalypse. You must believe!"

A chorus of "amen" went through the building.

"The signs are among us good people. Weather anomalies, disasters, how we treat our fellow man. Interpretation is key. Face value is the enemy of knowledge. The lost texts of the Bible contain many more signs of the coming end. Too many to have transcribed them all. Who is with me?"

Another wave of "amen" rippled through the church.

Rachel frowned. On television, the priest seemed less evangelical. Why did his followers believe in this stuff?

"I've seen enough." She stood, causing everyone to turn to look at her.

"Rachel, sit down until the sermon is over." Sarah gave her a stern look.

"You stay. I'll be waiting outside."

She pushed through the double doors and out into the cool evening air. Despite the nonsense the priest was spewing, the others didn't follow her out. How long would his lies last? She thought about heading back to the bar to wait for them, but they would probably want to talk to the priest after his sermon. She should be there for that to poke holes into his story.

Thirty minutes later, Leah poked her head out the door. Parishioners streamed past her.

Rachel took the stairs two at a time, stepped inside again, and let the warmth of the church settle over her. She hadn't realized how cool it had gotten. She would need to start wearing a heavier coat.

"What other lies did he tell?"

"How do you know they're lies?" Becky asked.

Rachel rolled her eyes. "How has he seen the lost books? They're lost."

Leah shrugged. "There's been speculation for years surrounding what they supposedly say."

Rachel couldn't argue with that logic, but she couldn't believe this priest had read lost texts of the Bible either.

"How could he know what they say? More people would have been talking about them if just anyone could read them," Rachel added.

"Not if evil has stopped all mention of them. If they need people not to know what the texts say in order to succeed," Leah countered.

"More than one overzealous man of the cloth would have read them if they were accessible," Rachel said.

"You don't like being wrong, do you?" Becky asked.

Rachel sighed. "It's not that. I can't believe He

wouldn't have let us read them. Especially before sending us here."

"Maybe other angels have read them," Sarah suggested. "Just because we haven't doesn't mean others are in the dark, too."

"Fine. We'll go on the assumption the priest isn't a total crackpot and ask him where these texts are. See if we can determine if what he's seen are real or fakes."

Rachel marched to the front of the church to take her place in the long line of people waiting to speak to the priest. Flashing her badge and moving to the front of the line crossed her mind, but she dismissed the idea. If she appeared overeager, the priest might clam up. Or maybe he would open up more about his predicted end of the world. It was hard to judge humans and what they would do. A lot about how they acted made no sense to her. She hoped she wasn't on Earth long enough for emotions to rule her judgment.

She watched him chat with each member of his congregation, tapping her foot. A few of them had tattoos on the inside of their wrists, partially visible when they proffered their hands for the priest to shake. She turned to her sisters.

"Did you see that?"

Leah nodded. "The tattoo?"

"Looked like the bottom of the omega," Sarah said.

Rachel filed the information away for now. While it was odd for more than one person to have the same tattoo, it wasn't unheard of. Friends sometimes had them of shared experience. Fraternity or sorority members might have them, and it did look like an omega.

When they finally got to the front of the line, the priest greeted them with a wide smile. His eyes twinkled.

"Bless you. I haven't seen you in my church before. Newcomers are always a delight."

He shook their hands, then folded his in front of himself.

"You gave an excellent sermon tonight, Father," Rachel said. "I'm interested to learn more about these so-called lost texts of the Bible. Where might I view them?"

He gave her a sharp stare. "Impertinent, aren't you? They are not *so-called*. They are *so*. Saw them with my own eyes. The words within their pages scared me like nothing ever has before. I was compelled to share my knowledge so that many can be saved."

"Saw them where?" Rachel persisted.

"Rachel!" Becky admonished.

"What? It's not a hard question. If he actually saw them and they caused such an impression, he would remember where he saw them."

A sad smile crossed the priest's face, like he'd lost all hope for Rachel's soul. She almost laughed at that. Little did he know, the four of them were the real experts on God. Of course, they couldn't tell him that and had no way to prove the claim even if they did.

"I remember it well, my child. I was on a pilgrimage that brought me to the Vatican. Housed within those walls are relics, artifacts, art, and books that would put the love of God even in a non-believer."

"So, nowhere else, then?" Rachel asked.

"No. The Vatican does not let such priceless documents out of the Holy City. Imagine the disaster if that happened."

"If you remember more about these 'texts,'" Rachel said using air quotes, "give me a call." She shoved her business card into the bewildered priest's hand.

Becky shook his hand while Sarah tugged on Rachel's sleeve. "Thank you for your time, Father."

She followed the angels outside again. "He's crazy."

Sarah shook her head. "No matter what you believe, if the texts he read are the real deal, we need to find them. We need to see what they say."

"Fine. They might have the actual words of the Bible before the countless translations corrupted their meaning."

"Then we're agreed that we'll look for them?" Leah asked.

"Yes. But I still don't think we'll find anything." Rachel shoved her hands in her pockets and headed for their apartment.

Father Ianetti hurried through the rest of the parishioners, ushering them out as quickly as he could. How far away had the women gotten from the church? Would he be able to find them? Damn his devout flock. They wanted more and more of his time. Usually, that didn't bother him. He was eager to talk about the Lord and what his sermon meant, but he had important God's work to do now that most of them wouldn't understand. Not yet, anyway. The others, who like him, belonged to The End, a sect started decades ago, knew what needed to be done.

He smiled and shook hands as he hurried through the nave of the church. His bewildered flock stood there open-mouthed and stunned. How many of them would still be waiting there when he returned?

No time to grab his coat, he burst through the doors of the church and ran down the stairs. He spotted the women at the end of the street before they turned the corner. Making sure to keep a safe distance behind them, he followed. He turned the corner thirty seconds after them and stopped abruptly when he saw them talking to a homeless man. He recognized the man from his sermons. Recognized him as a member of The End from the tattoo the man had on his wrist. He'd wondered what had happened to the man when he'd missed sermons for two months. What had happened in his life to cause this decline? It was unfortunate that his current circumstances made him a liability.

Was that how they found him? Three months ago, the man would have never compromised The End's mission. Normally, he welcomed all newcomers, no matter how they found their way to his church. But these four made the hair on the back of his neck rise. He stood against the wall as far out of their sight as he could get. Perhaps he'd said too much during his sermons. The one who appeared to be in charge of the group didn't believe what he'd said, though. There were always non-believers who needed to be swayed to see the truth.

Had the homeless man said something to send the women to his church? He had recognized Becky as a TV personality, but the others were a mystery to him.

The man nodded a few times, and one of the other women gave him a twenty-dollar bill.

He couldn't risk following them all the way to wherever they were going. He needed to get back to his church, to his work. But he needed to know what to do about them. The little bit he had told them might help them stop what should be inevitable. He needed to be more careful. The detective had no way of getting more information about the texts, nothing that would help, anyway. There might be mentions of them, but the actual text wouldn't be floating around the internet for anyone to stumble across. The Vatican was careful with their relics.

Still, it wouldn't hurt to do some damage control. He needed to keep an eye on the homeless man as well. Father Ianetti didn't want the guy to be sending even more people to his church who might try to get in his way.

He would deal with the women later if needed. Right now, he had to contact Conquest to make sure things were moving forward.

He hurried along the sidewalk back to the church. A few of his parishioners milled about at the bottom of the steps. If he detoured around the building and went in the back, he wouldn't have to make inane small talk with them. Not that he minded any other time, but he was too busy right now to be the priest he wanted to be. The priest he would be again when the end came and not only his flock but the rest of the city needed him.

Before the group of people saw him, he crossed the street and walked down the road parallel to the street where the church sat. When he got to the cross street, he hurried across, not waiting for the light to turn green. At any time of the day, you took your life in your hands when you crossed against the light, but he didn't have time to spare. Luckily, traffic was lighter than usual.

He made it to the church and passed through the back door. The quiet of the place soothed him. When everyone was gone for the day, he sometimes sat in the center pew and listened to the silence. On sunny days, the beams of light passing through the stained-glass windows caused halos to form on the floor.

Back in the rectory, he pulled out his summoning supplies for Conquest. If he needed to keep contacting the horseman, he would have to get more organized. Supplies to summon any of the horsemen weren't exactly bursting off the occult shop shelves.

Using the same pewter bowl as before, he went through

the ritual, ending with the slice of his finger. Hoof beats filled the small room. The air chilled.

In a flash of light, Conquest appeared out of thin air. This time, he wore jeans, a T-shirt, and a leather jacket that had seen better days.

The horseman glared at the priest. Despite calling the horseman, the priest backed away. Summoning didn't necessarily mean control. They wanted the same thing, but he didn't believe for a second that the horseman wouldn't snuff him out if he got in the way.

"What do you want? I can't return at the drop of a hat. I am busy now."

Father Ianetti filled him in on the detective and her questions.

"Yes, I've seen her. I suspect she'll be a problem, but don't worry. The gang will keep an eye on her."

"Gang? You're running a gang now?"

"You question my methods?" Conquest glared.

"No, not questioning anything. It's probably good being in the gang. They have a hand in almost everything that goes on in the city. What do I call you now?"

"It's Victor. Next time you need me, text or call." Conquest pulled out a smartphone and punched in some numbers.

The priest's phone on the table buzzed. He shuffled over and looked at the message that flashed on the screen.

"I will do that. Hopefully, I won't need you again until we're in the final stages. How is it going?"

"It's underway. You worry about getting the rest of the horsemen here. Let me worry about everything else. Don't forget who is actually in charge here, Father."

"Of course not. I serve you and your brothers."

"Good. Don't summon me again."

Father Ianetti took a deep breath. He knew he was

pushing his luck, but problems had to be dealt with. "There's one thing that would help. A homeless man is talking far too much for his own good."

"I'll take care of it."

With another glare, the horseman disappeared again. The rectory was silent. Father Ianetti sighed and shuffled over to the cabinet to see what he still needed for summoning War.

Chapter Six

Monday morning, Rachel sat at her desk at the police station, going over reports from all the robberies that had been prepared by the robbery unit, while she listened to the tech guy on the phone tell her about the cameras at the gas station. She didn't want to miss anything, but nothing popped out at her.

She hung up the phone and growled.

"That good?" her partner asked.

"There was nothing on the video." She took a sip of her now lukewarm coffee. With the way her day was going, she should have ordered a triple-shot espresso on her way to work.

"It didn't record?"

"It recorded, all right. But it recorded nothing, apparently. It was like nothing was going on. The screen starts off with a view of the entire floor, then when the gang members come in, it's snow."

"Did you check the cameras at our crime scene?" Detective Williams asked.

Rachel shook her head as she picked up her notebook.

"But I did talk to a crime scene tech before we left, and she confirmed there was no tape placed over the lenses and nothing spray painted over them either."

"What about the other gas stations?"

"This is where you're not going to believe me."

Detective Williams leaned back in his chair, closed the folder on his desk, and raised an eyebrow at her. "You're not saying…"

She blew out a pent-up breath. "Yep. All of them were like that."

"At six different gas stations. At the same time?" He shook his head.

"Hard to believe, I know, but there it is."

She called up a document on her computer and perused it before continuing. "I also checked to see if any of the stations were owned by the same person. Or same family. There's no connection."

"We already think it was a coordinated attack but why? To what end?" Williams picked up the half-eaten breakfast sandwich on his desk and took a bite. "So far, there is no connection between the stations. The ones in Scarborough aren't even associated with a local gang. The Esskays run The Annex."

Rachel sighed and pushed away the files. She picked up her coffee again, but before she could take another gulp, Detective Sergeant Reyes marched onto the floor.

"Malak, Williams, you're needed at Harbourfront Beach. A jogger just found the body of Bruno De Luca. Detective Nathan Littman from the gang task force will meet you on scene."

Rachel and Williams bolted out of their chairs. Rachel took a step away from her desk before she turned and yanked her coat from her chair on the way to the elevator, pulling it on over her blazer, further stifling her wings.

"The Grange isn't going to like this," Detective Williams said, pressing the button to call the elevator.

The bell dinged, and the doors slid open. Rachel jabbed the button for the lobby. "Do you think it was a gang hit? I know the Grange and Esskays have been drawing lines in the sand and pushing boundaries, but they haven't been killing each other. That we know of."

"If it was a gang hit, you know the Grange is going to retaliate." Williams's expression hardened.

If they had two gangs running amok in the city trying to kill each other, there could be a lot of civilian casualties. Gangs didn't care who got caught in the crossfire. They only cared about payback and not appearing weak. If it wasn't a gang hit, they would have to prove that theory as early as possible.

The ride to the lakeshore took longer than usual. Mid-morning traffic snarled the streets. Rachel pulled her coat tighter around her body, not liking her newfound ability to experience cold. She didn't relish having to spend hours by the water with the wind blowing cold mist in her face.

As they approached the beach, she spotted Dr. Padma Malani, the Forensic Pathologist who did most of the autopsies in Toronto, and a man she assumed was Detective Littman chatting to one side. Dr. Malani's black hair was pulled back into a bun. The doctor bent over the body during her exam, and her horn-rimmed glasses slid down her nose. She pushed them back up with the back of her wrist. A gust of wind came up, prompting the doctor to pull her long coat tighter.

The man towered over the petite doctor but stayed out of her way. A bulky coat left unzipped flapped in the breeze. Was it a breeze in the winter? He had broad shoulders and large hands that dwarfed the notepad in his palm. He gazed up, spotted them, and waved them over.

A woman with her dog huddled closer to the street, talking to a uniformed constable. The body sprawled face-down on the sand was definitely Bruno De Luca. Even from this distance, she could make out his distinctive tattoos.

"I have a bad feeling about this. I hope there isn't a gang war in the works," Detective Williams said.

Based on her research, one was brewing. Was this the first stage of the supposed apocalypse prophesized by Father Ianetti?

"I thought I was the one with the bad feelings." Rachel smiled.

"Maybe they're rubbing off."

When they arrived at the body, they flashed their badges. A constable held up the crime scene tape that cordoned off an area around the corpse all the way to the water.

They introduced themselves to the gang task force officer. Even though they all worked on the same police force, he worked out of a different division.

"Detective Nathan Littman," he said, extending his hand.

"Good to meet you," Rachel said. "What can you tell us? Is this a gang rivalry gone bad?"

"Too soon to tell. Dr. Malani has ruled it suspicious based on contusions on his face and the fact that he washed up on shore."

Dr. Malani snapped the latex gloves off her hands and stood. "It will be hard to get an exact time of death on him. Based on preliminary findings, I'd say he died at least four days ago. He was beat up severely. Put up a fight himself based on the cuts and bruises on his knuckles."

"The fight didn't do him much good. He still ended up dead. Are we thinking body dump?" Rachel asked.

"It's likely. I'll know more once I've done the autopsy, but it could have been a fight that killed him."

Crime scene unit officers were already bagging anything that might be evidence, including a sample of the water and the sand around the body. Anything useful had probably been washed away by the lake.

"Do they have a new gang leader?" Detective Williams asked.

Detective Littman shrugged. "We haven't heard anything yet."

"They can't function without a leader, though, right?" Rachel asked.

Nathan nodded. "Not for long. They need structure, even if to the rest of us it looks like chaos. No one has come forward to take credit for the murder, either. If it had been a rival gang, they would have bragged about it by now."

"That's a little bit of a relief, then. Are you going to have a press conference stating it likely wasn't gang related?" Rachel asked.

The man frowned. "We can't do a press conference yet. We don't have anything conclusive. A rival gang could still come forward to claim the killing. It might have been a family member of a gang violence victim. We just don't know enough yet."

"What can you tell us about the gang violence in the city lately?" Detective Williams asked.

"It's gone up. Recently. And I'm not just talking about those six robberies. Whether that has anything to do with Bruno's death or not, it's too soon to tell."

Rachel put up a hand to stop him from continuing. "Do you think that's what those robberies were? New leader, new way of doing things? Recruitment, maybe?"

"Anything's possible in this city," Detective Littman said.

Rachel frowned. "I was afraid you'd say that."

Rachel followed Detective Williams up the dilapidated steps of the Grange's headquarters. How they could call it anything but a dump was beyond her. She lifted a foot over a crack in the stone steps and shook her head. If getting into the house didn't kill you, the mold, asbestos, and lead in the paint on the walls probably would.

She rolled her shoulders, itching to take off the blazer she wore. It smothered her wings. As much as she liked doing police work, she couldn't wait to get back to the loft and stretch out her wings for a while. Envy that the others were able to cloak theirs made her wonder if that had been her sin. It had to be one of the sins that got her kicked out of Heaven.

At the top of the steps, Williams rapped heavily on the door. After a few moments, he raised his hand again, but the music blaring from inside suddenly stopped. Scrambling noises, like large rats scurrying to find holes to disappear into, made Rachel smile. Whatever they were attempting to hide didn't matter. The gang task force knew most of what went on, and when they had enough evidence and warrants, the gang would fall. Until then, there was still a murder to solve.

"Police," Detective Williams said. "We have questions about Bruno De Luca. We just want to talk."

After a few seconds of silence, heavy footsteps sounded from inside. The door swung inward with a loud creak, swaying on the hinges as if any more force would yank it away from the frame. If they ever needed to raid the place, it wouldn't be too difficult to get inside.

A blurry-eyed man with dark hair blinked at them. He sported the gang colors on his arm in the form of stripes on his T-shirt. The blue jeans he wore looked to be years old. Faded in the upper thigh and knees. Suspicious white dust lightly coated the top of his shoes.

"I'm Detective Williams and this is Detective Malak. And you are?"

"We aren't doing anything wrong," he said, eyeing them with suspicion. "And you don't need to know my name."

They flashed their badges. She guessed no less than two felonies were going on somewhere in the house, but that wasn't the reason for their visit. At least, not yet.

"We're not here about what the gang has or has not been doing lately," Williams said. "What can you tell us about Bruno De Luca?"

The man shrugged. He leaned against the door in a nonchalant manner he couldn't quite pull off. He crossed and re-crossed his arms over his chest, then finally let them fall to his sides.

Another gang member joined them from the hallway, his gaze traveling up and down Rachel until she wanted a shower. A dark mop of greasy hair covered half his face. He wore the leather jacket given to the higher-ranking gang members. On the shoulder, she noticed the three stripes.

"What's going on, Manny?"

"They're asking about Bruno."

"We ain't seen him in a few days." He grinned at Rachel. "I'd like to see more of you, though." He tugged at the bottom of her blazer.

She swatted his hand away. With no angel power, she

didn't have to remind herself not to smite him, but she tucked that away for later, when she did get her gifts back. "And that doesn't worry you? Mister?"

"No mister. Just Chris. Why the hell should it? He's a grown-ass man. Can do whatever the fuck he wants."

The first gang member—apparently Manny—chuckled.

"Because he's dead." Rachel waited for a reaction. Anything to indicate surprise, sorrow, satisfaction.

Chris shrugged. "We didn't kill him."

Manny gripped the door tighter. "Esskays will pay!"

"What makes you think it was the Esskays? We said he was dead. Not what happened," Williams said.

"You telling us he was in an accident, then?" Chris asked.

"No, he was murdered. It was interesting that you assumed that first, though."

"Then, they'll pay. It had to be them. Lots of people wanted him dead. Who else would have the balls to do it?" Manny nodded.

"You're saying you didn't know he was dead?" Rachel asked.

"How would we?" Chris asked.

Rachel thought back to the gas station robberies. At least one member of the Grange had been at every station. If Bruno had already been dead for at least a day, he couldn't have coordinated the attacks. But if not him, then who?

"You don't have a new leader, then?" Rachel asked.

Sadness flashed across Chris's face so fast, she almost missed it. "How would we have known we needed one?"

"How indeed," Rachel said.

"That all?" Manny asked.

Hoots and hollering erupted from a room at the back

of the house. Without a warrant, they couldn't check the place out, and it didn't appear the gang members would invite them in.

"For now," Detective Williams said. "Unless you let us come in to talk more about where you last saw Bruno."

"Nothing more to say." Chris crossed his arms over his wide chest, Manny following suit.

Rachel pulled out a business card and placed it in the man's hand. "If you think of anything odd, give us a call."

The gang member nodded. "I'll be sure to do that." He went through the motions of putting the card in an upper chest pocket that didn't exist. The card floated to the ground.

Later that night, Rachel sat at their usual table at Baron's with Sarah, Becky, and Leah. She'd been nursing the drink in front of her for an hour. Her plate of fries remained half finished. The gang stuff was getting under her wings, and she didn't like the feeling. If she had to solve the gang leader's murder to earn some of her power back, she didn't like her chances. No one would talk. She'd get more information out of a cat.

The TV flashed the local news. Headlines gave little information about the robberies, but it was enough to pique someone's curiosity. The sound bites never revealed much, either. Viewers had to tune in at eleven for the full story from the sister network.

A waiter popped over to their table to replace Leah's glass with another pop. When he hustled to the next table, she took a sip and sighed.

"The sugar rush is amazing," she said.

Rachel smiled. "You can try something a little stronger."

Leah wrinkled her nose. "Not on a school night. I need to teach these kids important things. Can't do that without a clear head."

Right now, even a little gave Rachel a buzz, so she couldn't argue with Leah for wanting a fuzzy-free head.

She turned to Becky, who was still working on her onion rings. "Have you heard anything about the gang violence in the city?"

"No more than usual. The robberies are still a big story. When is the robbery unit going to hold a press conference?"

"Good question. They're still gathering information. I'm sure they'll make a more formal statement soon."

Becky narrowed her eyes.

"Your news station doesn't have any information about what might be going on in the city?" Rachel pressed.

Becky dipped an onion ring in ranch dressing and took a bite. "Nope. If the gangs are up to something, they're keeping a lower profile than usual."

Low profile. Rachel smiled bitterly. Until they pounced, you didn't see them coming, but if you looked back, the signs were there that they'd been up to no good. She'd studied past reports of the gang activity in the city after first arriving on Earth. Since her jurisdiction crossed paths with a few of the gangs, she wanted to know what she was up against. Sometimes, their actions appeared to make no sense, but there was always a reason for what they did. It usually had to do with money, revenge, or power.

She snagged one of Becky's onion rings and took a bite. Greasy goodness, mingled with the sweet taste of the onion, exploded across her taste buds. Becky shot her a dirty look and pulled her plate closer for protection.

Rachel turned to Sarah. "What about you? Are you seeing a greater number of violent injuries than usual at the hospital?"

Sarah cut off a piece of her steak and dragged it around the plate to pick up the juices. "It's hard to tell. We haven't had any more gunshots than usual. As for other injuries, if the patients don't tell us the truth, we don't know how they acquired them."

"So, there's been nothing odd in the city except for the robberies," Rachel said.

"The school is fine, too," Leah said.

They all turned to look at her.

Tension eased from Rachel's shoulders. "That's good to know. At least they aren't hanging around trying to recruit kids."

"You think they're recruiting?" Becky asked.

"Maybe," Rachel said. "But that is off the record for now."

Becky pouted. "Fine."

"I mean it."

Becky glowered at her. "I said fine."

Rachel took a sip of her drink. "What about the research into the lost books? Did you find anything more about that?"

Over the weekend, they'd followed every crumb they could find on the internet regarding the books. Most accounts talked about them being at the Vatican as Father Ianetti had indicated.

Becky and Leah shook their heads.

"My intern is still looking into it," Becky said.

"You passed it off to your intern?" Rachel shook her head.

"What? She's good at research. She can find just about anything."

Rachel turned her attention to Leah. "No luck for you either?"

"Not much. I found a few possible sites that might help. I was also looking into the tattoos. Nothing definitive on those yet either, but I'll keep looking."

The TV on the wall behind Becky caught Rachel's attention. A picture of Father Ianetti flashed on the screen. A waiter was walking by, and she snagged his arm.

"Can you turn that up, please?"

He fished in his short black apron and handed her a remote. She studied it for a moment to find the volume, then pointed the device at the TV.

"The end is nigh," Father Ianetti said. The reporter standing beside him did her best to hide a smile.

"Can you tell us more about why you think that?" The woman put a microphone under his lips.

"Becky, one of yours?" Rachel asked.

Becky nodded. "I've seen her around the building. She's good."

Sarah took a sip of her drink. "But not as good as you?"

"I have a better intern." Becky picked up another onion ring and popped it into her mouth.

They focused on the TV again.

"I've read the prophecies. I've studied the good book. I've done the calculations. We are at a critical time in human history! And the Earth shall be purged to start anew." Father Ianetti's face turned red, his eyes wild.

The reporter kept a straight face. "Can you tell us when, exactly, this apocalypse will happen?"

"It is already upon us! The end has started. The rapture will take the chosen and leave the sinners in three months' time."

"Thank you for your time, Father." The reporter smiled at the camera and did her sign off.

Rachel rolled her eyes. "Your station needs to stop giving him airtime."

She didn't see any reason to pander to the priest's delusions. And they had to be delusions. Either that or he was trying to get attention for the church and would somehow explain it all away when the apocalypse didn't happen as predicted.

"People are seeing this priest's predictions and they want to know more," Becky said.

"So, people can prepare for the end?" Leah asked.

Rachel smiled sadly at the newest angel. Leah hadn't been there long enough yet to know which priests actually knew The Word and which didn't but put on a good show. Rachel had no doubts about Father Ianetti's deep belief in God and the church, but she didn't for a second think he was one of the chosen who actually spoke to their Father.

"It won't be the end," Sarah said. "We're supposed to stop it, remember?"

"We think we're supposed to stop it," Becky corrected.

"Yes, but why else would we be here? It's not supposed to legitimately happen for centuries. Someone is moving up the timetable, if Father Ianetti is right and it's nigh," Leah said.

"Not just someone. What if it's Father Ianetti?" Rachel took a quick sip of her drink, waiting for one of her sisters to argue with her.

Becky's eyes widened. "You really think it's him?"

Rachel absently stuffed a few fries into her mouth and nodded. "Why else would he be so sure this time that his calculations are correct? I watched previous footage of him talking about the end of the world. He was never this adamant. For the record, this whole thing sucks. How are we supposed to stop the end of the world without our powers?"

"We all have to try harder to figure out how to get those back. You more than the rest of us," Becky said.

"Maybe you should get that star intern on it." Rachel grabbed another of Becky's onion rings.

Chapter Seven

On his way home from work, Caleb paused in front of the gas station at Adelaide and Spadina. The police tape was gone. Lineups for the pumps indicated no one even remembered what had happened there three days ago. Didn't remember or didn't care. Or had no choice.

He pushed himself to move forward. Paralyzing fear didn't help him get home on time. The thought crossed his mind that he should go to the police. Talk to them again about what had happened that day. About what he knew, what he saw.

Would finding the people who did it make the city any better? Any safer? He was safer out here than he was at home.

He shoved his hands in his pockets and kept walking. No one was killed, but something about Victor nagged at him. The robbery was a lesson—he was sure of that. He had seen that same look in his father's eyes that Victor used for the two attackers. But a lesson in what? What purpose was there in beating up the clerk and random customers? It taught fear, not respect.

Guys beating people didn't teach anyone anything. Images of his father's angry face as he rained punches down on him flashed through his head. The bruises on his body tingled as if to remind him what it was like to be beaten on for no reason.

Not that it would make him change his mind about going to the police. Minding his own business kept the bruises to a minimum if his father was in a good mood. And no one else used him as target practice because he kept to himself.

Despite his resolve, he glanced down the street, in the general direction of the police station. It wouldn't take him long to get there, but how long would giving another statement take? He scanned the area around him. Were there members of the gang mingled in the crowd watching him? Making sure he didn't go to the police? No one stood out. He shoved the thought aside and picked up his pace.

Victor made him feel safe that day in the gas station. That there was promise that he wouldn't always be like those clerks and customers. He wouldn't always be someone's punching bag. He wished he knew when that time was.

He pulled out his phone and hit the home button to check the time.

"Shit."

He shoved past ambling pedestrians. Squeezed through a group of university students heading to a bar to celebrate cheap beer night. Or the end of class. Maybe the end of exams? He had no idea. He left school and exams behind when he turned sixteen.

Finally at his building, he took a deep breath before opening the door and tromping into the entryway. His heart beat faster, and his hands, slick with sweat, slid off the handle to the lobby. Legs wobbled on his way to the elevator.

His father liked dinner on the table promptly at six. Fifteen minutes after the hour wasn't a huge amount of time, but for Karl, it was fifteen minutes to stew in anger. Every minute Caleb was late would make the beating worse. He thought about turning around and running. But where would he go? He only had the clothes on his back and the money in his pocket, which wasn't enough for a hot meal. If he left and some day came back, the beating would probably end up killing him.

When the elevator doors opened on his floor, he almost pushed the button to close them again. Almost rode the car back down to the lobby and went anyway. But as bad as the beatings could be, he knew he couldn't survive on the street. After work the day of the gas station robbery, he'd come home to his father passed out on the sofa again. Thankfully, the anger of that morning had gone. Since then, Caleb had been careful not to raise his ire again.

He pulled out his keys from his pocket, cringing at the loud jingling sound they made in the quiet hallway. Scents from meals being prepared teased his nose and made his stomach roil. Whatever his father had intended for dinner would be late. There was nothing Caleb could make that would be ready in ten minutes.

He unlocked the door and pushed it inward. Bright lights illuminated every corner of the small apartment. Nowhere to hide.

Shutting the door behind him, he took a deep breath. Prepared himself for the onslaught of verbal abuse. Mentally readied himself for the physical assault. He didn't tell anyone about the beatings because he knew what they would all say. Fight back. A man, even a young man, shouldn't put up with that shit, especially from a parent. But they hadn't met his father.

Where he was tall, lanky, scrawny, his father was taller, all muscle. Caleb had watched him once pick up a car to prove he could. The lift lasted only a few seconds, but that was all Caleb needed to know his father could squash him like a bug if he wanted.

"Boy!"

Caleb cringed at the word. No matter how old he was, his father would always call him *boy*. Always make him feel less than everyone else.

"Sorry I'm late. Rick started his shift late, and I had to cover until he got there."

It was hit and miss whether the excuse would work or not. It depended on how long his father had been drinking. How hungry he was. How long he'd been stewing even before dinner was ready because he expected his son to disappoint him.

"That's Rick's problem." His father stood in the kitchen, hands clenched at his sides. "Your job is to get home on time to make dinner."

Before Caleb could dash to his bedroom, his father crossed the floor and pushed him against the door.

"I'm sorry."

A large fist landed on Caleb's upper arm. "Not good enough."

Caleb put up his hands to ward off blows to his face, though his father was usually careful about where he left marks. That left his midsection vulnerable. His father punched him repeatedly in the stomach. Finally out of breath, his father paused.

Caleb inched away from the door, toward the living room. Closer to his bedroom. If he could get in there, shut the door, wait it out until his father drank enough to pass out, he might get away with only a little damage.

The booze on his father's breath choked Caleb. He coughed. His eyes watered.

Before he got any closer to safety, his father punched him in the ribs. Sharp pain raced through him. Aggravating already bruised bones. He tried to pull in a breath, but it hurt. He clutched his side. His ribs were probably broken. How much more damage would his father do before exhaustion overcame him?

With his face unprotected, his father landed a few blows to his cheek. Caleb's head spun. Spots danced in front of his eyes. His eye stung when blood dripped into it.

He crouched down, making himself as small as possible. His father, breathing heavily, staggered. Caleb stood, shoulder angled to hit his father's chest, and pushed as hard as he could. His father stumbled, then fell against the sofa. He'd pay for that later if his father remembered, but he didn't care. All he could focus on was escape.

Caleb grabbed his father's wallet from the coffee table and raced out of the apartment.

Caleb stumbled out of the building, not sure which way to go. His friends, what few he had, were all busy. Most were still working. The police station wasn't far. He could walk there, despite his injuries. They might be able to do something about his father. But that's not what the gang would do. He wasn't an idiot. He knew Victor was part of the Grange. Anyone living in the area for more than a few months knew the colors of the Grange.

He wanted to be strong. Be feared. He couldn't do that

if he went and tattled to the police. The gang would take care of it themselves.

He shuffled down the sidewalk, looking over his shoulder to see if his father decided to follow him this time. One of these days, he was sure his father would burst through the lobby doors, chase after him.

Outside a pub, he spotted Tony counting a large wad of bills. Rumored to be the Grange's enforcer, the guy towered over the other members of the gang who followed him. Talk of the protection money most of the area businesses paid to the gang were true.

He followed the gang members at a distance. They walked along the sidewalk, most pedestrians giving them a wide berth. The ones who didn't weren't paying attention, too busy on their smartphones to see who was walking toward them. For their trouble, they were shoved out of the way.

One of the men stumbled off the curb from the strength of Tony's shove, and a car screeched to a halt.

The hair on the back of Caleb's neck rose the longer he followed them. Trailing them away from the crowds and the overpowering night lights of the main streets brought him to a street with old, dilapidated houses. Streetlights flickered in spots. Some patches of the street were shrouded in darkness where the lights were blown out.

Counting the shadows in front of him, he stopped when he realized there were two missing. Tony was still there. He was unmistakable. But a couple of the other members were gone. Had they run ahead?

A strong hand clasped the back of his neck. Though he couldn't see the guy, he knew he was taller than him. The grip tightened.

"Caught him!" the voice yelled.

The gang members in front of him turned. They stalked over, glaring at him in the flickering light.

"I say we make an example of him," the voice behind him said.

Tony grinned.

Please don't let me wet myself.

Though his legs shook, his stomach clenched, he looked Tony straight in the eye. Show weakness and they wouldn't let him join them. They were his only hope of getting away from his father.

"Would love to, gentlemen, but you heard what Victor said. For some reason, this pipsqueak is off-limits. We can't touch him." Tony leveled him with a hard stare. "Yet."

Another gang member at his side grabbed his arm. He grimaced as shooting pain raced through his body. The two of them hustled him forward until they were at a rundown old house.

The lighting inside wasn't much better than outside. At least, not in the entryway of the crumbling house. A glow of light from the back of the house was accompanied by hoots and hollers of triumph after video game sounds of a character dying. From the glow, Victor emerged. He stood in the doorway, the light surrounding him like a halo. And he was Caleb's savior, if he agreed to let him in the gang.

The gang members at his back and side shoved him forward.

"Found him outside sneaking around," the guy still holding his neck said.

The noise from the room stopped. The clunk of game controllers on wooden tables replaced the video game soundtrack. Gang members crowded around Victor, blocking out the light.

Victor snapped his fingers, and the room Caleb was in flooded with light. A few of the gang members jumped as if they weren't expecting that outcome. Others looked at Victor for guidance. The ones holding Caleb gasped so softly; he was sure he was the only one who had heard their surprise.

A parlor trick. That's all it was. It was easy to wire the house so lights turned on at a command or noise.

"What are you doing here?" Victor walked forward.

Caleb took a deep breath, then blew it out. "I want to join you."

Uproarious laughter erupted all around him. The gang members holding him let go. The members beside Victor clutched their sides, doubling over in hysterics.

Victor put up a hand, and the house fell silent again except for the barely discernible hum of electricity that ran through the building. Caleb wanted that power. To be feared, respected like that. Victor stood directly in front of him now. Towering over him like his father. But there was something about the man in front of him that didn't illicit fear. Tony had said Victor didn't want him harmed. Caleb had no idea why, but he was glad the gang leader saw something in him.

"You can't just decide to join and have that be it. Boom, you're a member."

Sadness crawled through him. It hadn't occurred to him that Victor would reject him. The gang was his only hope.

"I'd be a good addition to the group." He hated the desperation in his voice, but he was desperate.

"You have to be worthy. There's an initiation. The next step is killing someone. Your first step was loyalty, and so far, you've proven that by not going to the cops about the robbery."

Caleb straightened slightly as hope renewed. "How did you know I didn't tell the cops anything?"

"Please. I run this city. No matter what the Esskays think, the Grange controls everything. We've been watching. Listening."

Killing someone wasn't the task he expected, though he should have. Gangs were notorious for crimes he wouldn't normally consider. But the Grange was different now. He didn't know how, or why, but Victor ran the gang with a purpose.

"I can kill my father." His fingers tingled. His stomach fluttered. Would his father be shocked? He needed to see the look on his father's face when the life ebbed out of his body.

Victor looked him up and down, his gaze stopping at every bruise. A vague hint of pity crossed his face. "Too easy. I'll pick the right target for you."

Chapter Eight

The next day, Rachel sat at her desk at the police station, scanning through her notes from the interview with the gang members. If you could call it that. Not surprisingly, they'd been unhelpful on the surface, but what they *didn't* say told her a lot. She needed to figure out who the new leader was, and she didn't think she had to look much farther than the guy at the gas station.

"Hey, you remember the guy at the gas station wearing the leather jacket with the colors?" she asked Detective Williams.

"Yes. Seemed to be hovering around a young man at the back of the station."

"Did he seem odd to you?"

She didn't want to tell Williams her theory yet. That the guy was the Grange's new leader, because she hadn't been able to see all the stripes. The new gang leader could be anywhere, and they didn't know for sure if Bruno had been dead at the time of the robberies or not. They wouldn't know that until the autopsy results came back.

She shifted in her chair to rub her wings against an

itchy spot on her back. She sighed. When she first arrived, she thought being exiled had been the worst thing to happen to her. But no, her missing abilities was the greater handicap. Without them, she couldn't even blend in properly unless she wore these cumbersome blazers. She hated the way they felt.

For some reason, it was also unusually warm most days for the time of year. The station had automatic timed furnaces, programmed to turn on in early November. Heat blasted from the ceiling vents even though it was still T-shirt weather outside. It felt like she was somewhere in the tropics, not Toronto.

"Aren't you hot in that thing?" Williams loosened his tie and undid his top button.

She picked up the bottle of water on her desk and chugged it. "I'm fine."

"Whatever you say. It's okay to be a little more casual in here, though, you know. You don't have to wear that all the time."

"I like it," she lied.

The ringing of his phone distracted him. She wanted to get another look at the surveillance video even though most of the information had been magically wiped out. Was it magically? She would think on that more later. She wanted to watch the relationship between everyone in the station before the video went wonky.

Williams hung up his phone. "My informant says we can find the Esskays' headquarters at a house in The Annex. I have the address."

"What are we waiting for? Let's go." She sprang out of her chair.

Williams smiled. "You're eager."

"I want to close this case. There's lots of crime in the

city, and we need to focus on the people who need us the most."

On the way out of the police station, she stopped at the vending machine in the lobby and bought two more bottles of water to take with her. It was always good to be hydrated.

A blast of cooler air hit her when she exited the building. The sun was shining brightly in the sky, warming her face. She breathed a sigh of relief. This kind of weather, she could handle.

It was a short walk around the building to the parking lot. She waited at Williams's car, then yanked open the door as soon as he unlocked it. She climbed into the passenger seat. The console in the middle still held the morning's empty coffee cups.

"Really, Williams? Don't you clean this car out?"

He shrugged. "When you start cleaning yours, I'll start cleaning mine." He closed the top button of his shirt and tightened his tie.

She grabbed the cups and marched over to the garbage bin near the entrance of the lot, right before the sidewalk. Back at the car, she deposited the bottles of water and settled into the passenger seat.

Once Detective Williams started the car and put it in drive, she pulled out her smartphone. She swiped to unlock the screen and went to her email. Just because she'd been exiled didn't mean He would ignore her prayers for a quick autopsy. She scrolled through the messages, frowning when she got to the end.

Detective Williams took a right onto a side street. "What's wrong?"

"Still nothing from Dr. Malani."

"And here I thought it was the end of the world by the look on your face." He smiled.

The thought had occurred to her that the gang leader's death had something to do with this supposed apocalypse, but there was nothing concrete yet. And she couldn't bring it up to Williams. He would tease her like there was no tomorrow.

They arrived at The Annex. Williams parked a few houses away from the gang's headquarters. This spot was in a rundown neighborhood with homes that were at least seventy years old. Back in the day, it might have been nice, but time and gang activity had left it degraded and broken. How many of the houses were actually occupied? It would be difficult to sell once the gang moved in.

They jogged across the street and marched up a chipped stone walkway. Some stones were broken in two, others ground into dust with an outline of where they used to be. The Esskays weren't too worried about curb appeal.

Williams knocked on the door. At this place, there was no loud music from inside. She glanced up at the power lines around the house. Not surprisingly, the Esskays were tapping into their neighbor's electricity. She craned her neck up to look at the second-floor windows, then checked the bottom windows. Nothing covered them except thread-bare curtains.

Loud footsteps rang from inside. A tall man with a sleeve of tattoos on both muscled arms opened the door. Where Manny had been annoyed, this man looked amused at their appearance at his door.

"Something I can do for you fine officers?"

Rachel looked at Williams. "We look like police? And we were trying so hard not to."

"We're here about Bruno De Luca." Williams flashed his badge. Rachel followed suit.

"Why would you come here asking about him? The

Grange doesn't come past Spadina, if they know what's good for them."

He puffed out his chest and stood straighter. Rachel noted the Chevrons on his wrist. Detective Littman said six of the markings meant gang leader.

"What does that mean, exactly?" Rachel asked.

She pulled out her notebook, pen poised to capture anything he said that was of any value.

"It means whoever sticks their nose in our territory can kiss all parts of their body goodbye. I'm sure you get my meaning."

It was possible Bruno had ventured past the border between the two gangs. But he wouldn't have done it on purpose.

"And you would expect the same if you crossed over into their turf?" Rachel asked.

"Damn straight."

"What if you need to talk to each other or something? Coordinate business, divvy up new business?" Williams asked.

"We'd meet up then. Either here or there."

Rachel held up a hand. "Wait. I'm confused. You said you couldn't go into each other's territory."

A slight flutter sloshed in her stomach and spread to her wings. Something was different. She didn't dare hope, so she ignored it for the moment.

"We can if there's been something set up in advance. You know what? That's all I'm saying. You got no reason to be here harassing us."

"We do have a reason," Williams said. "Bruno is dead."

"And you think that fool came into our territory and one of my boys popped him?"

"Did they?" Rachel asked.

"Hell no."

"Of course you would say that," Detective Williams said.

"Well, yeah, in this case, it's the truth. If it was us, you'd know. We're not cowards who'd hide it. But you'd never be able to pin it on any of us."

Rachel flipped the page in her notebook. As much as she hated to admit it, she didn't think the rival gang was responsible. Littman would have heard something during their surveillance of the gangs. It was unlikely that an informant would come forward pointing the finger at anyone in the gang, but stranger things had happened.

The niggling feeling in the back of her mind that everything so far with the gangs pointed to the apocalypse wouldn't leave her alone. When she got back to the loft, she would have more research to do. They were getting closer to finding out about the lost books and summoning an apocalypse. Hopefully, Becky's intern had been able to fill in some gaps of knowledge.

"Fine. If you find out anything or decide to confess, let us know." Rachel handed over a business card.

She and Williams walked back to the car.

"That went well," Williams said, yanking open his door.

"It's not like we thought he would cooperate, but I don't think his gang is responsible."

Williams raised an eyebrow, and they got into the vehicle. "Another feeling?"

"Maybe. I think something else is going on, and it's not good."

He threw the car into drive, and it surged away from the curb. "It's almost time for lunch. Your pick this time."

She rattled off a diner that was usually empty this time of day. Her wings brushed against the seat of the car, reminding her of the flutter that passed over them earlier. When they arrived, she opened the door and practically flew out of the car.

"Hungry?" Williams asked.

"Can you order me the usual? I need to hit the ladies' room."

He hid a smile as she raced into the diner. She held the door for him and tapped her foot impatiently. When he grabbed it, she beelined for the back.

In the bathroom, she checked the stalls to make sure she was alone. She pulled out her phone. With a deep breath, she shrugged out of her blazer. She swiped the phone, put it in selfie mode, and turned around to look at her wings in the mirror. Nestled in the dark limbs near her left shoulder, a small patch of white gave her hope.

She kept her eye on the source of her power and cloaked her wings. The patch got smaller, but it was still there.

With her blazer folded over her arm, she left the bathroom.

Rachel popped the last fry in her mouth, chewing contemplatively. Now that she was full and her wings were cloaked, she had a second wind. She crumpled up the empty burger wrapper and dropped that and the fry container into the plastic bag their lunch had come in.

She went over everything in her mind for the hundredth time since gaining the spot of power. What had she said or done to be rewarded? How could she duplicate it if she didn't know why power had been returned to her? After so long of nothing working, why now?

Williams crumpled his wrapper and tossed it over his

shoulder into the back seat, pulling her mind away from her musings. The wrapper bounced off her blazer, then rolled to the floor.

"Hey, watch it. I don't want it stained."

"Sorry, not used to it being back there. I don't remember ever seeing you without it. Are you really you? Were you replaced by an alien pod while you were in the bathroom?"

Rachel laughed. "Don't be ridiculous. Aliens aren't real."

She turned to face her partner directly. They needed to make progress on both investigations. Right now, Bruno's murder was going nowhere.

"I think we should switch gears for a little while and do more investigating into the robberies. I know it's not our job, but the robbery unit is swamped. I'm sure they'd appreciate the help. Plus, I think learning more about that case might help with the De Luca homicide."

Williams took a sip of his drink. "You really think they're connected? The robberies and Bruno's death."

"Don't you? It's too much of a coincidence that they happened so close together. The robberies could have only been sanctioned by a new leader."

"I think you're right."

"Then we should focus on those right now. We don't have any reports back from the coroner on Bruno, so we might as well work on the case that has more evidence. Though, not by much."

"True. At least those have witnesses," he noted.

That was another thing that bothered her. The witnesses. Since arriving on Earth, she'd watched the gang activity with a morbid fascination. Haphazardly organized, they managed to run a lot of drugs and weapons through the city. Their hands were in many pockets. But they rarely left witnesses when one of them blatantly committed a crime. Video cameras were smashed, victims silenced before police could get there. Yet, this time, with six robberies across the city, no one died.

"I think we should start with the kid at our scene." She flipped through her notes. "Caleb."

He put the car into drive. "You think he knows more than he's telling?"

Rachel nodded. "He saw something. Knows something. I hope we can get through to him."

She put in two quick calls. One to the robbery unit and another to her boss. Grudgingly, both agreed to let her and Williams conduct more interviews.

"We need to give Detective Vargas copies of all our notes when we're back."

They pulled up in front of Caleb's apartment. Though old, it wasn't run-down. The bricks needed a good power cleaning to get the grime of the city off. The windows hadn't seen a cleaning product in ages from the look of the dirt on them. The lobby had a desk for a guard, but no one sat there to greet visitors.

She pushed the button for Caleb's apartment.

"What do you want?"

The slurred words, harshly muttered at the intercom, made her feel bad for Caleb. The voice was too old, too gravelly to be his. It must be the young man's father.

"Police. Detectives Williams and Malak. We wanted to speak with Caleb if that's possible," Rachel said.

"Turn around and show your badges." The drunken words were followed by a hacking cough.

They turned to the camera positioned above the locked lobby door and flashed their badges.

"May we see Caleb?" Williams asked.

"Why do you want to see him? What did he do?"

Where Rachel would expect fatherly concern, the question was laced with disappointment. She shrugged at Williams.

"He didn't do anything wrong, Mr. Bishop. He might have been a witness to a crime, and we need some information from him," Williams said.

She waited for the buzz of the door, but nothing happened. The connection with the apartment was still live. She could hear the man grumbling under his breath.

"He's not here. He won't be able to help, anyway. Good for nothing asshole. You'd think at twenty, he'd have a better job. Help out his old man more."

"Do you know where he is?" Rachel asked.

"Of course I fucking know where he is. What are you saying? I'm a bad father?"

"That's definitely not what I meant." Rachel took a deep breath. She hated dealing with angry drunks. Why wasn't he working midday? "I just wanted to know where we could find him."

After a heavy sigh and a long pause, he said, "At work."

"Thank you. Sorry to bother you, Mr. Bishop," Williams said.

Rachel held the entryway door for Williams. "I've got his workplace in my notes."

The man was obviously angry about something, and she suspected he took it out on Caleb. Often. Her heart broke for the young man. Without knowing why his father was so hostile, she couldn't do much to fix that. The best she could do was offer to listen, offer to help him find somewhere else to live. If he wanted help.

Back in the car, she buckled her seat belt. Williams put the car into drive and pulled away from the curb. She retrieved her notebook from her pocket and flipped to the day of the robbery. She scanned her scrawl until she found the information she wanted. She rattled off the address of the warehouse where Caleb worked.

"Why don't you drop me off at his work and you can go to the hospital. We'll get things done faster if we divide and conquer."

He gave her a side glance as he maneuvered through traffic. "Your sister works at the hospital. Wouldn't it be better for you to go there?"

She closed her notebook and shoved it back in her pocket. "She does. But that's exactly why you should go."

He laughed. "I don't get your logic."

"We don't want anyone to think she's giving me more information because we're sisters, do we? I think she'd be more willing to talk to you, anyway."

"Okay. I get the sibling rivalry thing. My brother was always one-upping me through high school. Thank God we went into different professions."

Rachel smiled. "Great. I can take a subway back to the station when I'm done, and we can compare notes."

Rachel waited in the break room of Caleb's work for the floor foreman to get him. She paced behind the table, unfurling her wings wide, moving them around now that they were cloaked. With a sigh, she sat in a chair facing the door. Would he come into the room or take off? He wasn't a suspect; he had no reason to run, but that didn't stop people. The police scared a lot of people, made them nervous. She wished they would understand police were still like everyone else. Regular Joes or Jills doing their job. Their job was just law enforcement.

She had thought only of the good she could do in this job, not about the inherent problems with the bad apples in the department. Since she'd been here, the bad apples had come out to play a lot. Rachel still couldn't figure out how to fix what was wrong with law enforcement. And there was so much wrong with it. It was a problem that could be all-consuming on the best of days, but she had other more pressing problems. She had to focus on the gas station attacks and stopping the apocalypse. Fixing the police department would have to wait.

A few minutes after requesting to see Caleb, he pushed through the door. The smile on his face died when he saw her. He walked into the room and sat in the chair on the opposite side of the table with a wince.

The welts from the morning of the robbery had turned to bruises that covered the left side of his face. Those marks had started to heal, but fresh, angry, purple ones covered those. A cut above his eye should have had stitches.

He held his side as he leaned back in the chair. Not happy with that, he sat on the edge of the chair, wincing again. No position would be comfortable to him. She suspected cracked ribs, if not broken ones. She doubted any of his injuries happened on the job.

"You're the detective from the robbery. I told you everything I knew then."

"I know, but I thought after a few days, you might remember something else. Even the tiniest detail might be able to help us."

He shifted in his chair and winced again. Sweat popped out on his forehead. What little color his face had drained. She didn't know what he did at the warehouse, but if it involved lifting anything, every day would be agony until his ribs healed.

"I don't. Can I go now?" He tapped his foot.

She sighed. He was holding back. Hiding something.

Protecting someone. He wasn't a gang member, but the neighborhood clammed up for fear of gang retribution.

"Look, I can't even pretend to know what you're going through. Those bruises look painful. I want to help. I really do."

Sadness crept into his eyes. "But you'll only help if I tell you something?"

She put her notebook away. "No. That's not how I work. Regardless of what you can tell me, I want to help you. I don't know what it's like living with someone like your father. You don't have to keep doing that."

A tingle in her wings made her pause. The feeling spread outward. This time, she didn't need a mirror to check her wings. In front of her, a pale glow surrounded Caleb. And a low, pleasing hum reached her ears. A sound she was sure only she could hear.

He sucked in a breath and winced.

Before she'd known for sure, she'd suspected Caleb had a soul. Now it was more important than ever to get through to him.

She touched his hand long enough to see the new power from her wings flow into him. The light was so imperceptible, a human wouldn't see the exchange.

He suddenly sat up straighter—took a deep breath and let it out. His face didn't contort in pain; he didn't wince. She smiled. The aura around him was gone now. Not gone, but she couldn't see it anymore. Couldn't hear the sound of his soul anymore either. It was worth sacrificing her newly gained power to heal him. She understood why Sarah was so frustrated at the hospital every day now.

Caleb snatched his hand back and stood so fast, he knocked his chair over. The few people in the break room who had been doing their best to mind their own business looked over at them.

Caleb grabbed the chair to right it. "You don't know anything about me, lady. My life is fine." He pointed to the bruises on his face. "These are from a fight I was in. I won, too." He grinned. "You should see the other guy."

She nodded. "My mistake."

"Ya, your mistake. I don't know anything more than what I told you at the gas station. Stop hounding me."

She wished she'd kept a little more of her power. She suspected the hum of his soul had faltered. That the light of his soul was a little dimmer. Sometimes, free will sucked. But the rules were clear. Angels could give the choices, offer the right thing, whisper in a human's ear what their options were, but humans were always free to choose what they wanted.

"I can't promise that, Caleb. This is an open investigation and you are a witness."

"I didn't witness anything." He stood straighter and took another breath. A deep one. "Even if I did, what makes you think I'd tell you?"

"I would hope you would do the right thing."

She watched as conflicting emotions crossed his face. Regret, fear, annoyance. After the robbery, she'd checked out everyone present. The victims had no criminal records. The guy standing with Caleb didn't have anything listed either. And Caleb had a few shoplifting charges from years ago, but that was it. He'd kept his nose clean since then. There wasn't even a sealed juvenile record for him.

"The right thing for me is what I'm doing. I didn't see nothing."

Rachel stood abruptly. A fleeting cringe crossed Caleb's face. The man had been beaten up too many times. She wanted to put a stop to that. Despite what he said, she knew his father used him as a punching bag. When she'd been alive the first time, over a thousand years ago, she'd witnessed beatings. She'd been lucky to have avoided them, especially back then, when it was a husband's right to do what he wanted with his property.

"I hear what you're saying, and for now, I'll go." She pushed the chair back into the table. "You still have my card. Please call me if you remember anything. Or if you just want to talk. We don't have to talk about the robbery. It can be anything."

She looked at his bruises again. It was too bad she didn't have enough angel power to heal those. The ribs would have to do. At least he could continue his shift without that pain.

"Whatever." He stormed away from the table.

She watched him leave the break room, then followed him out. He had her information, again, but she couldn't force him to ask for help. She just hoped he did before it was too late.

Chapter Nine

"You don't know what you did to get some of your power back?" Becky asked.

They were in the loft after work, choosing, for a change, to eat in and discuss the research everyone had been doing. Becky and Sarah were at the stove while Leah sat on a stool at the island, overseeing their progress.

Becky stirred a pot of pasta. "At least you don't have to wear that blazer anymore," she said over her shoulder. Beside her, Sarah added cream to a bubbling pot of tomato sauce.

Rachel sighed heavily, tapping her fingers on the island. "I want to know *why* I earned some power back."

"After dinner, give me all the details and I'll create a spreadsheet to help analyze the data so we can all figure out how to get our power back."

"Thanks. I will."

"What are you making today?" Leah asked.

"Becky's intern found this recipe for rigatoni in a blush sauce that sounded really good."

"Do you get her to research anything else for you besides what recipes you want Sarah to try?" Rachel asked.

Becky spun around and frowned. "Yes. She's helping me with the background for a story I'm working on right now. And research about the horsemen."

"What excuse did you give for that?" Rachel asked.

Becky went back to stirring the pasta. "I told her I was doing a follow-up on Father Ianetti's assertion that the end of the world is coming."

"You think the increased violence, especially the gang violence, has to do with the prophecy?" Sarah asked.

Becky nodded.

"I think it does," Rachel said.

Leah jumped off her stool and went to the fridge. "Didn't the city have a gang problem before we got here?"

Leah pulled bottles of water out of the fridge, plunked them onto the island, and settled in her seat again.

Rachel opened one and took a sip. They didn't keep a lot of alcohol at the loft, so evenings in meant teetotaling. If they were going to be here a while, maybe they should stock up a little better. But they needed clear heads.

"They've been getting more and more out of control lately. Violence, in general, all over the city is on the rise."

"If the apocalypse is ramping up—and judging by the weather anomalies I've been studying it is—there has to be at least one horseman here," Becky said.

"At least one, yes. When it's time for a full-fledged apocalypse, the horsemen need to be present, but I don't think all of them are here yet. Things would be much worse. Which means we have a chance of dialing it back." Rachel walked over to the stove to dip a spoon into the sauce Sarah was now stirring.

Sarah slapped her hand away. "Not all, I agree. With the threat of a gang war, do you think War is here?"

When Becky sat at the kitchen island and Sarah turned her attention to the pasta, Rachel got her taste of the sauce. "That's good." She put the spoon down. "Who else could it be?"

Leah shook her head. "I don't think it's War. The first horseman is Conquest. White horse, bow, crown. Went forth conquering."

Rachel took a seat at the kitchen island again, her mind whirling with the events of the past few days. "Yes! It makes so much sense now."

Sarah frowned. "How does that make sense? Conquest and gang war."

"He's conquering the neighborhood. Building a little army for when the rest of his brothers get here. Collecting souls. The more people on his side of lawlessness, evil, and disinterested in what's right, the better the chances that the horsemen will win."

"Okay, that makes sense. We have no idea who it is, though. It could be anyone," Becky said.

"I have a hunch on who it might be," Rachel said.

All eyes turned toward her. "Who?" Leah asked.

"The guy from the gas station robbery. And we have to assume he has all of his power." Rachel took a sip of water to squelch the burning anger in her throat.

"Yes, because why would it be an even match for us?" Sarah asked.

Rachel put a hand to Sarah's head. "No fever."

Sarah swatted the hand away. "I still believe in His plan, but it would have been nice to have things even down here."

Becky's eyes lit up. "I found out something else! I looked into the Omega tattoo."

Rachel raised an eyebrow. "You looked into it?"

Becky shrugged. "Okay, Laura looked into it. Anyway,

she found reference to some sort of doomsday cult dating back to sixth century Europe."

"That's good information. We'll have to keep looking into that. What progress have we made with finding the lost books of the Bible?" Rachel asked. "If the priest was telling the truth and he actually read them, we'll need them to figure out how we can stop the end of the world."

Leah jumped up from the island and hurried to the living room area. She pulled out her laptop from her computer bag and brought it back to the counter. "I found more crumbs, but I'm getting close. I'll keep at it after dinner."

Rachel pushed away her plate before giving in to the temptation of a third helping. She didn't remember food tasting this good the last time she'd been on Earth. A lot could change in over a thousand years.

"Delicious again, Sarah," Becky said.

"I don't think Rachel liked it at all." Leah grinned.

One more small portion wouldn't hurt her. Rachel reached for her plate, but Sarah grabbed it off the table. "You need to be able to chase the bad guys."

A buzzing in her pocket drew Rachel's attention. She fished in and pulled out her phone.

"Detective Malak," she said.

A voice on the other end sighed. "Thank you for picking up, Detective. This is Constable West from 52 Division. We were called to a scene a few minutes ago. A woman was thrown from a car in the middle of University Avenue."

"That's horrible for her, but why are you calling me? I work homicide."

"I realize this isn't your usual case, but the EMT found your business card with her. She said you helped her once."

Rachel's stomach tightened—the pasta suddenly a stone in her gut. While she'd given her card to a number of people since arriving on Earth, there was only one person she thought might be the victim of such a crime.

He rattled off the address, and she scribbled it on a card. "I'll be right there."

She hit the end button and stuffed her phone back into her pocket.

"Who was that?" Becky asked.

"Duty calls. I think that working girl I saved last Thursday is in trouble again."

Leah jumped off her stool. "I remember that! Well, not really remember like I was there, but the image of it flashed in my head."

"That can happen. I remember you there now, too, even though you weren't. The prostitute will remember you, too. The memories the magic plants feel real enough, but it feels odd sometimes," Sarah said.

"Do you want us to go with you?" Becky asked.

"No, it shouldn't take long. I don't think there's much of a story there for you, Becky."

Becky glared at her. "I'm not always after a story. I do care, you know."

"Sure, you do. And it wouldn't hurt to have a breaking story either, would it?"

She hardly thought a prostitute being dumped by a john was a breaking story, but sometimes, Becky's choice of career pushed all of Rachel's buttons.

And, she had to admit, it annoyed the hell out of her that Becky got back some power before her, for the silliest of reasons. Cats were cute and all, but to be slightly redeemed for saving one didn't make sense with all the people Rachel had helped since they'd arrived. More frustrating was the fact she'd earned some power back and had no idea how. What had she done that deemed her worthy, cat saving worthy, of an angelic power gain?

She didn't wait for Becky's comeback. She grabbed her purse and her gun and left the loft.

It took twenty minutes to get to the scene with the evening traffic. She could have walked there in the same amount of time. She parked her car across the street and behind a police car that had cordoned off part of the road. When she reached the officer on scene, she flashed her badge.

"Victim is over there," he said with disdain.

"She's like any other victim, Constable, have some respect."

One of the EMTs broke away from the scene and approached her. In his mid-thirties, with brown hair, cut short, his face dripped concern. His cheeks were flushed from the evening chill. A large coat hung on a muscular frame. He was easily over six feet tall and from the look of him, worked out. Often.

"Detective Malak?" he asked.

"Yes, are you the person who found my card?"

He extended his hand. "Jason Hickey. She's pretty shaken up. We're treating her injuries and will be taking her to the hospital as soon as you talk with her."

Rachel surveyed the crowd as she walked to the EMT bus. A few ladies of the night huddled together, watching the scene unfold. Most of the rest of the bystanders were businessmen and women, or university students out for the evening. Off to the far left of the scene, almost at the next intersection, a few familiar gang members milled about.

At the ambulance, she smiled at the woman. "Hi, remember me?"

The woman nodded. "Sorry I took off like that without saying thanks."

"No need to apologize. I never got your name."

"Darla."

"Can you tell me what happened here? Was it the same guy who I helped you with in the alley?"

Darla looked around, her eyes darting to every face in the growing crowd. An EMT dabbed at a cut over the woman's eye, and she swatted it away. Another attempted to bandage the woman's wrist. "No, ma'am. Different guy. I haven't seen Tony in my area since that night." A shudder racked the woman's slight frame.

"Was it for the same reason? I'm not here to judge what you do or arrest anyone. I just want to find the person who did this to you and put them in jail."

The woman nodded. "Says I owe extra for protection 'cause of last week. Collecting his pound of flesh, he said."

Fear crept into the woman's face. Her eyes widened, and the color drained from her face. In her lap, her hands trembled, and she gripped them so tight, her fingers turned white.

"Can you describe him to me?"

The woman shook her head so hard, Rachel thought she would hear a snap. "If he knew I told you, I would get a lot worse than what he did."

Rachel looked the woman over, her stomach knotting in anger as she cataloged the injuries. Besides the cut above the woman's eye, her lip was split, and welts on her face promised to blossom into bruises. Jagged scrapes ran down the woman's legs, most prominent in her knees. Possibly from being thrown out of the car.

Rachel wanted to teach the perpetrator a lesson. Use him as a punching bag to give him some of his own medicine. But if Darla wouldn't even give a description, it made it hard to look for anyone. She had no doubts it was the gang again. The man who had attacked her before wore the Grange's colors and she recognized him as Tony, their enforcer.

"Okay, that's fine for now." Rachel reached into the ambulance and pulled out a wet wipe. She then tugged the bloodied, crumpled business card from Darla's hand. Rachel smoothed it out, wiping the blood off it as best as she could. "This is just in case you remember anything or want to tell me something you might have forgotten."

The woman glanced around, then clasped Rachel's hand, moving the card to her own palm before anyone else noticed.

Rachel backed away and let the EMTs continue their care of the woman. There were a lot of bystanders she could talk to, but the only ones who might actually know something were the prostitutes congregating right across the street. She doubted they would be any more forthcoming than Darla, though. If this was meant as a message to teach them a lesson, they would keep their mouths shut.

Rachel walked back over to the constable who had called her.

"She wasn't only thrown from the car, was she?"

He shook his head. "You saw her face. The EMTs say it looks like she was beaten pretty badly. They're also going to do a rape kit at the hospital."

The anger festering in her stomach grew. Would it have been better for the woman if she hadn't helped in the alley? No, what would have made things better was if she'd taken the guy into the station and arrested his ass. But would this have still happened? She'd said it wasn't the same guy. If the gang was using another enforcer, she didn't know who it was. Maybe the gang task force could tell her about any new players.

Despite her workload, she did not want to let this woman down. If she had to work the case in her off hours, she would. The sex workers in the city deserved to be protected as much as any other resident. In some cases, they were more vulnerable. She doubted Darla would have called her or reported the incident. The only reason it was a police matter now was because Rachel had given her a business card after the first incident. Without that connection, the police might have been too overworked to properly investigate the crime, let the woman go to the hospital to be checked out, and washed their hands of the whole thing.

"Thanks. Did she say anything to you about who did this?"

He shrugged. "I assumed it was a disgruntled john."

"I hope you don't ever want to make it to detective, Constable."

"Why?"

"You never assume anything. She's a person. Give her a little respect."

With the constable still trying to come up with a retort to her parting shot, Rachel stalked over to the prostitutes huddled together on the opposite sidewalk. If she'd been his guardian angel, she would have whispered more about sympathy and not judging people by their circumstances. Maybe he was one of the soulless.

As she approached the group of women, she pulled her coat aside to show her badge clipped to the belt loop of her slacks. Not that they didn't know exactly what she did, but it was a habit any time she wanted to talk to a witness or suspect.

"Ladies, did any of you see anything tonight that might help us catch the person who did that to Darla?"

The closer she got to the group, the more her stomach tightened. Standing underneath a streetlight, the soft yellow glow made their bruises look darker, the streaks of their tears deeper. Under this light, it was easy to see the fingerprints ringing a wrist or a throat. She suspected if a full exam was performed on any of them, they would all be riddled with bruises in varying degrees of healing.

Every woman shook her head.

"She was thrown out of the car. That's all we saw." The woman speaking stood a little taller than the rest. She was a bit older than the other girls and stepped out in front of them, like a protective mother pushing a child behind an apron. Her bruises were almost gone.

"Do you know why she was thrown out of the car? Was it a customer?" None of the ladies looked at her, their gazes avoiding eye contact. "I'm a homicide detective, but I'm looking into this because I believe it deserves justice."

The woman pulled out a cigarette and lit it, taking a long drag before shaking her head. Smoke billowed upward. "Whatever she did to make the person angry, she won't do it again."

"Is that what you all think?"

The other prostitutes nodded. Either they thought they deserved the treatment their customers or pimps dished out, or they were too afraid to say anything. Helping the police might get them more severe beatings than they'd suffered recently.

Makeup could cover a lot, especially if the bruises were on the face, but contusions in other places were harder to conceal unless they kept the lights off with their customers. Maybe the customers didn't care as long as they were getting off.

Anger boiled in her stomach. No one deserved to be treated like cattle. They were some of the most vulnerable in the city, and most people treated them as if they were part of the scenery. Ignoring them for the most part, residents didn't do anything to rock the boat if something went wrong. Sex workers went missing all the time and no one even noticed unless a body turned up. As soon as the paramedics drove away and the police left, the bystanders would go back to what they'd been doing and completely forget what had happened by the time they went to bed.

Rachel sighed. She couldn't force help on people. And she couldn't make them talk to her, either. Despite their lack of cooperation, she pulled out a few of her business cards from her pocket. She handed one to the woman in front and the others to a couple of the women standing closest to her.

"If you think of anything, no matter how small, call me."

Out of the corner of her eye, she spotted a person get out of the white SUV that idled at the intersection right by the curb. All the women tensed in unison and promptly dropped her card. Except for the spokeswoman. She tucked the card into her bra, but fear still skittered across her face.

"No one's gonna call you, lady. Sorry, Detective." The spokeswoman for the group hugged herself so hard that her fingers turned white.

"I understand that. But if you won't do that, at least go to the hospital and get checked out. Some of those bruises look serious." She looked each woman in the eye. "Talk to my sister, Dr. Sarah Malak. She'll help you out and won't ask questions you aren't comfortable answering."

Some of the women nodded noncommittally. It was the best she could do now that the person who threw the prostitute out of the car had made himself known. She couldn't be sure, of course, and she couldn't arrest him based on a gut instinct, but the prostitutes' faces told the story their lips refused to utter. They weren't just afraid of the man who stepped out of the SUV. They were terrified.

She turned to look at the newcomer. She recognized him immediately as Victor from the gas station when the attack happened. He'd been protecting Caleb. At least, at the time, she'd *thought* he'd been protecting him, but now, she wondered.

She walked to the end of the block, keeping her gaze on the man. Gang colors were prominent in the group, but he didn't even wear a jacket that indicated his rank. A black T-shirt hugged a muscular chest. The sleeve on the shirt barely touched a tattoo on the guy's arm. A tattoo of a crown over a crossbow.

Her eyes widened.

The man turned his gaze to her and grinned.

The vehicle's door opened, and Manny got out, holding a leather jacket. Conquest took the jacket and shrugged into it, turning so she could see the sleeve with the stripes. Six of them. Conquest was the new gang leader.

Rachel pushed through the door of the loft, wishing the warehouse had an operational elevator. Why hadn't they worked that into the magic when they'd set up their identities?

Exhausted but bubbling with new information the other angels required meant bed had to wait for at least an hour.

Sarah was the first off the stool. "What happened? Is everything okay with the sex worker?"

"Okay in that she'll live, but not okay."

Sarah guided her to a stool. Leah put a steaming cup of tea in front of her.

"It's decaf," Leah said, looking up at the clock above the sink in the kitchen.

Rachel took a grateful sip. The island stools helped with their posture, but she wanted to slump back into a warm, cushiony chair.

"Thanks."

"Do you know what hospital she was taken to?" Sarah climbed up on the stool beside her. "She was taken to one, wasn't she?"

Rachel nodded. "I'm not sure which one. It happened on University, close to Queen Street West."

"I'll check around tomorrow before rounds. See if I can find her."

Rachel took another sip of the tea. "If she's still there. I got the feeling she wouldn't be staying very long. She's afraid. They all are, and now I know why."

"Why?" Becky grabbed a tub of ice cream from the freezer and held it up. They all nodded.

"We need to step up our investigation into how to stop an apocalypse. Crumbs here and there aren't good enough. Conquest is definitely here. I was right. He is the guy from the gas station robbery. And he's the new leader of the Grange."

Sarah gasped. "You think he's the one who harmed her?"

"He's got to teach them a lesson, and he's always been hands-on." Rachel shuddered.

She knew they were all cogs in the universal wheel.

The horsemen, though, were going to be hard to stop. Could they even kill a horseman?

Becky placed bowls of vanilla bean ice cream in front of them. Rachel scooped up a large amount on the tablespoon tucked into the side of the treat. "I know the horsemen are needed when the actual apocalypse gets here, but there has to be a way to send them back to limbo. We need to double down on finding those lost books of the Bible."

Leah raised her hand. "Sorry, used to the classroom." She pulled her arm back down. "Crumbs hit pay dirt while you were gone."

She hurried into the living room and returned with her laptop. She put it on the counter so they could gather around the screen while she scrolled. She stopped at a picture that looked older than Methuselah. Clicking on the photo brought up a larger image.

It was a picture of a scroll, safely ensconced under glass, with faded ink marks scrawled across the page. It looked like a worm had been dipped in ink and left on the parchment to crawl around.

"That's gibberish. You can't even make out any words."

"This one, yes. It doesn't say anything. I think it's fake. However, there are others that look more promising."

Leah clicked the X to close the large image and continued to scroll down the page. She stopped at another photo of a parchment under glass. The caption under the photo proclaimed the location of the photo to be The Vatican.

"That one is more promising. But there's no way anyone in The Vatican would have allowed someone to take a picture of anything remotely rare. And if it's a lost book of the Bible, it will be priceless," Becky said.

"I know. It's possible they took it furtively. There are apps now that could have helped them."

Rachel raised an eyebrow. "Apps, you say? You've been playing with your smartphone."

Leah grinned. "So many options. I love it. Anyway, back to the picture. See the writing?"

"My Enochian is a little rusty," Sarah said.

"Mine is perfect." Leah clicked to bring up the larger image. "This looks like it comes, or would have come, right before Revelation, but it's only a piece. There are a lot of other pictures on the site I'd need to look at to put it all together."

"Send it to the printer and we'll try to put the puzzle together," Rachel said.

"It would go faster if we divvied them up," Leah said. She clicked the URL in the address bar and sent a group message.

Phones pinged in unison. Sarah and Rachel jumped down from their stools. Sarah went to the sofa to grab her laptop. Rachel ducked into her bedroom to get hers.

"Can someone get mine, too?" Becky asked, shoveling another spoonful of ice cream into her mouth.

Rachel sighed but stopped at the love seat to pick up the angel's laptop. They opened their computers and clicked on the link Leah had sent.

"There are twenty pages of the photos. I suggest we each take five pages. I'll do the first five." Leah hit the print button.

After gathering the pages from the printer, she divvied them up and handed them out. Rachel forced herself to skim through the pages first. Enochian didn't usually appear on Earth anymore. And she missed the angelic language. Sarah had preferred to study other ancient languages, and not having used the angelic language in centuries, it was no wonder she was rusty. Maybe Leah being a teacher of history with an eidetic memory could help them with stopping the end of the world.

Almost an hour later, they sat around an island covered in printed photos of the scrolls. Some were ancient text, while others were nonsense, possibly put there to confuse people. She doubted The Vatican would admit any of the scrolls were lost texts of the Bible. Everything they were about would have to change.

A quickly growing pile of fakes was building on the floor beside Leah's stool. She tossed another photo over her shoulder with a disgusted sound.

"Why are these under protective glass when they mean nothing?"

Rachel shrugged. "You'd probably have to ask The Vatican."

"Noted. I'll get around to that." She pushed a bunch of pictures together as if they were puzzle pieces. Some of the text at the bottom connected perfectly with the scrawled letters at the top of the next.

"You found some that go together," Becky noted.

"I don't like what they're saying," Leah said. Her already pale face grew paler.

Rachel's stomach tightened. If the optimistic angel was afraid, maybe the Earth was doomed. No, she couldn't think like that. They were fucking angels. They were sent here for a reason. He wouldn't have sent them if He expected them to fail. He loved his humans too much for that.

"What exactly do they say?" Rachel asked.

Leah riffled through the pages, putting others together to create long sheets of photos. "Death killed souls in purgatory. A lot of them. Well, not so much killed, because you can't kill a soul, but sent them off to Hell. Humans think souls are created when the body is created. But they're not. They were created at the beginning of time and there is a finite number of them, barring miracles."

"When you say a lot, how many do you mean?" Sarah asked.

"Enough so people have been born without souls for years, probably decades."

Rachel stood abruptly, knocking over her stool. "That explains a lot."

"Explain it to us, then," Becky said.

Rachel righted her stool and sat again. "Haven't you felt that people are a little off since the last time you were on Earth? Like kindness has taken a holiday? Maybe that's why. Leah was here most recently and even then it was the early 1900s. The horsemen can only control the soulless."

Leah nodded. "Yes, but if they can turn a souled person to evil, they'll gain even more power. When the soulless outnumber the souled on the planet, the Earth is in a spell of hot water."

"We have to make sure we turn it around," Sarah said.

"Do the scrolls say when Death started killing souls?" Rachel asked. "How many soulless are we talking about?"

"It doesn't say, or I haven't found it yet."

Rachel nodded. "Keep looking."

"I will. In the meantime, Becky has found more information about the signs of the apocalypse," Leah said.

Becky opened her laptop. All on the same side of the island now, huddled around the computer, Becky pulled up reports and video footage.

"I had my intern looking into a few things for me," she admitted. "I won't even go there with the most horrible stuff."

She brought up a report on the racial violence in the city to the front of the documents. Rachel skimmed it as

Becky scrolled through it. Footage of riots in the surrounding cities. Violence breaking out at picket lines. Racial slurs, misogynist slurs hurled at women in fast food lines. Video after video of customers abusing retail clerks. Pages and pages of internet "warriors" whose words encouraging suicide resulted in the desired action by the person being bullied.

Becky stopped for a moment and went to the fridge to grab a bottle of water. She took a long gulp before speaking again. "And it's getting worse."

Back at the laptop, she pulled up graphs, weather patterns, Doppler images.

"What's this?" Rachel asked.

"Forecasts from all over the world for the next month. Severe weather expected in a lot of places." She pointed to a swirling mass in the middle of the Atlantic Ocean. "That's one huge hurricane headed toward the East Coast. Pacific islands are expecting typhoons. Earthquakes have been happening in places not usually known for the ground shaking."

"Let's clear our calendars after work. We have a lot of research to do and not a lot of time to figure out how to stop the end of the world," Rachel said.

Chapter Ten

Wednesday afternoon, Caleb hung back, watching the gang members from a safe distance. Since the gas station, he'd thought of little else except joining the gang. The thought of killing someone other than his father didn't sit well with him, but if it was someone who deserved it, he could get on board with that.

They walked past the HQ he'd been in with them before, continuing down the sidewalk until they reached a warehouse. Lights were on at the back of the building that he'd thought was abandoned. One of the members stopped at the door and turned, looking directly at him.

So much for stealth.

Before he could retreat, the presence of someone behind him raised goose bumps on his arms. He turned to see Victor regarding him with a piercing look.

"You found the new place. Good for you. Shows initiative. Now what? What do you want?"

He looked longingly at the warehouse. His ribs were healing, but the bruises on his face still hurt. He didn't want to go back to the apartment again, ever. "I want to join you. You need young up-and-comers."

"What have you done to prove yourself? Kill anyone yet?"

Ice went through Caleb's veins. Victor couldn't take this hope away from him. "Not yet. I didn't want to kill anyone not approved by you."

Victor eyed him appraisingly. Not in the disappointed way his father looked at him, but a thorough gaze that saw his potential. His father only saw a loser, which was funny because Karl was the loser.

Caleb straightened, hoping if he looked taller, stronger, the gang leader would at least let him inside. Even a night in the warehouse would be better than going back to his apartment.

"You think you have what it takes to be a Grange member?"

He nodded. "I do."

Victor raised a hand to Caleb's face, and he couldn't help flinching. "Your face and your actions say otherwise. I'm going to guess and say your father did that."

Caleb looked down at his feet. The weight of failure made his heart beat faster. Panic at being turned away forced him to look up at Victor, his eyes pleading. "He won't do it again."

"Can you even fight? Do you know how?"

Caleb thought back at all the times his father had hit him. He'd tried fighting back once, but the beating afterward was far worse than any that had come before. It was easier to sneak out of the apartment until whatever rage had a hold of him disappeared.

At school and at work, no one bullied him or beat him.

"I can learn how to fight. With your help."

Victor leaned closer, inhaling the air. Caleb frowned. Odd behavior for a gang leader, but he stood his ground. If he didn't convince the man to teach him, he'd end up living on the street, because one of these days, the beatings would be too much and he wouldn't go home.

"We have a decent gym now. Me and the men could teach you some moves."

Hope soared. Caleb smiled. "I can start now."

Victor nodded to the man guarding the door, then stalked over. The guard swung the door wide, and Caleb followed Victor into the gang's new headquarters.

Upon entering, it looked like a typical warehouse. Stacks of boxes lined the back wall. Metal shelves formed rows directly to the left. They were filled with boxes of varying sizes with labels on the front. On the right, a hallway branched off that at one time probably led to offices.

"Nice place."

"We like it. This way."

Victor turned right and stopped at a door halfway down the hallway. He opened it and stood aside for Caleb to enter the room. The gym was huge, at least the size of four medium-sized offices. None of the usual gym accoutrements distracted from a workout. No TVs were mounted on the walls. Even the windows were painted black. A heavy bag at the far end of the room hung from the ceiling. Treadmills, exercise bikes, rowing machines lined the wall facing the windows with no view. On the right was a door. He nodded to the door and looked at Victor.

"Target practice. We'll get to that eventually, but you need to be able to handle yourself with these weapons first." He grabbed Caleb's hands.

Caleb pulled his hands away from Victor and took a step back. He'd never been good at defending himself. Never wanted to hit anyone except his father. But the gang leader was right. If he didn't want to be pushed around anymore, he had to do something about it.

"Teach me," he said.

Victor's hand flew toward his face and clocked him in the jaw before he could move. His head pounded, and he saw spots for a second. He shook his head to clear it.

"I wasn't ready!"

"Boo hoo. You think a rival gang member is going to wait until you're ready for them to hit you?"

Caleb put his hand in front of his face, preparing himself for another blow.

"Keep your eyes on your opponent at all times. Don't lose focus."

From behind him, Caleb heard the shuffling of other members. Their snickers reached him loud and clear, even though they whispered among themselves. They didn't feel he was worthy.

Anger straightened his spine. He put his shoulders back. He kept an eye on Victor, but his ears trained behind him.

This time, when Victor threw a punch, Caleb blocked it. He swung back, missing the gang leader by inches.

They danced around each other, tossing blows back and forth. Some landed, some didn't. He would be bruised again in the morning, but this time, it was worth it.

"I've picked a target for you," Victor said as he threw another punch. "A sweet woman who frequents the convenience store nearby."

Caleb side-stepped and put up a hand to block the next blow. "Shouldn't it be a rival gang member?"

Victor leaned in and delivered an upper cut to Caleb's jaw. "And start a gang war before I'm ready? No."

The pounding returned to Caleb's head, and he shook it. Needed to watch for those out-of-nowhere punches. "Then shouldn't it be someone who deserves it?"

Victor stopped moving. His hands fell to his sides, and he regarded Caleb with a raised eyebrow. "Do you want to be in this gang?"

"Of course I do. I wouldn't be here letting you beat the crap out of me if I didn't."

"We do things for a reason. Someone who deserves to die won't cause fear. People need to fear you."

Taunts from the other members reached his ears. The whispering grew louder until shouts of "Pussy!" couldn't be ignored.

He turned to glare at the bystanders, then fixed his attention back on Victor. He watched the man's every move, anticipated where the punches would come from, what he would leave vulnerable. It helped that his father had beat him so much. It was easier to predict what was coming.

He landed more punches than he missed. Victor, too busy blocking, threw a couple of punches that missed the mark. After another thirty minutes, Victor held up a hand.

Caleb stopped punching and waited.

"You're getting better. There is hope for you. But first, killing the woman is only the start. If you can do that, you'll have promise."

Nerves clenched his stomach. Killing an innocent woman didn't sit well, but he had to get out of the apartment. He couldn't stay at the gang headquarters indefinitely until he was a full member. Maybe he could pretend to kill her. He dismissed that almost as soon as he thought of it. Victor would check, make sure he'd completed the task.

He nodded.

Hoots and hollers followed him down the corridor. He still heard them when he left the warehouse, Victor by his side. The walk to the convenience store was too short. His hands trembled. His stomach knotted. The reassuring weight of Victor's hand on his shoulder chased away some of the doubt, but not all of it.

Inside the store, a few customers milled about. A clerk behind the counter smiled at a petite woman in the dairy aisle. She had long dark hair and an olive complexion. Her smile at the clerk could light up an entire room.

Victor pointed at her and nodded.

Caleb took a deep breath and stepped into the store.

Rachel sat at her desk, the hum of activity from the police station a balm on her nerves, absently taking a sip of cold coffee. She clicked her email refresh button for the twentieth time in ten minutes. Still no autopsy report on Bruno. Without that, she didn't know the exact time of death. Or as exact as possible. She needed that to piece together what had happened to him.

Dr. Malani estimated the time of death to be Thursday so until she received the report she would work with the coroner's estimate. People in the neighborhood had to have seen something. Bruno was an imposing figure, easily memorable, even if you wanted to forget him.

She pulled out her file for the homicide and scanned the notes she had so far. Not much to go on. Obviously, he wasn't killed on the beach where he was found. Only the killer knew exactly where the murder took place. She needed to find that crime scene, though any evidence the killer might have left behind was probably long gone by now.

She closed the folder in frustration. The hurry up and wait of police work annoyed her. How could she be productive if she wasn't doing anything?

"Do you have any ideas on how we can get a timeline on Bruno's murder without the report from the forensic pathologist?" she asked Detective Williams.

"Well, I know you're probably not going to like it, but we can't do a whole lot except go interview people in the neighborhood."

Usually, she would send a constable to do that while she chased down other leads and talked to more reliable witnesses. But she was at a standstill right now.

"It's better than nothing. I'll get the car. Meet me out front."

He raised an eyebrow. "Sure. I'll grab some fresh coffees."

A few minutes later, she pulled the car to a stop in the parking area of the gas station.

"Why are we at the robbery scene?" Her partner put his now empty coffee cup in the cup holder.

"I'm sure the station is in the Grange's territory. All the businesses around here pay protection money to them. It's as good a place as any to start. We'll work our way back toward the neighborhood."

He shrugged and got out of the car.

Inside the station, the blood in aisle three had been cleaned up, but there was a faint staining on the tiles. If you didn't know it was there, you probably wouldn't notice the difference in color.

Food was back on the shelves. It looked like nothing had happened. At least it hadn't ended in death. The victims of the beatings were still recovering in the hospital, but they *would* recover.

They walked over to the man behind the counter. He fidgeted when he saw them, his eyes darting to them and the door. His bald head shone under the fluorescent lights, like a beacon in a storm. "Good afternoon. I'm Detective Williams and this is my partner Detective Malak. Are you the manager?"

He nodded. "What can I do for you?"

"We were wondering when you last saw Bruno De Luca in the area," Rachel said.

The man screwed up his face in thought. "Been a while. I think it was Thursday afternoon."

Rachel made a note of the date in her book. "Thanks."

They turned to go.

"That's it?"

Detective Williams flashed a smile at the man. "Is there something else you wanted to tell us?"

"No, I just thought you would ask more, that's all."

The jingle of the door followed them outside. Back in the car, Rachel grabbed her coffee and took a long sip.

"That was odd. You think he was worried we were there?"

Williams shrugged. "Maybe. Let's check with some of the businesses around here."

Two hours later, back at the station, after checking in with over ten businesses, they had a timeline of events for Bruno. No one had seen him after the night she saved Darla in the alley beside a pub. The owner of the pub said Bruno used to come in after his enforcer made the rounds collecting from everyone.

"I bet Bruno thought the pub owner should be flattered that he chose that pub to count his money and toss back a few drinks," Rachel said.

Williams looked up from his notes and grinned. "Probably."

Gnawing in the pit of her stomach had Rachel calling up the CCTV footage from around the pub. She scrolled through the dates and found the one from the night she saved Darla. Then she checked the times until she found the correct one.

She pressed the play button on the screen and watched as Tony, the guy who had been assaulting Darla, walked along the sidewalk. It was odd seeing herself on screen, running to the alley. Even though she knew what happened next, she left the footage rolling.

A few minutes after she entered the alley, her sisters arrived, and Darla ran out. She expected the guy to leave as soon as he got the air back in his lungs. After she and her sisters left, the footage was fine for a minute, then it went fuzzy, like the gas station footage on the day of the robberies.

She called up another angle of the street. She spotted Bruno walking toward the pub on his usual route. That camera's footage also went fuzzy.

It didn't take a genius to figure out Conquest had been in that alley some time after she'd left. Killed the gang leader and took over. She needed to get back to that alley to see if there was anything there that would help her with Conquest. If they couldn't kill a horseman, maybe putting him in jail would be enough to stop or at least slow down the approaching apocalypse. She rewound the footage to the part where Bruno appeared on camera.

Detective Sergeant Reyes approached her desk. When he looked at the notes and the footage on the screen, he beamed. "Good work!"

Rachel nodded at Williams. "He deserves the credit. It was his idea to check with the businesses in the area."

Reyes clapped Williams on the back. "Great idea. Now catch the guy. I don't want the city thinking a vigilante is responsible for killing a gang leader. And I want to rule out a rival gang."

A tingle went through Rachel. She felt different. Stronger. More herself. She made a mental note to let Becky know exactly what she'd said and done so she could add it to the spreadsheet Becky had started last night before they'd all gone to bed. Rachel's entries were sparse compared to the others, but at least she had data to contribute.

Williams' phone rang. He answered right away, balancing the receiver between his ear and shoulder while he wrote something down. After a brief conversation, he hung up and stood, waving the piece of paper in his hand. "We're up. There's been a homicide at Bob's Convenience and Gifts."

A large crowd gathered on the sidewalk in front of Bob's Convenience and Gifts, spilling onto the street. A uniformed constable stood outside, waving people away as more curious onlookers tried to peer inside. Rachel's first thought was Conquest finished off Darla. The store wasn't far from the alley where Rachel had first met the woman. Maybe Sarah hadn't been able to keep Darla at the hospital.

Anger at the loss of life, any life, careened through her. She'd chosen detective as a job when she got here so she could make the city safer. Clean up the streets enough so people were confident walking alone at night, even downtown. Since arriving, she didn't feel like she'd made much of a difference in the city. How the fuck was she supposed to stop the apocalypse?

Off to one side, a different group of people huddled against the wall of the store. Surrounded by police, most people in the group wore horrified expressions. Tracks down some of their faces from tears marred once perfect makeup. Others stood with blank expressions, shaking their heads. Witnesses. She hoped they could tell them something useful this time, but she didn't think the interviews would be much different from the gas station interviews.

She and Williams dug out their badges as they approached the store. The constable nodded and pulled open the door. The bell jingled. Every person in the store glanced up briefly, then went back to work.

A CSU team took pictures and bagged evidence. At the back of the store, a woman in her thirties lay sprawled on the floor. Blood mixed with the milk from a carton full of bullet holes. The carton lay on the floor next to her. Dark hair spread out around her head. If it weren't for the red blooms of color on her beige coat, someone might think she was sleeping.

The glint of a ring on her wedding finger caught Rachel's eye. Shit. A spouse, maybe children. Almost everyone had someone in their lives, but it was always harder for her when the victim was married.

Another officer talked to a man at the back of the store. The man, with a shock of white hair, looked ancient. She'd seen him in the neighborhood before. The heinousness of the crime added years to the man's face. His gaze darted to the woman on the floor. He wrung his hands, nodding every so often at the constable's questions.

She followed a path designated for walking, to the back of the store. Williams trailed behind her. When they reached the man, the constable made the introductions.

"This is Robert Cregg. He owns the store."

"Hi, Mr. Cregg. I'm Detective Williams. This is Detective Malak. We'd like to ask you some questions if you're up to it."

Rachel watched the tremble of the man's hand get more pronounced. He took a shuddering breath. Sadness flooded his face. He shook his head, as if denying anything bad had happened, but then he nodded.

"I'll try to help as much as I can," he said.

Rachel pulled out her notebook. "Did you know the victim?"

The man nodded. "Not well, you understand, but she came into the store around this time every day on her way home from work. Always picked up a few treats for her son. Sometimes, like today, a few essentials. Her name was Felicia Newman."

Rachel looked over at the woman as she wrote her name in her notepad. The milk seeped into the woman's hair, moistening the ends. Gunshot wounds in the coat were clustered together around the heart. Nothing about the woman screamed gang ties. But it looked like a gang hit. She wasn't wearing rival gang colors, either.

"Do you know if she was having trouble with anyone?" Williams asked.

"Everyone around here liked her. She helped the drama club paint their props for their school play. She bought cookies from Fort York Collegiate students when they were doing fundraisers. I can't imagine anyone not liking her. Especially not enough to do this to her."

His eyes glazed with unshed tears.

"Did anyone take anything out of her purse?" Rachel asked.

The man shook his head. "After the shots, everyone scattered."

That made her wonder how many of the people outside were actual witnesses. How many of them had fled the scene before police got there? Most people wanted to help any way they could, but others wanted to get away from any source of danger.

She looked around the store, above the entrance and the door to the back offices. "Do you have working security cameras?"

"Yes, they record all the time even though we're not open twenty-four hours. To be on the safe side, you understand. Every day's video gets put on the store's cloud account."

She didn't want to hope that they'd get something useful out of the footage, but she did hope. She clung to that with all of her being.

"We'd like to see that footage as soon as possible," Williams said.

The man nodded. "I can create a new admin login and send you the details."

While Williams gave the owner their cards, Rachel made her way to the front of the store. She pushed open the door and pulled in a deep breath of the crisp early evening air. Most of the crowd still lingered, pushing past the person in front of them to see into the store.

She smiled when she got to the group of witnesses.

"When can we go home?" one woman asked, pulling her coat tighter around her shoulders.

"Soon. We just need to ask you a few questions about the incident here," Rachel said. She turned to one of the constables. "Is it possible to get these people something warm to drink?"

A man pushed to the front of the group. "I don't want something to drink. I want to get home."

"Did anyone see anything? Anything at all?"

Heads shook in unison. Rachel sighed. More people jostled to the front demanding to go home. At the back of the group, she spotted a familiar face, and her heart sank. It couldn't have been a coincidence that Caleb was present at two crimes and have nothing to do with either.

"Caleb, can you come here?"

He shrugged and shuffled to the front of the group.

"Did you see anything?"

"Why do you keep asking me that? I saw nothing. I was minding my own business, outside, when I heard gunshots."

"Did you know the woman?"

"How many times I gotta tell you? I didn't know her. I didn't see anything."

The way his gaze flicked to the street, the shuffle of his feet, his hands shoved into his pockets, sent off alarm bells. He was lying. But she hoped that was the worst of it.

"Constable, make sure you get everyone's contact information and give them my card before you release them." She handed over a stack of cards. "Could you also get us an address and next of kin information for the victim?" She wrote the woman's name again on the back of a business card and gave it to the constable.

"Yes, ma'am." He shoved the card with Felicia's name on it in his pocket.

She turned to see Williams talking to Detective Littman at the curb. His arrival at the scene confirmed her suspicions about gang involvement. She hurried over.

"What do you think?" she asked.

"You're not going to like it," he said.

"I already hate it. Lay it on me."

"This screams gang initiation. The Grange hasn't recruited in a long time. The last time they did, there were several civilian casualties. The Esskays didn't fare so well, either. Their violent acts are ramping up, too. If the Grange is recruiting, The Esskays will follow."

"Great. And in your experience, what is the next step?"

"If that's the case, you will end up with a gang war on your hands sooner rather than later unless we can stop it," Detective Littman said.

<u>Chapter Eleven</u>

A commotion from the right pulled Rachel's attention away from the store. Cordoned off by police, the area at the corner of the street sported a group of people vying for a spot to see the action. Not much action going on now. She suspected they'd run for the hills if anything happened. But now that the police were there, it was safe to return and pry.

A van with CTBN, Canadian Television Broadcasting Network, emblazoned on the side pulled up to the curb in front of the police tape. Bystanders moved out of the way so they wouldn't get hit. Henry, her sister's usual camera-man, emerged from the driver's side. He paused, half in and half out of the van to grab his video camera. Rachel groaned.

Becky alighted from the passenger side. Her makeup and hair perfect, a somber expression on her face perfectly suitable for reporting a homicide live on camera.

"This day just keeps getting better," Rachel said.

Williams chuckled beside her. "It could be worse. They could have sent Kevin Moore."

The police would do their job and not let Becky through the police tape, no matter what excuse she used. The sister card only worked for certain things. Special access to a crime scene wasn't one of them.

Grudgingly, Rachel plodded over to the crime scene tape.

Becky fluffed her hair and pressed her lips together to blot her lipstick. Her eyes lit up when she spotted Rachel.

"Couldn't they have sent someone else?" Rachel asked.

Becky bristled. "No. They couldn't have sent someone else. I am the senior journalist at the station."

Rachel leaned closer so Henry couldn't hear them. "Only because you used magic to give you that position."

And no one at the station even knew that Becky was the newest person there. Kevin Moore had been at the news game longer, not just at CTBN, but in the city, period. Before Becky had used the last of her angel power to set herself up as a reporter, he had been the face of the evening six o'clock news. At least she made him her co-anchor.

"Can't argue with you there. The fact remains that I am a senior journalist. I asked for this story."

"Because you knew I'd be here?" Rachel asked. She turned to the crime scene, longing to get back to work instead of verbally sparring with her sister. Williams jogged over, a smile on his face at the grimace on hers.

"I'm covering the increasing crime in the city for one of the major news reports I'm working on. This qualifies."

"Fine."

Becky nodded to her cameraman and thrust the microphone at Rachel. "Detective Malak, what can you tell us about this crime? This is the two hundred and eightieth shooting in the city this year that has resulted in an injury or death. And the five hundred and thirty-fifth incident of a shooting or firearm discharge. Is this gang related?"

Rachel stood a little taller, pasted a neutral expression on her face, and looked directly at Becky. "I can confirm there was a shooting. For more, you'd have to talk to our media relations officer."

Becky's sympathetic smile faltered for a split second. "You can't tell us anything else? Anything about the victim? Any suspects?"

"We have not formally identified the victim and their next of kin also needs to be informed. When we know more, you'll know more."

The only sign of anger Becky let slip was the glare she gave Rachel. She quickly softened her gaze and directed her next question to Williams.

"Detective Williams, what can you tell us about the scene?"

Williams glanced at Rachel. She gave him a warning look and imperceptibly shook her head.

"We're still investigating. Our media relations officer will be setting up a press conference. We'll have more answers for you then." He looked at her again for approval.

Rachel smiled. Williams disliked the media encroaching before they had time to do any investigating as much as she did. It didn't help that it was usually her sister accosting them at crime scenes, asking questions she knew they couldn't answer yet.

Maybe she did that on purpose, to see how much they would reveal. There was always a chance they might let something slip that they shouldn't. Though not likely, it could happen, especially with one of the rookie constables.

Detective Littman approached the crime scene tape. He guzzled a cup of coffee like it was a lifeline. His hair was tousled as if he'd been running his hands through it all day, trying to make sense of things. Becky's eyes lit up, like a lioness who had spotted easy prey. She motioned to her cameraman, who shifted the camera on his shoulder into a more comfortable position.

Before he could duck under the tape, Becky thrust the microphone at him. "Detective Littman, is this gang related?"

He looked at Williams and Rachel, then back at Becky. Unsure what he would reveal, Rachel yanked the microphone away and spoke into it clearly, "No comment."

Becky glared at her again. She didn't care. Her sister should know better by now. She had all the knowledge of years of experience at her job, even though she didn't actually live through it all.

"Sorry about that," Rachel said to Littman. "My sister is a bit pushy."

"Sister, huh? I get it. Thinks she can get the inside scoop?"

Rachel nodded and walked a few feet away from the tape. She jerked her head to the left so Williams and Littman would follow.

"I think we should keep the gang angle out of the papers as long as possible. Williams and I will go inform the husband."

Littman nodded, then escaped under the tape before Becky could stop him.

Rachel watched Becky talk into the camera, her back to the crime scene. The light on top of the video camera illuminated her sister and the immediate ground surrounding her. After thirty seconds, her sister nodded, the light went off, and the cameraman lowered the camera.

Rachel and Williams walked back over to the tape.

"Now that you have your sound bite, you can go back

to the studio and let us do our job," Rachel said.

Was she pushing her luck treating her sister this way because they were sisters? If it had been another reporter on the scene, she wouldn't have been so rude. Guilt tightened her chest and churned in her stomach. But another reporter wouldn't be an angel who could have picked a better profession to help stop an apocalypse.

Becky glared at her.

"I'll meet you at the car," Williams said.

Rachel nodded.

"I know you hate my job, Rach, but this is what I do. It will help stop the apocalypse, and then, you'll have to get off your high horse and apologize to me."

The constable from inside the convenience store emerged from the building and strode over to Rachel. He handed her a piece of paper with a name and address on it. "The information you asked for."

Rachel nodded and took a deep breath. The part of the job she hated never got easier. "I'll see you at home, Beck. Right now, I have actual work to do."

Williams expertly maneuvered the car through downtown traffic, throwing questioning glances at her when he stopped for a red light.

"What?"

"You're always stonewalling your sister. You hate when witnesses do that to us."

"Light's green." Rachel pointed at the red light that suddenly turned green. She'd have time to regret using her power later. How much that little trick cost her might come back to haunt her, but she didn't like talking about Becky.

Williams stepped on the gas.

"Malak, I'm your partner. Talk to me."

She shrugged. "You think she should get special privileges because her sister's a cop?"

Williams took a left turn, pointing them toward the residential area of the city, away from the hustle and bustle of the downtown core. "No, but you'd give more to any other reporter. It's just her you won't talk to when she's on the job."

The truth was she did think police work was more important than what Becky did. It was more important than what Leah did. As a cop, she saved lives by keeping the city safer. Catching the bad guys. Sometimes stopping crimes before they happened. Sarah's job was important, maybe on par, or slightly higher than being a cop. Sarah saved lives every day. How did a reporter and a teacher save lives? Now that they knew the apocalypse was coming, how would either of them be able to help stop it? Preventing the end of the world would fall to Sarah's and her shoulders.

"You're right. I don't agree with her choice of profession, but I shouldn't make it even harder for her to do her job. I'll talk to her tonight."

She knew as soon as she got home, Becky would lay into her. Now that she thought about it, how others saw their "working" relationship, she couldn't blame Becky for being angry. She vowed to try harder not to show so much disdain for what her sister did.

Williams pulled the car up to the curb on a middle-class street. The houses were all shapes and sizes, telling her the neighborhood had been around for decades. None of the cookie-cutter houses with the same yards, same color brick, same size on this street. Every house was slightly different than the next.

He'd stopped at a red brick house with the clichéd

white picket fence. A pristine lawn, devoid of fallen leaves, was marred only by the toys pushed discreetly against the wall of the house. The pathway up to the front door was unspoiled. No grass or weeds seeping through the cracks.

Rachel knocked on the dark green door and took a deep breath. This was the worst part of the job. She hated doing notifications, even though she knew the people were going to a better place. Home. Where she wanted to get back too.

But were they going anywhere? The soul went to a better place, the body went back to the Earth. With so many souls siphoned out of purgatory, did Felicia have a soul before she died? If she hadn't used her newly gained power to change the traffic light and fix Caleb's ribs, she'd be able to tell if Mr. Newman had a soul. If her son had one.

The door swung open and a smiling man in his late thirties greeted them. Laugh lines around his eyes spoke to the life he had with his family, and now, they were about to ruin that happiness.

"Mr. Newman?" Williams asked.

"Yes. What can I do for you?"

They pulled out their badges. "I'm Detective Malak and this is Detective Williams. We're here about your wife."

The light died in his eyes. He shook his head but moved aside so they could enter. He walked into the sitting room off the main hallway. Curtains on the bay windows were pulled aside to give a view of the lawn outside.

He slumped into a chair facing the windows. Rachel and Williams took seats on the sofa against the right wall. A table in the middle of the room held coffee table books. Three huge photo books. Possibly of places they'd been or wanted to go.

"Why would you be here about Felicia?"

Rachel shifted in her seat. "I'm sorry, Mr. Newman. Felicia is gone."

"What do you mean gone? She's dead? I saw the news. It was her?" His hands turned white in his lap from the strength of this grip.

Rachel nodded. "I'm sorry, Mr. Newman."

"How did the news station hear about this before I knew? When they talked about a woman being shot I never in a million years thought it was Felicia."

"I'm so sorry." She didn't know what else to say.

Rachel wished in that moment that she had the ability to take away his pain. Make him feel serene, like things would eventually be okay, but she didn't know if the little angel magic she had left would be enough. And false closure wouldn't help him in the long run. As much as it pained her, he needed to work through the grief on his own.

"Do you know anyone who would want to hurt your wife?" Williams asked.

He shook his head. "Everyone loved her."

They would get the formalities out of the way when it came to his whereabouts later. Despite the husband almost always being the first suspect, Rachel knew he hadn't had anything to do with his wife's murder. Not unless he was in a gang. She believed Detective Littman when he said it might have been an initiation. What better way to strike fear into the city than kill someone at random who everyone liked?

"Daddy!" a little voice from deeper in the house called.

Mr. Newman sighed and shook his head as a tear rolled down his cheek.

Little footsteps echoed in the hallway. A boy of about four burst into the sitting room, barreled toward his father, and held up a large paper. "I drew this! When is Mommy coming home?"

The boy turned in his father's lap to look at Rachel and Williams. He smiled. It turned his cute cherub face into an even more adorable angelic face. He brushed the mop of dark brown curls out of his eyes, then thrust the picture toward them.

In a child's scrawl, there was a picture of a house, with a white fence around it. Dark green lawn with no leaves. In front of the house were three stick figures. Two larger ones, one with long dark hair. And a little figure with circles around the head for the mop of curls.

He reminded her of a child from ages ago, when the world was ancient. The child she'd never see again after her Earth body died.

She blinked back tears that threatened to spill. "It's adorable."

Anger coursed through her body.

"Why don't you go to the kitchen while Daddy talks to the nice people? I'll be in soon to get you a snack."

The boy slid down his father's lap and raced out of the room.

"We'll do whatever we can to find out who killed your wife," Rachel assured him.

She was drawing a line here. Right now. The gang violence in the city would stop. She did not want to make any more of these visits. No more innocent people would die on her watch. If Conquest was behind this, she would stop him and all the horsemen. They'd been exiled for a reason, and she was damn well going to stop the end of the world from happening.

Rachel glanced at her watch, then turned the key in the loft's lock. Not even nine o'clock meant all of her sisters would still be up. She took a deep breath and pulled open the door.

Sitting at the island, facing the door, Becky frowned when Rachel came in. Rachel couldn't blame her. If others were calling her out about how she treated Becky, her sister deserved some sort of apology.

"Hungry?" Sarah asked from the kitchen.

Without waiting for an answer, she placed a plate on the island beside Becky.

Rachel hung up her blazer by the door and made sure the lock was secured before taking her spot at the island. The scent of garlic mingled with onions teased her nose; her stomach grumbled. Sarah was becoming a great cook. If she'd added that as part of her background, the culinary skills would make sense, but she hadn't. All of the cooking had happened naturally once they'd chosen their professions.

Rachel dug into the fluffy jasmine rice smothered in spiced beef, taking a few bites while Becky steamed at her side. Admitting she was wrong was the hardest thing she ever had to do. By all standards, Earth and angelical, she was the oldest. She should have been the wisest, but she hadn't seen how treating Becky was hurting them all.

She put down her fork, turned to look directly at Becky, and took the angel's hands in hers. "I'm sorry about stonewalling you at the crime scene."

Becky eyed her suspiciously and pulled her hands away. "You always stonewall me at a crime scene."

"I know. And I'm sorry. I need to get over your chosen profession. We'll just need to work with it."

"Gee, thanks."

"You know what I mean." Rachel turned her attention back to dinner.

"You think you're better than us," Becky accused.

"Not better. Really. That's not the point." She took another bite of the beef dish and chewed slowly, savoring the hint of cumin. "You were right. We think the murder was gang related. But you can't report that yet until Detective Sergeant Reyes is ready to make it public knowledge."

"Okay, I can sit on that information for now. Was it some sort of initiation?"

"I wish you'd waited to air the convenience store piece. Mr. Newman saw it on the news before we could tell him."

Becky cringed. "Sorry about that. We can be more vague with the details in the future so you have time to get in touch with next of kin."

Sarah and Leah pulled up stools to the island. No plates sat in front of them. Most likely, they'd been home for hours, already eaten, and now could focus their full attention on her and Becky.

"Thanks. Detective Littman thinks it was an initiation. The woman didn't have any gang ties. She was a loving mother and wife. She didn't deserve to die like that."

"We need to work together, Rach. Some people are more willing to talk to reporters than they are to the police. We're on the same side. Small scale and big scale. I want to stop this apocalypse, too."

Leah and Sarah nodded.

"We all want to stop it," Sarah said.

"I know. I promise I'll do my best to be better at accepting help."

Sarah squeezed Rachel's arm. "Good. You're a whiz at delegating, but you can give us some of the heavy lifting, too. Not just tasks you don't want to do."

Rachel's cheeks warmed. "Deal."

Chapter Twelve

The next morning, Rachel reached for her coffee cup, remembered it was already empty, and frowned. It was her second cup since arriving at the station over an hour ago. She put it back and scrolled through her email, looking for anything from the forensic pathologist. Anything on any of the many cases they had going would help move the investigations forward. Investigations looked so fast on television. Waiting had never been her strong suit, not even when she was human.

Her mailbox pinged as another email popped up. This one from the store owner.

"Did you get the email from Mr. Cregg?" she asked Williams.

"Just now."

At least the CCTV footage from around the convenience store had been sent to her and Williams. "Divide and conquer?"

"Sure. You want the interior of the store and I'll take the surrounding area?" Williams asked.

"Sounds good. Holler if you notice anything."

Not that she thought much would come of the footage. If her suspicions were right and Conquest was behind this, the video would be fuzzy like the gas station robberies.

She hit refresh on her email one last time, hoping Dr. Malani was finally done with the autopsy on Bruno. Now she needed to wait for Felicia Newman's autopsy. Not that there would be any surprise there.

She clicked the email from the store owner and followed the instructions to log into the cloud service he used for his security camera. Once they were done with their investigation, he said he would delete the temporary admin credentials.

"Get everything squared away with your sister?" Williams asked.

"If you weren't a cop, would you have gone into counseling or something?"

He grinned at her. "Kind of rubbed off from my mother, I guess."

She searched her planted memories of Williams and found the ones about his family. It took a while before the magic filtered everything to her of her new life and the people in it. Less important tidbits were more likely to remain buried.

"Right. She's a psychologist."

"Best in the city." He smiled again. "I could be biased. So, did you talk to Becky?"

She nodded. "Yes, I talked to her. We're fine. Promise." No need to go into lots of details no one had time for, but in time, they would be fine. It was easier to let Williams think everything was roses.

"Good."

She pulled up the first video from the convenience store with the time stamp around the time of the murder. The angle was from the front of the store and didn't show her much, except who was already in there. Felicia Newman was walking toward the back to the dairy case. The images of the blood and milk mingling on the floor crowded into her mind.

She clicked another video file. This was taken from the back of the store and showed everything in the front of the place. Felicia was out of frame now. At the door to the store, she spotted a familiar face. She paused the video and leaned closer. The door opened, and Caleb stepped inside.

As soon as Caleb crossed the threshold, the footage went fuzzy. "Shit."

"No luck?" Williams asked.

"Same as the gas station robberies. What have you got?"

She slid her chair around her desk so she could see Williams's laptop. He had three videos paused on the screen. He dragged one of the videos to the center of the screen and clicked play.

Cars crawled by on the street. Pedestrians hurried along the sidewalk, huddled into their coats. Late November winds pierced through you if you didn't have the proper outdoor attire. Tomorrow, it might be sweater weather again based on the recent weather shifts in the city.

Five minutes into the footage, he hit the pause button and pointed at the screen. Caleb stood right outside the store, Conquest by his side. The horseman had a hand on the young man's shoulder. From this angle, she couldn't tell if Conquest said anything or not, but Caleb nodded, then stepped into the store.

She wanted to know what the horseman had said. Wondered if any of the angles would clearly show his mouth. There had to be someone they could find to read lips.

"I knew it! I'm always right. Caleb had something to do with it." She leaned back in her chair but pointed in the direction of the screen toward Conquest. "And he is the new gang leader."

"Really?"

The footage went fuzzy like all the other footage Conquest was around. Williams scrolled it back to when the pair had first arrived at the store. He clicked the icon to make the video fit the entire screen.

"See the stripes on his jacket? There are six of them."

"You're right."

"Of course I'm right. Aren't I always?" She grinned.

A sudden tightening of her stomach made her gasp. The sensation felt different from the times she'd gained power. She stood abruptly, sending her chair into the desk behind Williams.

The bang caused people in the immediate vicinity to glance over at her. She shrugged an apology and pulled the chair back over to her desk.

"I'm going to get a coffee. You want one?"

The startled look on his face might have been humorous if she weren't in crisis mode.

"Sure."

She dashed to the bathroom. After a quick check to make sure she was alone, she turned her back to the mirror and looked over her shoulder. The white patch she'd been steadily building had shrunk.

"Fuck! So not fair."

Keeping her back to the wall, she left the bathroom and snuck down the hall to the locker room. A quick check of the area confirmed there was no one else there.

She yanked open her locker and retrieved her backup blazer. After her first stakeout, she'd kept the blazer in her locker in case she spilled anything on her every day one.

She hadn't realized how much gravy could stain a blazer until she'd spilled an entire portion on herself in her attempt to get out of the car to pursue the bad guy. Shrugging into the blazer, she adjusted her wings into a reasonably comfortable position. Better safe than exposed for what she was.

The measly amount of magic that helped glamor her wings enough to fit under a blazer without any noticeable bumps might disappear. Being a detective wasn't something she could do from home. And it was well past Halloween, where claiming it was part of a costume would do more than raise eyebrows. How had she lost power sitting at her desk talking about the case?

Halfway back to her desk, she remembered the coffee. She hurried to the pantry area and poured them both coffees in to-go cups. They had a gang leader to talk to.

Under any other circumstances, the room Rachel and Williams sat in would be considered an office. The oak desk in the middle of the room held a laptop and an office caddy full of pens and highlighters. A two-drawer oak filing cabinet with a printer on top stood against the wall behind the desk. A multifunction printer with scan and copy capabilities.

Across from her, Conquest sat behind the desk, hands folded in front of him, looking like someone masquerading as a businessman. Inside gang headquarters, he let the leather jacket hang on the back of his chair. The T-shirt she'd seen him in before was gone. Now he wore a crisp white business shirt with the top button undone. The sleeves, folded to just below his elbow, covered the tattoo that revealed who he was.

"Nice digs," she said, waving her hand in the air.

He leaned back in his chair and grinned. "All legit. Look at the paperwork if you don't believe me. With a warrant, of course."

She glanced over at the filing cabinet. She would love to get a look at any of the paperwork the gang kept on their various activities. Even if they had figured out a way to make it look legitimate, she could always trace it back. Laundered money never came completely clean.

She wanted to throttle him right there. Demand to know where Caleb was. Beat answers out of him if necessary. But she couldn't do any of that with Williams there.

The grin on Conquest's face told her he knew what she was.

She scowled. "I'll believe that when I see it. There's nothing legit about gang activity."

"Now, now, Detective Malak. That scowl mars that angelic face."

"Mr. Tosto, can you tell us what you were doing outside the convenience store yesterday?" Williams asked.

"Victor, please. And is it a crime to stand in front of a store?"

"No, but it is a crime to kill someone in the store." Rachel held her hands to keep them from shaking. So close to a horseman and she couldn't do anything but ask ridiculous questions. It didn't matter what he said; she knew he was, in part, responsible. A horseman's gift, one of their gifts, was the ability to manipulate the soulless. Caleb had a soul. He would be a huge gain for side apocalypse if he could be turned.

"I had nothing to do with that poor woman's death." He schooled his face into a mask of sympathy. "If you have video footage, you know I didn't even go into the store."

"But you were in the gas station when it was robbed," Rachel said.

Williams shot her a questioning look. Her interviews weren't usually all over the place, but she couldn't help it. The bitter taste of anger in her mouth needed answers.

"Also, not a crime," Victor reminded her.

"I will connect the murder of Felicia Newman, Bruno De Luca's death, and the robberies to the gang eventually. Maybe even directly to you."

Conquest grinned. "Don't do anything that will tarnish your halo, Detective."

Heat flushed through her body, warming her face. Body tense, she stood. "Let's go," she said to Williams.

"My men will see you out," Conquest said.

As they walked down the hall, a couple of gang members followed them. Williams touched her arm to stop her. "What was that about?"

It would be so much easier if she could tell him everything. Tell him about being an angel, the impending apocalypse, all of it. If he knew the end of the world was imminent, maybe he would be able to help her stop it. But telling anyone what she and her sisters were was a psych eval waiting to happen.

"It's a feeling. And you know my feelings are rarely wrong."

"Okay, but it's not like you to get rattled. Don't let him get under your skin."

"You're right. Let's get back to the station and piece more together. I am going to nail this guy for all of these crimes."

The gang members behind them chuckled.

"Good luck, lady," one of them said.

Even though they didn't have access to Victor's files, they could talk to real estate agents in the area. Check the recent listings to see who had the commission on the warehouse. When they'd gone in, she'd checked everywhere she could for stray power lines to indicate they were siphoning electricity from a neighboring building. They weren't. So, the lights were on legitimately. Cosmetics didn't matter. What mattered was what was underneath.

One of the gang members slipped past them when they reached the door. He pushed the heavy metal bar in the center, swinging the door wide. Rachel stepped into November's dying light and rolled her shoulders to release the tension from her body.

A black four-door sedan careened around the corner at the top of the street. It slowed when it approached the warehouse. Too late, she spotted the barrel of a gun. The muzzle flash brightened the street. Pain seared through her shoulder. She dropped to the ground, clutching her arm. Williams ducked down beside her.

The car sped away.

The warehouse door banged shut.

She pulled her hand away from her arm. It was wet and sticky.

"What the fuck! I'm bleeding!"

The screeching of the ambulance sirens made Rachel want to bury her head under a pillow. Her temples pounded, and her arm throbbed in time to her heartbeat. Jostled left and right as the ambulance careened through the city streets, Rachel's anger festered. Was that what was causing the woozy feeling in her head? It had been ages since she'd been a flesh and blood human, vulnerable to mortal injury. Now she remembered why she didn't like being human again. The pleasure of food and alcohol didn't make up for the fact she was bleeding.

A figure above her blocked out some of the light in the back of the bus. Her gaze traveled upward until she saw the concerned face of a young EMT who looked vaguely familiar. He peered down at her with knitted brows, his hand gently encircling her wrist as he looked at his watch.

"I'm Jason. How are you feeling, Detective?"

"Like shit."

He smiled, revealing a crack in his front tooth. "You'll be feeling better soon. You've lost some blood, and your blood pressure is a little low."

"How's Williams? Is he okay?"

The ambulance took another turn, and she gripped the side of the gurney with her one free hand.

"He's fine. The bullets missed him. He's worried about you, though. He's going to meet you at the hospital. Do you know what day it is?"

She huffed out a breath. "Thursday."

"Good. Any nausea?"

Rachel shook her head. "I feel fine. I didn't hit my head. I got shot."

Built-up anxiety flushed out of her. At least the gang members were a bad shot. She didn't know who or what they were aiming at, but it didn't matter. There would be retaliation. The Esskays couldn't have known that police detectives were at the warehouse, so that ruled out her and Williams as targets.

"We can never be too careful."

She shouldn't be giving him a hard time. He was doing his job. "Thanks." She closed her eyes to stop the spinning of the small enclosure.

"He called your sisters. They'll likely be at the hospital, too."

The ambulance pulled to a stop in the emergency entrance. The sound of the front driver's side door slamming closed made her jump. The back doors opened, and Jason jumped down to help his partner get her out of the ambulance.

With him beside her constantly checking her vitals, his partner took the bottom of the gurney and pushed it through the sliding doors of the emergency room. Quiet chaos ensued. A large group of people sat waiting to be seen by the triage nurse. Others stood against the wall. Because of the gunshot wound, her EMTs pushed her through the triage door into the actual emergency room. Beds with curtains drawn around them to provide a modicum of privacy lined both walls. A desk stood directly in front of them. Two nurses sat behind it, entering patient information into a computer.

Sarah rushed up as soon as Jason engaged the brake on the gurney.

"Rachel! Are you okay?"

Before she could reply, Jason rattled off her vitals, time of the wound, how coherent she was, liquids they'd given her en route.

"I'm fine, Mom," she said when the EMT was finished.

Sarah smiled. "Bed eight," she said to the EMT.

He rolled the gurney down the hall, and he and his partner, with the help of a nurse, expertly transferred her from the ambulance gurney to the hospital bed.

"Thank you. I'd like to speak to the patient alone for a moment," Sarah said.

Everyone filed out of the small curtained in space. Sarah waited until she saw the shadows against the curtain disappear before regarding Rachel. Under her sister's scrutiny, Rachel wanted to shrug off the injury.

Sarah lifted the gauze on Rachel's wound and grimaced. "Looks painful."

"It is. As a doctor, you can prescribe something for that, right?"

"I can work something out." She replaced the bandage. "You know what this means."

Rachel nodded. "If we can bleed, we can die."

She hadn't liked dying the first time, what she could remember of it. Heaven was good about wiping those kinds of traumatic memories from your mind, especially if you were going to get angel duty. Couldn't have PTSD afflicted angels helping people.

Sarah peeked through a crack in the curtain, then turned her attention back to Rachel. She placed her hand on Rachel's arm. A pleasant warmth spread out from her wound. She jerked her arm back.

"You can't do that," Rachel said. "We need to keep our power." She lifted her arm as proof. "If I'd had more of mine, this wouldn't have happened."

Sarah tugged on Rachel's arm a little more forcefully. Rachel winced. "Sorry. But we can't afford to be an angel down. I'll help it along instead. So the healing time doesn't take as long."

Rachel glared at her but settled back against the pillows. "Okay, but not too much. I don't want to make anyone suspicious."

Sarah placed her hand over the wound again. This time, Rachel didn't pull away from the warmth, the itching. The longer Sarah's hand was on Rachel's arm, the less her wound throbbed.

A shadow appeared on the curtain. "Knock, knock." Williams's voice, while jovial in tone, held a note of worry.

"Come in," Rachel called.

"You look fine." He grinned and took a seat in the

uncomfortable chair beside the bed. "Window curtain, you must have some pull here."

Sarah laughed. "Nice to see you again, Detective Williams."

He dipped his head. "How's she doing?"

"I'll live. I don't suppose you caught the guys who did this?"

"No. Car took off too fast. Got the plate number, but I'm sure that will come back as a stolen vehicle. It was the Esskays. Even they aren't dumb enough to use a car registered to one of them to shoot up a warehouse."

"Fuck."

Sarah gasped. Williams laughed.

"Potshots at the Grange's headquarters means the city has a gang war to look forward to." Rachel clicked the button on the bed to raise the back.

"Afraid so," Williams said.

The curtain rungs screeched as Becky shoved it aside. Becky and Leah filed into the enclosure, Leah pulling the curtain closed again. Sarah jumped out of the way to allow her two sisters to swarm the bed, one on either side. They both leaned over and hugged Rachel. She winced from the slight pinch in her wound.

"Glad you're not dead," Becky said.

"Wouldn't that have made a good story for the six o'clock news?" Rachel asked.

Becky glared, but her bottom lip quivered, and her eyes shone with unshed tears.

Williams also glared at Rachel.

"I'm sorry. I didn't mean it." She held out her arms to pull Becky in for another hug.

Becky perched on the edge of the bed, and Leah took a seat in the other chair at the foot of the bed.

"How much time should Rachel take off, Doctor Malak?"

Sarah opened her mouth, but before she could say anything, Rachel raised a hand. "I can't afford to take any time off. Not now." She gave Sarah a pointed look.

Williams sighed and rubbed a hand across his chin. "You're a great detective, Rachel, but we can do without you for a few days."

If they were dealing with anything else, she would agree with him. But the police were not equipped to handle an apocalypse.

"It's not that. I don't want to leave things unfinished. I won't get any rest anyway. I'll be thinking about our cases. I know they're all connected."

"I've got no problem with you coming back right away as long as your doctor doesn't." Williams glanced at Sarah, who shrugged. "But Reyes will expect you to go see a counselor and be on desk duty until you're cleared to go back into the field."

"Totally fine with seeing someone to talk about my 'feelings' if that's what it takes to get back on the job sooner." Rachel made air quotes to punctuate feelings. "Once the investigations are over. I can't be off the job during these homicide investigations."

Williams shrugged. "You know it's policy."

Rachel shot a frantic look at Sarah.

She had her sisters if she needed to work through emotions. Though the wound initially scared the shit out of her, she knew the angels would be there for her. They would talk her down if needed, so she could stop Conquest.

Sarah pulled the gauze back to see how the wound fared after a little angelic healing. Rachel glanced down at her arm. A small red hole that looked like it had been healing for almost a week marred the otherwise smooth skin.

"Turns out it was a flesh wound. She's okay to return to work after a restful weekend."

"Flesh wound? It looked a lot more serious than that." Skepticism crept into Williams's voice.

"There was a lot of blood loss because of the angle the bullet hit, but she'll be fine on the job on Monday."

Williams stood, and his shoulders sagged with relief. He smiled at Rachel. "Good to know. But Reyes will still require you to see a counselor and be cleared."

Sarah touched his arm, and a glow passed between them. Without another word, he left the curtained area. Then she touched Rachel's arm. The glow was brighter, and during the short time Sarah's soft hand touched her skin, images from the incident careened in her mind, different from what actually happened.

Becky, her gaze glued to Sarah's wings, gasped. Leah's eyes widened.

Sarah pulled her hand back, and as far as Rachel could tell, the doctor's wings not only still had white in them, they had more power than before she'd used some.

"I altered your history so I wouldn't have to make a trip all over the city touching anyone involved. As far as Williams and the police force, and anyone associated with the incident are concerned, you weren't shot. The bullets missed both of you. But I know better, and you're going to take it easy over the weekend."

Chapter Thirteen

Saturday morning light streamed through a crack in the blinds, warming Rachel's hand. Sarah had made her stay home from work Friday, so she'd told Williams she was working from home for "reasons." She kicked her leg out from under the covers, turned over, and hugged the extra pillow on her bed. Groggy, she blinked a few times to bring the room into focus. If it was past eleven, she would get up. Before eleven, she would snooze a little longer.

She turned to her other side, a low throb in her arm reminding her of the shooting. Her heartbeat kicked up a notch, the unpleasant sensation causing her to pull in a deep breath. She concentrated on getting it back to a normal pace.

She wasn't used to the fear. She'd never feared dying. Not even when she died as a human, but now fear that they could be killed raced through her. If Conquest knew they could be eliminated as easily as any human, he might send out hits on all of them. She was sure he'd seen her with at least one of her sisters. Maybe all of them. As a horseman, he had to know if there was one angel there to stop them, there would be three more.

What if they didn't stop the apocalypse? Getting their angel power back was the only thing that could prevent them from dying.

She grabbed her smartphone from the bedside table and hit the home button to check the time. Twelve fifteen. So much for more snoozing.

Rachel stretched and flexed her arm. Every movement worked out a little more of the pain until her arm felt almost normal again.

Since it was the weekend and the doctor ordered her to rest, she left her pajamas on, shoved her feet into bunny slippers, and padded to the living room.

"You're up!" Sarah bolted off the sofa, clicking the remote to turn off the TV at the same time. She hurried over to Rachel and lifted the gauze on her arm.

"I can't believe I slept so long." Rachel smothered a yawn.

"It was the sedative I put in your tea yesterday."

"I feel like it wants to pull me back to sleep." Rachel yawned again.

"Maybe this will help." Becky shuffled over with a steaming mug of coffee.

Rachel took a sip and savored the rich flavor. *Do your magic, caffeine.*

With Sarah by her side like a worried mother hen, Rachel eased herself onto the sofa and put her feet up on the coffee table. She took another fortifying sip of the coffee.

"How much damage did you do to your powers?"

"Not much. Don't worry about it."

"I do worry. If Conquest figures out we can die, we're all as good as toast. It's important that we keep what we earn back. Now more than ever. That means no more miracle healing in the ER."

Sarah twisted a blond lock around her finger, then let it go. "You have a point, so I'll do my best."

Leah, who had been in the kitchen when Rachel woke up, rushed into the living room with a bagel on a small plate. She offered it to Rachel. "Onion and chives cream cheese."

Rachel's stomach grumbled. She smiled her thanks, took the bagel, and bit off a huge chunk, then washed it down with a large gulp of coffee. "Loving the attention but stop mothering me now."

Becky and Sarah took seats on the sofa on either side of Rachel. Leah plopped down into the chair beside her.

"Since you have orders to rest this weekend, we thought we could all do some research." Leah grabbed her laptop from the coffee table and put it on her lap.

"While you were sleeping all day yesterday, we were trying to figure out when Death siphoned the souls in purgatory to Hell," Becky said.

"Let me finish my breakfast and wake up a bit more and I will help." Rachel finished her bagel and chugged the last of the coffee.

Her mind was starting to clear, but she'd need another jolt of caffeine to fight off the lingering effects of the sedative. She took her plate and mug to the kitchen. After putting her plate in the dishwasher, she poured another cup of coffee and added in a generous amount of cream and lots of sugar.

"Don't push yourself too much," Sarah said.

"I love you guys. Stop worrying."

They all looked at her like she was someone else. Even though they weren't real sisters, the bonds of sisterhood were there. They'd all built those into their histories with the magic they'd had left when they first got here. And they were sort of sisters. All angelic beings were brothers and sisters, created by Him. It was a shame it took her getting shot to realize she loved them. And they loved her. Despite sleeping all day, she knew Sarah had stayed home with her while Becky and Leah went to work.

"We love you, too," Becky said.

Leah grinned, happily typing away on her laptop. "I knew she loved us."

Deciding a shower could wait, she retrieved her laptop instead and joined them in the living room for research. The sooner they learned more about what Death had done and when, the better. Knowing when he'd purged the souls in purgatory would help them extrapolate how many people on Earth didn't have souls. At least to a degree. They wouldn't be accurate, of course. Once a person died, if they had unfinished business, their soul was reformed in purgatory to await the next person being born. And if there had been genuine miracles over the years, a new soul could be formed, but those were rare.

Before checking on the Death stuff, she pulled up a browser and did a quick search for real estate in the area of the Grange's HQ. The listing for the warehouse was still up, but a big LEASED banner was splashed across it. Another search turned up numerous listings with the same real estate agent. *Serving business in the downtown area*, according to his tagline. She clicked the link for his website. He'd been in the real estate business for over a decade. Apparently, he had no qualms about helping out criminals. She copied the links and sent them to her work email address to add to the case notes.

After a few hours, Leah sighed and put her laptop on the table. She stood, stretching from side to side. "I found a few leads to libraries that might have actual books with information about the purge in purgatory, but I can't be sure. Everything is vague."

Rachel closed her laptop to give her eyes a break from the glare. "I found some, too. One mentioned a parchment in the Library of Alexandria. No chance of getting a look at that. What have we learned so far about the purge of souls?"

Each one of them had a different web page up. Leah was looking at documents about history. Sarah was looking up birth and death rates going as far back as she could.

Rachel leaned over to see Becky's screen. She was looking up political parties and peace talks.

"Beck, stay focused."

"I am, but you guys have everything covered right now. What else is there for me to check?"

"Fine, follow the signs for now," Rachel said. "Sarah, what have you got on the birth and death rates? Was there a time when the death rates were higher?"

Sarah shook her head. "Most recent birth mortality statistic I can find is that for every one thousand births there are only seventy-nine deaths."

Rachel let out a low whistle. "That's a lot of soulless people walking around."

"Leah, do we know how many souls purgatory actually had?" Sarah asked.

The teacher shook her head. "I'd need to find texts referencing the number it had, but I don't think there is mention of it. Unless the lost book reveals how many there were and we haven't gotten to that part yet."

"Great," Becky said. She shuffled through the printouts of the lost book they'd been able to find. "This doesn't tell us even half the story."

Rachel took a sip of her drink, still non-alcoholic as per doctor's orders. "We'll have to find more of those photos so we can get a better picture of the lost book." She hoped there were more photos out there. They needed the entire book to be able to figure out exactly how much damage Death had done.

"I thought I saw it somewhere, though," Sarah said.

Becky handed her the pages, and she flipped through them.

She cycled through them twice and was on her third when she stopped at a page that didn't look different than any of the other pages to Rachel. She pulled it out of the pile and waved it in the air.

"In this page from the lost books, it says there were a hundred and nine billion souls total in purgatory, not counting ones created due to miracles."

"Those would be negligible, anyway," Rachel said.

Sarah nodded. "Agreed."

"We extrapolate that back, using the birth and death rates, to see when people started being born without souls," Leah said.

"That's too much math for me right now," Becky said.

Leah laughed, held up a finger, then typed in something on her computer. "Based on my calculations, that means people started being born without souls around 1951."

None of them had been Earth side since the early 1900s, choosing cloud duty over spending endless days on the planet. It wasn't as prestigious a job as being a guardian angel, but for her at least, after almost a millennia of guiding humans, she'd been ready for a change.

Rachel sighed. "So if some souls are recycled to purgatory because they still have unfinished business, and new souls are created with miracles, it's possible that people born after that could have a soul."

Leah nodded. "It would be rare, but yes."

"We should take a break for a late lunch," Becky suggested.

"I'll order pizza." Sarah already had the website open for the pizza place around the corner.

Rachel nodded to Leah. "What have we got on Father Ianetti? There is something seriously off with him and I need to know what."

"He was born in 1950 in Toronto and has been here ever since."

Becky frowned. "He hasn't lived anywhere else? At all?"

Leah shook her head. "Nope. To get more detail about where he's visited, I'll need some angel power. Haven't mastered hacking without it yet. I'll work on that later."

Rachel leaned closer to the screen to look at the picture of the priest from a religious website. "He's known in religious circles. For his predictions?"

Leah nodded. "He's been predicting the apocalypse for over ten years. The math was never right."

"He seems awfully confident this time," Sarah said.

"I'm telling you, it's because he's summoning the horsemen. As long as signs are present, all someone needs is the arrival of the horsemen to kick it off. And if he was born in 1950, he has a soul."

"Based on what I'm seeing at the hospital, on my way to work, just walking around with other people, it's pretty bad already," Sarah said.

"Think about how bad it's going to be when they're all here," Rachel said.

"We can do something about that." Leah pulled out a few sheets of paper and waved them triumphantly in the air. "Summoning and vanquishing rituals including ingredients for all the horsemen."

Rachel's pulse raced. "That's great!"

Leah frowned. "Except, there are some things on here that are going to be difficult to get, especially for the vanquishing."

"Concentrate on getting the stuff to summon and send back Conquest since we know for sure he's here."

When the buzzer on the website went off indicating the pizza was on the way, Becky hurried to the kitchen and pulled out plates. She arranged them on the kitchen island, two on either side.

Five minutes later, there was a knock on the door.

"I'm up! I'll get it." Becky ran to the door and yanked it open. "Must have moved too fast. I feel a little odd."

From the sofa, Rachel watched as a patch of white bloomed in Becky's wings. She stifled the annoyance that answering the door earned the angel some power.

"Beck, is there anything different about the delivery?" Rachel asked.

Becky was smiling at the delivery guy, a sixty-something Middle Eastern man with a thick mustache. He smiled as he handed over the boxes.

The man handed her the bill, and she pulled money from her purse. From their usual orders, Rachel could tell Becky gave him a fifty percent tip.

"Thank you so much," Becky said, shoving the money in his hands.

He grinned. "Thank you, ladies."

When she'd closed the door again, Becky listened for a moment, then turned to them. "I saw and heard something!" Becky said. "The pizza guy has a soul!"

Hours later, taking a break from the research, they sat in the packed bar doing a little investigating of a different kind. While they waited for their order to arrive, Becky squeezed through the patrons to see who had a soul and who didn't. Their waiter did. The group of people at the table behind them didn't. Would knowing the exact ages of the people with souls help them figure out when the last soul left purgatory?

After ten minutes away from the table, Becky finally returned, jumping up on her seat with a sigh. "It's bad."

"How bad?" Rachel asked.

"From the people in here, it looks like less than a quarter have a soul." She wrinkled her nose. "They smell like death and decay."

Sarah frowned. "That few?"

"It's only going to get worse," Leah said. "If there are no souls left in purgatory, every birth will be soulless."

Their waiter appeared with their dinner. They waited until all the plates were on the table and he'd left.

Rachel picked up a fry. "The only way to change that is a miracle, which none of us can perform right now. Or more souled people need to die than soulless are being born."

"When has the death rate been higher than the birth rate? I'll tell you. Almost fifty years ago." Sarah snared a fry from Rachel's plate before digging into her pasta.

"They are fond of reproducing," Leah said.

Rachel picked up her juice and regarded Sarah. "Couldn't I have at least had a shot of vodka in it?"

"Doctor's orders. Juice or water only for now. You lost a lot of blood. Alcohol can wait."

As much as she despised being human again, Rachel liked being able to enjoy food once more. And tonight, she had a whole plate of comfort food she was surprised Sarah hadn't vetoed. Surely, the fat and calories of her meal were just as bad for her. She didn't care. The poutine and mac and cheese made her feel better. Maybe it was the cheese.

The jazz music from the stage at the front of the bar soothed her, too. There was something about live music. She tapped her foot, for the moment, enjoying the beat. Life would intrude soon enough, and she'd need to catch killers, stop gangs, try to persuade a beaten, desperate young man with a soul that gang life wasn't for him.

Instinct told her Caleb was more involved with the Grange than she'd previously thought. Not from the beginning. But now, he was involved. Maybe not a full member, and that's what worried her. Initiations.

"Beck, can you get us any information from the TV station about the gangs?"

Becky took a sip of her drink while she thought, reaching back to planted memories of her life at the station before they arrived. "A few years ago we did an exposé about gangs in the city. And a couple months before we were exiled, they did a piece on the guns and gangs summit in Ottawa. I'll see if I can get my hands on the recordings."

"We need to see that footage," Rachel said. Anything they could get that would help them understand where the gang was headed. What Conquest might have in mind for them would help.

"On it when I get back to the station on Monday," Becky said.

A ruckus from the front of the bar drew their attention. Rachel stood to get a better look. Tony and Manny pushed their way through the crowd. Her stomach knotted.

"Shit."

"What is it?" Leah asked.

"Speak of the gang and they will appear."

"How many of them?" Becky asked.

"Only two that I can see, but that doesn't mean there aren't more outside waiting."

The two gang members got to the bar and spoke to the bartender. She couldn't make out what they were saying, but the look of fear on the bartender's face was all she needed.

Before she could move, Tony and his companion slammed through the swinging door that led to the back office. Steve was usually in there doing paperwork if he wasn't on the floor schmoozing with customers. She hadn't seen him all evening.

"Be careful." Sarah grabbed her arm.

Rachel turned, the look of concern on her sister's face reminding her what they were fighting for. Not just getting back home but saving everyone they could.

"Aren't I always?"

She took one last fry covered in gravy and melted cheese curd, popped it into her mouth, then stormed over to the door leading to the office. The relief on the bartender's face was all she needed.

Inside the kitchen area, she spotted Tony, arm poised above Steve for a punch. Another one, by the looks of Steve's cut lip.

She cleared her throat. Loudly. "I wouldn't do that if I were you."

Tony's hand dropped to his side, and he let go of the owner. He turned. The grin that spread across his face when he saw her shot adrenaline through her.

"I know you."

"And I know you. Let him go unless you want a repeat of the first time we met."

He grabbed Steve's shirt again. "Things will be very different this time."

"Really? You want that humiliation in front of your fellow gang member?"

Manny clenched his fists and leaned forward. Tony pierced him with a stare. "No. She's mine."

Tony let the owner go. Steve rushed past her, to the bar. Smart man. She wondered vaguely if he had a soul. Not that it mattered. She saved people who needed saving. The soulless were more easily influenced, more easily corrupted, but they could be good, do good if they wanted.

When the door swished open with his departure, the strains of another jazz tune drifted into the back. She liked this song. Now she was angrier at Tony for ruining their night. Their soul recon. Becky didn't have to check these guys out for Rachel to know they were soulless. Although it would be nice to get confirmation.

"I'll let you go with a warning this time if you're a good boy and leave."

Anger flashed across Tony's face. His hands twitched at his sides like he had pent-up energy that was coming out whether he wanted it to or not.

Confronting them in the back without witnesses wouldn't help the patrons of the bar. She turned her back on the gang members and walked back into the bar area. Probably not her smartest move, but from the quick glance she'd done, Tony didn't have a weapon. And he liked beating his victims. A flash of Darla's battered face popped into her mind.

She smiled at Steve, who was now behind the bar with the bartender. The door swished open behind her. Patrons in the immediate vicinity turned to see what was going on. Music still filled the bar. From the corner of her eye, she spotted her sisters standing at their table, ready to help if she signaled them.

Tony lunged toward her. She stepped out of the way,

kicking out her leg so he tripped into a table. The people at the table grabbed their drinks and quickly fled into the crowd. Others watched the scene unfold from lowered heads, gazing up every so often.

Sadness crept into her. No one thought they could stand up to the gang members. Bullies. That's what they were when it came down to it. Criminals, murderers, but bullies, too.

She turned to Tony, who was shaking himself off from the stumble. "You know what happened last time. Save face and leave. Now."

Though rage contorted his face, a muscle in his jaw twitching in time to the music, he gave a brief nod. "This isn't over, bitch."

"No, it's not. Tell your new leader that this bar is off-limits. I see you here again and you won't like the outcome."

Manny rushed to stand beside Tony. The man's stunned face was almost comical. Anger for the prevalence of the gangs seared through her.

The two gang members hurried out of the bar, a clear path made available to them by patrons who parted as they approached before they moved back into place again. She wiped her hands in front of herself, dusted imaginary lint from her pants, then sidled back to the table.

The TV above the bar showed the weather on one side and a video clip of Father Ianetti on the other with the caption, "The end is still nigh." The ticker below him, giving the latest breaking news, said world peace talks were to start in a week.

Chapter Fourteen

M onday morning, Rachel sat at her desk, her third cup of coffee cooling beside her, going through the preliminary report the forensic pathologist had sent over the weekend concerning the death of Bruno. A more thorough report would make its way to her inbox later, but the cause of death looked like a blow to the head.

As much as she hated the gangs, she hated even more that Conquest had killed the man. That was the only way he could have taken over as gang leader. It also confirmed to her, without Becky's official seal, that the gang members were soulless. If they had a soul, Conquest wouldn't have been able to manipulate them into not killing him when he killed their leader. That was assuming any gang members witnessed the leader's death.

"What did your wife say about the shooting?"

"She was worried, of course. She knows what the job entails, though. And she was happy the guys were such a lousy shot."

Satisfied that Sarah's magic worked and he had no memory of her being shot, Rachel relaxed. "The gang activity over the weekend was too quiet. I'm worried about retaliation. Soon."

"Be thankful for now. If the gang task force hears anything, we'll be the first to know."

Detective Sergeant Reyes walked toward them, a somber expression on his face. The look he always wore when he was sending them to a violent crime. Her immediate thought was a gang hit. Retaliation had begun.

"Malak, Williams, we've got a body for you at an underpass near the lake."

Her stomach turned. "Gang related?"

"Thankfully, no. Old-fashioned homicide. Looks like a homeless man."

She grabbed her jacket and threw keys at Williams. "You're driving."

At the crime scene, ten minutes later, the stench of garbage assaulted her nose. Crime scene tape sectioned off an area closer to the lake. A few homeless people stood by, watching the police. A couple ventured away to panhandle at cars stopped at the red light on the other side of the underpass. The closer she got to the body, the more her stomach knotted. Though they'd been to the bar a few times over the last week, she hadn't seen the street prophet in days. She couldn't remember the last time she'd seen him. Sometime before she and her sisters had gone to the service at the church and talked to Father Ianetti afterward.

"What have we got?" Williams asked one of the uniformed constables.

"Man, mid-fifties, found by a jogger. Initial observations are stab wound."

"I've seen him before. He's usually up near Queen and University. Kind of far away from his usual stomping grounds. Why would he be down here?"

Williams shrugged. "Maybe the earnings aren't that great near the bars. Drivers down here might be more likely to hand over some change."

"Maybe. But I'm not convinced. I know his church. I'd like to go talk to his priest."

Williams raised an eyebrow at her. "Pulled that out of left field."

"Call it another hunch."

If she wasn't careful, she would play the hunch card one too many times and Williams would start asking for explanations. Explanations she couldn't give.

She snapped a picture of the man with her smartphone.

"Whatever you say."

They finished checking the crime scene and gave the constable their cards. CSU would need to finish gathering evidence before they could do much. Uniformed constables were taking statements from people on the scene.

She gave him directions to the church as they walked back to the car.

"Gonna tell me what this hunch is?"

In the passenger seat, Rachel shrugged. "Not yet. You'll think it's too out there."

When they pulled up in front of the church, she felt a longing for home. The church was the closest she'd get to Heaven for now. But this priest was not like talking to a favored uncle.

Rachel opened the heavy wood door for Williams. She followed him down the aisle. A few people sat in pews, silently praying. An elderly woman at the front of the church lit a candle, said a silent prayer, then hurried up the aisle.

"He's probably in the office," Rachel said.

She led the way, turning right at the end of the aisle.

Pictures of past priests of the church lined the wall in the hallway. Rachel scanned them as she walked, starting at the portrait of Father Ianetti until the end of the hallway and Father Power from 1842.

As they turned a corner, a woman came through a door at the end of the corridor. She let out a small gasp when she saw them.

"Sorry to startle you. We were looking for Father Ianetti," Rachel said.

"Of course. This way." The woman retreated through the door she'd just come through.

They followed her into an office. A large desk, the focal point of the room, sat in the middle of the space, with a leather office chair behind it. The desk was bigger than hers and Williams's put together. Two guest chairs were positioned in front of the desk—for ministering to his flock or providing marriage counseling. Bookcases, floor-to-ceiling, stretched across the entire back wall.

Father Ianetti stood at the bookcase, pulling a thick leather-bound tome off the shelf.

The secretary cleared her throat. "Father, these people would like to speak with you."

"Detectives," Rachel corrected.

When Father Ianetti turned around, he was smiling. The jovial look didn't reach his eyes. He gave her partner a once-over, then extended his hand in greeting.

"Nice to see you again, Detective Malak."

"Yeah, you too, Father. We're looking into that street prophet who sits a few blocks over, warning everyone about the apocalypse."

"Yes, disturbed fellow. I've tried a number of times to get him into the church's shelter, but he refuses. Is he okay?"

"Funny you should ask that, Father," Williams said. "He's pretty far from okay."

"That's distressing to hear." Father Ianetti pulled out his chair and sat, waving at the two empty chairs.

They sat, Rachel keeping an eye on the priest to gauge his reaction to what she was about to say next. She pulled out her phone, swiped to pull up the picture, and slid it across the desk. "The end came for him a little early, wouldn't you say?"

The priest's eyes widened, and his hand fisted at his lips. "Who could have done that to him?"

"We were hoping you could tell us, Father." Rachel pulled the phone back and shoved it into her pocket. "Maybe someone didn't like his end of the world proclamations. You know, the ones you keep spouting."

"Malak," Williams warned.

She acknowledged her partner's admonishing look with a shrug. Williams didn't know all the facts. Didn't know what the priest was capable of.

"The end is coming. There's no secret about that. You've seen the countdown clock in my church."

Ignoring Williams's warning, Rachel leaned forward, steepling her fingers in front of her lips. "Did he give too much information away? Your sound bites on the news don't have a lot of information in them. Remember when you saw that lost book yet?"

The priest's gaze went to his bookcase and back to her so quickly, she almost missed it. Did the priest have the ancient text in the building? There was no way they could get a search warrant for it. No judge would believe her theory on the death.

Father Ianetti looked at Williams with sympathy. "It's no surprise she's suspicious. She's not a believer."

"I'm a believer, all right, that's why I know the apocalypse isn't imminent. Unless someone was manipulating things to bring it early." She gave him a piercing stare.

"How can you be certain unless you've deciphered all the prophecies as I have?"

Realizing she'd gone too far, she leaned back in the chair and gave the floor to Williams. She'd have to answer questions from him on the ride back to the station.

"Was the victim part of your congregation, Father?" Williams asked.

"Yes, he listened every Sunday. It could have been a reason to get in out of the cold, but I think he got something out of the sermons."

Williams nodded. "When was the last time you saw him in church?"

"Must have been a few weeks ago. I saw him outside on the street a few days ago, though."

"Did he have any enemies?" Williams asked.

The priest chuckled. "He came off as a little eccentric, but no one disliked him that I knew. I doubt a random pedestrian would kill him because he asked for money."

"Thank you for your time, Father." Williams handed over a business card. "If you can think of anything else, please give me a call."

Williams jerked his head toward the door. Rachel followed him outside. At the bottom of the stairs to the church, he spun around on her.

"What the hell was that? You think a priest killed him over some prophecy? Do you even believe in the apocalypse crap?"

"I've had a run-in with the priest before. There's something about it that isn't right. As to your question about the end of the world, people have been trying to figure out the prophecies and work out the exact date of the apocalypse almost since the beginning. It annoys me that he's taking advantage of people. And others are jumping on board."

"People have been predicting the end of the world for centuries and it hasn't happened yet. Let's see if we can find some actual clues about who killed the homeless guy."

They got to the car, and she slid into the passenger seat, buckling her seat belt. In the window of the insurance company they were parked in front of, a special Rapture policy was on sale.

After smoothing things over with Williams as much as possible by claiming discombobulation from a hectic weekend, Rachel pushed through the glass doors of CTBN. She nodded to the security guard on duty, who nodded back. Though she didn't visit Becky much, he knew they were sisters and wrote her name down in the visitor's log.

"Official business or sisterly?" he asked.

"Sisterly. Thought we could have lunch together. It's been a while since we've done that."

He scribbled the note and handed her a visitor's badge. She tapped the card reader at one of three turnstiles. When the red dot on the corner of the black screen turned green, she pushed forward. The turnstile clicked over smoothly and locked again behind her.

At the bank of elevators, she hit the call button. Becky would be surprised, and when she gave her the news about the street prophet, not good surprised.

Riding the elevator up to the twelfth floor, she ran through what she would say. Nothing sounded right. As much as she harassed Becky for her choice of profession, her sister did care about the people of the city. They all cared.

Becky looked up as Rachel approached her office. The cautious surprise on her face spoke volumes about their relationship. And that was entirely her own fault. Rachel needed to treat Becky more like an actual sibling. A sister she'd grown up with, loved, joked with, mentored.

Becky stood and leaned over to give her a quick hug. "What are you doing here?"

"I thought we could have lunch. They do let you go to lunch, don't they?"

"Sure. Let me tell my intern." Becky unlocked the bottom drawer of a filing cabinet beside her desk and pulled out her purse. She slung the bag over her shoulder, then picked up the phone and told her intern they'd be in the cafeteria.

"I hope you don't mind eating there," Becky said. "We're working on a few big stories and I don't want to go too far in case she needs me for something."

Rachel shrugged. "Food is food. I could eat just about anything right now."

In the cafeteria a few minutes later, they sat by the wall of windows looking out into a park, with a view of the entire cafeteria in front of them. Since it was after one o'clock, most of the tables were empty. Rachel took a bite out of her hamburger while Becky pushed salad around her plate. Right after they'd settled in, Rachel had told her about the street prophet. She hadn't expected the news to steal her sister's appetite.

"Why would anyone want to kill him?" she asked finally, piercing a grape tomato with her fork.

"We're working on it. I can't tell Williams the real reason I suspect the priest has something to do with it."

"You didn't trust him from the beginning," Becky said.

"No, I didn't."

"But why would he have anything to do with killing a

homeless man? He was homeless. He literally had nothing."

Rachel shoved a fry into her mouth and chewed thoughtfully. "I guess you won't be doing a story on him, then?"

Becky dropped her fork and glared at Rachel. "Why do you always do that?"

Rachel shrugged. "It's so easy to push your buttons. I'm sorry. I'll try harder to be better."

Out of the corner of her eye, Rachel spotted a petite blond woman hurrying toward the table, her arms wrapped around half a dozen colored folders. Her long hair was pulled back into a high ponytail, making her look sixteen instead of twenty-six. Pink flushed her cheeks. When she arrived at the table, she pushed black horn-rimmed glasses up from her nose.

"Glad I found you here," she said.

Becky smiled at her. "Laura, you remember my sister Rachel."

"Of course. Nice to see you again, Detective."

"Please, call me Rachel. Looks like you have something for Becky." She nodded at the folders.

"Right!" She handed Becky a green folder. "This is the information you wanted on the peace talks that are set to start next Monday in Prague."

Becky took the folder, skimmed the contents, then put it on the table.

"And this"—Laura handed over a red folder—"is some research on that tip we got last week."

Becky put the folder on the table and smiled. "Thanks, Laura. I should be back upstairs soon."

Her intern hurried away, stopping at the cashier to grab a diet soft drink.

Rachel raised an eyebrow at Becky. "Tip?"

"Nothing much so far, but we got a tip that there was some government secret, a scandal. Something big. Anonymous, of course, so we have to do a lot of research to verify. They didn't tell us much but pointed us in a direction to start looking."

"Why didn't they say more?"

Becky shrugged. "The line wasn't good. I don't know where they were calling from. And the call ended abruptly. We haven't heard from them since."

"Why didn't you tell me this before?"

"It's not a police thing." Becky dove into her salad, apparently suddenly hungry.

"But if it becomes a police thing, you'll let me know?"

"Yes, if it comes to that. Honestly, there are always so many supposed government secrets, we usually do a cursory investigation and they end up being nothing. At least, nothing the public didn't already know."

"Do you know what the something big is?" Rachel asked.

Becky shook her head. "Laura is still working on it."

"And you can trust her?"

Becky looked around, then leaned forward. "She has a soul. And yes, I can trust her."

"Okay." Rachel pointed to the folders. "You look busy and I should get back to the station. Tell Leah and Sarah about the street prophet?"

Becky finished her salad, grabbed her purse from the chair beside her, then stood. "I'll let them know. With all these murders, you're pretty busy, too."

In the building's lobby, Rachel gave Becky a hug and waited until she was at the elevators before leaving. The walk back to the station wouldn't take long, but she needed to think. She turned right outside to take the long way around the block. Why was the prophet a threat? What did he know about what Father Ianetti figured out about the apocalypse? Man had been close to bringing about the end of the world a few times, but the horsemen had never left limbo except for the times right before each world war ended. And even then, it had only been Conquest and War. Now that they had the spells, all they needed were the ingredients and they could send whatever horseman was here back.

Chapter Fifteen

Tuesday morning at the police station, Rachel sat at her desk biting her lip, thinking about the priest. Was the homeless man's death her fault? She was doing her job, but in doing so, had she poked the bear who was now waiting until she was gone to strike? She couldn't check out the streets all the time. She had a job, a life. Well, okay, a job. That job involved helping everyone in the city. If she didn't accomplish her task, it wouldn't matter in the long run how many people she helped.

Williams shuffled papers, flipped through file folders, drawing her back to the cases at hand. She shoved her doubts out of her mind.

"Anything new, Williams?"

Her partner frowned, took a sip of coffee, and pushed away from his desk as if to get up. But he remained there, staring at the computer screen.

"Nothing so far. We already know Bruno was killed with a blow to the head of some kind. No leads yet on who did it. We've started a tip line. Detective Sergeant Reyes is going to hold a press conference later this week to see if we can generate any leads."

"I'm liking a gang member for it. But we need something concrete."

Something that showed Conquest killing the guy would suit her fine, but that wasn't likely to happen. Especially not since he had the ability to screw with the video footage.

A nagging feeling in the back of her mind made her pull up the CCTV footage from a week ago around the street where the homeless man warned passersby of the end.

She pressed play on the footage. After fast-forwarding through days of the same old stuff, she slowed it back to normal when the footage went fuzzy. Rewinding a bit, she stopped it again and hit play. The homeless man panhandled as he talked about the apocalypse. At least she assumed that's what he was talking about. He hadn't been spouting anything else as people walked by. After a minute, the footage went fuzzy. She pulled up a different angle, a few streets over. Her gaze focused on Conquest. Confidently walking down the street, he looked up at the CCTV camera and grinned. Anger made her hands shake.

She pulled up another file with another angle to follow him when he stepped out of range of the first camera. Crisp, clear images played out on the screen of Conquest walking. He seemed to be sniffing the air as he went. Every few steps, he lingered, watching the people who had just walked by. Looking for more recruits?

When she switched the feed again, with Conquest getting closer to the homeless man, the video was fine for a minute. Then it went fuzzy. She synced up that footage with the footage of the homeless street prophet. At the same time, both feeds went fuzzy.

"Williams, you need to look at this."

Williams rolled his chair over, and she hit play on the different feeds.

"If you follow the path and extrapolate, it looks like he might have at least seen the homeless man," Williams said. "But it's fuzzy and you can't actually see him on the sidewalk there."

"I know. This is so frustrating."

"It would suck if other criminals got the same kind of jammer. We should be looking into that, too."

"It's probably not widely available," Rachel said.

She couldn't tell him the interference had nothing to do with a jamming device. Unless he believed a horseman was a device. Did he even believe in that? Scanning her memories, both genuine and planted, she found none that told her whether Williams would accept her apocalypse theory. It would make her job easier if she could tell her partner everything. He would understand her need to intervene. But if she said anything about it now, he might chalk it up to trauma from the job. If that led to being taken off cases, put on desk duty, talking to a shrink all the time, she couldn't handle that. The Earth couldn't afford for that to happen to her.

"How much of the footage do we have for the surrounding area?"

"We have it all from University Avenue and Lakeshore."

She scanned the links their techs had sent over. Finding the ones around the church, she pulled up a video of the night they thought Bruno had died. Williams looked over her shoulder. She felt the frown on his face, the question on his lips, but he remained silent.

She pressed play. A few streets over, out of view of the camera pointed at the church, the prophet guy was sitting at his corner, warning people about the end. She knew that without pulling up that footage because he was there every night. He was there the night she'd helped Darla in the alley.

Members of the congregation spilled out of the church's double doors. Some lingered at the bottom of the stairs. One woman looked up at the door, turned in that direction, as if to go back, but then changed her mind and walked away. Nothing appeared to be out of the ordinary, but something in her gut told her Father Ianetti was part of the puzzle.

A few minutes later, rewarded for her patience, the doors to the back gate of the church burst open. It was too long after mass for it to be a church member. Though she supposed the priest could have stayed behind to talk to people. She clicked the icon to make the video a full screen.

Conquest sauntered out of the gate like he belonged there. He inhaled deeply, turned in the direction of University Avenue, then practically floated along the ground. None of the cameras were fuzzy as they followed him along the sidewalk to the street near the pub where Rachel had helped Darla.

"Hey, that's the new gang leader."

The deep rumble of a voice from behind her made her jump. She turned to see Detective Littman staring down at the footage.

"We think this was the night the original gang leader was killed," Williams explained.

"It was most likely him," Rachel said. "But we can't prove it yet. And right after this, all footage in the area gets fuzzy."

"We've been doing surveillance. Gang initiations are up. Big time." Littman pulled over a chair and sank onto it with a heavy sigh.

Felicia Newman was a gang initiation. They all knew it, even though they couldn't pin it on anyone yet. How many others would there be?

"Why haven't we heard more about it on the news?" Rachel asked. She made a mental note to grill Becky, nicely, about that.

"Our boss is planning a press conference about it. Try to keep the citizens calm. So far, no civilian casualties that we can prove, though we're pretty sure Felicia Newman was an initiation. The Esskays had their HQ shot at. No gang member casualties, either," Littman said.

Glad no one was hurt, gang member or otherwise, Rachel wondered how long that would last. The gangs didn't care who got caught in the crossfire. A twinge of pain in her arm punctuated her point.

"The Grange won't let it stay that way for long," Rachel said.

Conquest had the beginnings of a gang war brewing, and they had to put a stop to that. Get proof about who killed the street prophet and Bruno. And stop the end of the world. No pressure.

Chapter Sixteen

A day following leads that led to dead ends left Rachel annoyed and ready to punch something. She tapped her finger on the desk in time to the headache that had been developing all day. The bright lights of the police station didn't help. She closed her eyes, envisioning all the clues dropping into place, except none of them did. She blew out a long breath. It was almost time to leave for the day, so she locked her computer screen, grabbed her things, and headed for the locker room.

After changing into a T-shirt and shorts, she made her way to the gym in the basement. State of the art, with all the equipment of a high-end gym, it was usually packed. Why pay for a membership somewhere else when you could get to work early to work out? Or in her case, stay a little late to work out her frustrations.

It wasn't just the case. It was everything. Not knowing why she'd been exiled frustrated her the most. She wanted nothing more than to get back home, but she had to help humankind first. They deserved help. The species had potential. They were capable of great things, but none of those things would happen if Father Ianetti got his way.

The fact that there was nothing to tie him to any of the killings irked her, too. With Conquest on his side, though, it would be hard to pin anything on the priest.

Thankful the gym wasn't as busy as usual, she strode to the heavy bag, smiling at fellow officers as she went. After taping her hands and putting on gloves, she flexed her hands a few times before throwing the first punch. The satisfying thud eased the tension in her shoulders.

She pictured Conquest's face and punched the bag again. In a showdown between the two of them, who would win? She had to have hope that good would triumph, but they could bleed, which meant they could die. If the bullet had hit her heart or another vital organ, would she be here punching a bag? Sarah would have used what little power she had left to save her. Probably. She shook off the thought. She didn't want to find out how vulnerable they were.

Working out also helped to clear her mind. God knew she had a millennium of knowledge packed in her brain, most of it accessible to her. But some only revealed itself when her mind was clear and she was able to think of things in new directions. It helped her become more human again before going home to her "sisters." It wasn't their fault they were all stuck here, but she tended to take it out on them.

An hour later, workout done, she showered quickly and changed back into her clothes. Expecting missed calls or messages from her sisters, she retrieved her personal phone with trepidation. Nothing. She frowned, hoping the same wouldn't be true for her department-issued phone. She pulled out that phone and checked emails, praying a report had miraculously popped up while she'd been busy.

Nothing new drew her attention. Tomorrow was another day. Instead of phone calls, she would drag Williams out to interview more people. Maybe get permission for a stake-out. All this waiting was driving her crazy.

She left the station and walked the short distance to the loft. One of the reasons they'd picked the loft was its proximity to work. Leah hadn't been there at the time, though, so she had a little more of a hike than the three of them did. The business that had been there before they'd magically moved in was now in an even more prime location closer to the lakeshore. At the same rent. They'd had to magically alter the zoning for their part of the street, too, but it worked out well.

She took a deep breath and headed up the stairs. They had the whole building to themselves, for now. Maybe once they fixed things on Earth and were able to go home, they'd open it up for others to move in. At reduced rents. They shouldn't be the only ones to benefit from the location and the amazing view of the city.

At the door of the loft, she squared her shoulders. She needed a distraction from the cases that were slowly torturing her. If she couldn't piece them all together, Conquest could win. He could start a gang war that the city might not recover from. But more than that, the perpetrators of three murders would go free. She couldn't live with that.

She slid open the door. Inside, Becky, Sarah, and Leah were standing at the kitchen island. Papers and folders were spread out in front of them. They looked up when she closed the door. She dropped her keys on the table just inside.

"Don't say anything else until I get back." Rachel retreated to her room, locked her gun away, then returned to the kitchen.

She stopped at the fridge. "Anyone need a refill?" She shook a bottle of water.

"I could use more," Becky said.

Rachel brought enough bottles over for all of them. "What are we doing?"

"Going through the ancient documents and assembling a list of the ingredients we already have for summoning and vanquishing the horsemen." Becky crossed her arms over her chest.

"Let me help."

Becky's eyes widened. Sarah walked around the island and put the back of her hand to Rachel's forehead. Rachel swatted it away.

"You want to read through piles of Enochian?" Leah asked.

"I need to forget these fucking cases for a while."

Becky gasped. "You know I hate when you do that."

Later, she would examine why she swore so much in front of Becky. Now, she smiled. "I know. Sorry. Can't say I'll stop. I do want to help for a while. Maybe thinking of something else will spark something."

Sarah handed over a list. "These are some of the ingredients we've got. The ones marked with an asterisk are rare. Like the pure black candles with the inscriptions. Leah has called into all the occult shops in the area. According to Father Ianetti's prediction, the full-blown apocalypse will be here in less than three months."

Eyes glazing over, like going over reports at work for too long, Rachel forced herself to focus. These documents were worse, in an ancient language she barely understood. And Sarah's handwriting was typically illegible doctor scrawl. After ten minutes, she sighed and put down the paper she'd been studying. As she picked up another paper, her stomach grumbled.

Everyone looked up.

"I could eat," Sarah said.

"Me too," Becky and Leah said in unison.

Rachel pushed away from the island. "I'll go pick up dinner. Any suggestions?"

The three angels looked at each other, eyes widening. They nodded.

"Burgers," Leah said.

Becky jumped off her stool. "I'll come with you."

Rachel thought about arguing, but she forced herself to smile instead. She got along fine with the other angels. Yet, something about Becky always got her back up. In their magically implanted history, they were the closest in age. She didn't have a sister in real life when she'd been alive. Maybe having one so close to her own age meant you either got along well or you fought constantly.

"Play nice, you two." Sarah gave them a stern look.

"We'll be fine," Rachel said. "While we're gone, see if you can find anything else about the summoning ritual for Conquest or any of the horsemen."

She barely waited for Becky to follow her before she was out the door and halfway down the stairs. Becky huffed behind her when she caught up.

"So, you've got nothing for the investigations, huh?" Becky asked.

Rachel glared over her shoulder. "Nothing yet. What about you? What have you found out about anything?"

"Laura is on it. I'm sure we'll find something soon. As much as you annoy me sometimes, you are a great detective. You used a lot of magic to build that into your history."

"Thanks."

Finally at the greasy burger joint on the corner of their street, Rachel held the door for Becky. Inside, the sizzle of meat on the grill made Rachel's mouth water. Filled with customers waiting for their orders, she and Becky squeezed through the crush of people to the one till with a cashier. After placing their orders, they moved to one side to wait.

"Why didn't we just call in the order and have it delivered?" Becky asked.

"I thought a little fresh air would be nice. Too lazy to do even that?"

Becky glared at her. "That's why you think I picked the job I did?"

Rachel shrugged. "I didn't say that."

Before Becky could say anything else, their order was called. Rachel pushed back through the crowd to grab it, then shoved the door open, holding it with her hip for Becky. What kind of angel had Becky been for her human charges? Did she whisper only half an encouragement speech to them and have them fend for themselves? The angel had to be good at what she did. He wouldn't have sent Rachel down here with three angels who weren't worthy. Who couldn't help her save the world. At least, she hoped not.

"The cashier doesn't have a soul. The cook does."

Rachel filed that information away for later use, noting that the cashier was probably mid-twenties, and the cook looked to be in his sixties.

Back at the loft, she and Becky entered the room again, paper bags with growing grease spots in their hands, and Leah beamed at Rachel.

"Dinner is here!" Becky said.

Leah turned her computer around and pointed at the screen. "The shop on College called while you were gone. The holy basil is in!"

"That's great." Rachel smiled at her. "Get the stuff to summon and send War back too."

"Why?" Sarah asked.

"Because he'll be the next to be summoned," Becky said.

Rachel nodded. Becky was smarter than Rachel was giving her credit for. "Maybe we can stop Father Ianetti from summoning any more."

"You really think it's the priest?" Sarah asked.

"Yes, I do." It wasn't against the law to hold rituals and attempt to summon demons or horsemen to speed up the apocalypse, unless he killed someone in the process. Too bad she couldn't arrest him for having the accoutrements. She was sure he would spin it somehow. Claim it was a lesson for his congregation and that he didn't use it for anything.

Everything happening in the city for the past week with the murders was tied together. She knew it in her gut, but she couldn't prove anything. And she needed to come up with a non-magical, non-apocalypse explanation for Williams when she finally tied everything together.

Sarah grabbed a note from the counter. "Becky, your intern called. She said she had another tip."

Becky pulled out her cell phone and walked to the far end of the living room. After a brief conversation, she pocketed her phone and joined them at the breakfast bar again.

"This tip is about government secrets going back to the eighties."

"What kind of secrets?" Rachel asked.

The frown on Becky's face worried Rachel.

Becky popped a fry into her mouth. "Not sure, but I get the feeling it's going to be really bad. We're just scratching the surface."

Chapter Seventeen

Two days later, after a full day of chasing more leads and doing more interviews, Rachel sat in her car, ignoring Becky's many messages about getting a quote for her story on the gangs, instead focusing on watching the Grange's office. That's what it was now. The previous hideout was rough, dusty, inadequate. This new place gave the gang an air of legitimacy.

The reasons for Conquest wanting the Grange to be more businesslike mattered. When it was a regular gang, they were more predictable. Now, with a warehouse, probably ledgers, maybe even legit investments, a raid might only slow them down. Still, slow was better than full speed ahead. She had to believe they would be able to disband the gang once they had sent Conquest back to limbo.

The parade of members coming and going from the place didn't surprise her until she spotted Caleb. Her heart broke a little when he grinned at one of the members with him. A quick, probably "secret" handshake, confirmed her fears. If the new swagger, non-hunched-over posture didn't indicate he was a member, the handshake did.

She still had hope that he hadn't had anything to do with Mrs. Newman's death. If he wasn't in too deep, there was a chance she could help him turn things around. If he helped them bring the gang down, the consequences for whatever he'd done as a member could be reduced. A knot in the pit of her stomach bothered her. Maybe not all gang initiations were murder. If Becky were there, would her sister see a tarnished soul when she looked at Caleb?

Her phone buzzed in her hand. Instead of ignoring it, she glanced at the screen, wondering if thoughts of Becky had willed the reporter to call again. Leah instead of Becky.

She swiped to answer the phone. "What's up?"

"Good, you are there. Becky was worried."

"I'm sure she was. Is that why you called? I'm in the middle of something right now."

Not a lie, really. She was watching a known gang location to gather information. True, it was also an excuse not to go home yet. The Grange, Conquest, and the apocalypse were tied together somehow, and she needed to pick at the pieces until they made sense.

There would be no Rapture. They would stop the coming apocalypse. They had to. Any other outcome was unacceptable.

"I know your work is important, but you're off the clock now, right? You need to come home. We need to talk about a plan for vanquishing Conquest. And we still need a bow and arrow washed in holy water."

Hope nudged the knot in her stomach. "I'll be there soon."

She put the car into drive as Manny arrived. A lot of the members were showing up tonight. It was rare to see most of the gang members in one place at the same time.

If something was brewing, that would make a raid that much more important.

An hour later, Rachel pulled open the loft door, shrugged off her coat, and put it on the top hook of the coat rack. She dropped her keys on the table. She would stow her gun later. On the way home, she'd stopped at a sporting goods store to pick up a bow and arrow set, complete with extra arrows. She plunked that down on the island.

Leah sat at the island, her cell phone to her ear. Snippets of conversation told Rachel she was trying to track down the rest of the ingredients to summon the horsemen. If they could get their hands on it before the person doing the summoning, they might put a dent in his plans.

Becky sat opposite Leah, her laptop open, an almost empty pint of ale beside it. She pointed at the weapon. "We'll need to find a priest to bless that and give us holy water."

Rachel sat at a stool behind the island, facing the living room. The blinds were down, shutting out the dark.

"Yes. I'm not sure what I'll say. Maybe the truth."

Sarah sat opposite her, digging into a bowl of melting ice cream. "Things are getting out of control. Today, leaving the hospital, I saw a woman yell at a man for holding the door for her."

Rachel frowned. "That does seem odd."

"The woman's hands were full. She was trying to open the door with her elbow."

Becky nodded, draining her glass. "In the café this morning, a guy threw a hot coffee at the server because it wasn't hot enough."

Sarah drank the melted ice cream from the bowl and walked over to the dishwasher. She put the bowl in the bottom rack.

"Rach, are you going to eat?" Sarah asked.

Until then, Rachel hadn't noticed the pizza box on the top of the stove. Her stomach grumbled. "I could have a few slices."

Sarah got her a plate of food and placed it on the island.

"Same delivery guy?" Rachel asked.

Becky shook her head. "This one didn't have a soul." The angel's pretty face screwed up with a disgusted look. "The soulless really do not smell nice."

Becky turned her laptop so they could all see it. Three different documents with various graphs populated the screen. "My intern has been doing some research for me. This graph shows the instances of minor violence and road rage type incidents going up." She pointed to a bar graph.

Rachel leaned closer to read one of the tags. "Carjackings? Not exactly road rage."

Becky pulled the laptop closer. "We lumped everything else under road rage for now."

"Conquest's influence is spreading even without him trying to affect others," Rachel said.

Leah hung up the phone. The look on her face didn't bode well for their plan to stop the rest of the horsemen from being summoned.

"Since we have most of the ingredients, I was calling around to all the occult shops in the area to see if anyone else was looking for the same items. According to the clerk I just spoke to, Father Ianetti has enough holy basil to summon a hundred horsemen."

Monday afternoon, after a weekend of accumulating ingredients and items to vanquish Conquest and summon the other horsemen, Rachel sat at her desk, eyeing her empty coffee mug. At best they would delay Father Ianetti from summoning more of the horsemen that he didn't already have the ingredients to summon. Maybe he had them all and now they had more than they needed for the horsemen. She shoved the apocalypse out of her mind and turned back to the investigation at hand. Going over witness statements for the fifth time from the convenience store murder was making her eyes glaze over. She needed a jolt of caffeine. Stat.

"You want another coffee?" She pointed to Williams's mug. It sat precariously on the edge of his desk. One accidental gentle tap of anything would send it crashing to the floor.

He picked it up, saving it from a shattered fate, and drained the contents. "If you're getting it, sure."

She flashed a smile and grabbed his mug.

The coffee at the café around the corner was much better than the break room coffee at the station, but they had too many loose ends from too many cases to waste even a second. Second-rate coffee would suffice for now.

She finished pouring their drinks, adding a little more sugar to her own than usual, then hurried back to her desk.

"We're getting together for drinks next Thursday. You guys should come." She plunked his mug in the center of his desk. Not that having drinks at the bar with her sisters was new, but she should spend more time with Williams outside of work. The partnership bonding she implanted in his memory would be stronger if they actually bonded.

"Drinks? Special occasion?"

"Becky got it into her head that it would be fun. We haven't seen your wife in ages. Becky promised not to grill you about any cases."

He took a tentative sip of his coffee. "I guess we could

show up for a while. Tisha is always on me about going out more."

"You do work too hard. I should appreciate that more." The now familiar feeling of magic returning to her wings fluttered through her.

Later, she would mention it to Becky so she could put it in her spreadsheet. It couldn't be as easy as being genuinely nice to someone. She'd been nice and in some cases selfless a lot since arriving on Earth. Not everything got her a power boost.

"Back at you." He saluted with the mug and took another drink.

She turned her attention to the statements again. She shuffled them around, putting them in order of believability. The most believable at the top, working down to the least believable. Some of the witnesses had been girl-friends or ex-girlfriends of gang members. Others were regular citizens of the city, in the wrong place at the wrong time. It was always traumatic witnessing violence but watching a murder, seeing the life drain out of someone, haunted you.

As a guardian angel, she'd been around death a lot when she'd been on Earth. Before transferring back to cloud duty to observe from afar. Helped people in their final moments come to terms with what was about to happen. Held their hand reassuringly when the Angel of Death came to take them. Or one of his servants did the job in his absence. Earthbound most of the time, Death couldn't be everywhere at once. His presence was found where big death counts happened. For the individual, everyday passings, an army of reapers ushered the souls home if their business here was done.

Even if people related to the gang had been lying, there had to be a ring of truth to something they said.

Anything. She would grasp at any straw if it meant finding out who killed Felicia Newman.

"I know this convenience store murder is gang related," she said. "The problem is proving it. I think we should go talk to Caleb again."

Williams drained the rest of his coffee and plunked the mug on the desk. He tidied a pile of folders, then closed the lid of his laptop. "Let's go. According to my notes, Caleb should still be at work right now."

Outside the warehouse where Caleb worked, Rachel scanned the surrounding area, up and down the sidewalk, the street. At that hour of the afternoon, the early commuters milled about in their attempt to reach Union Station on time for their evening trains.

Caleb's boss told them he was in the locker room. Raucous laughter greeted them when they pushed through the doors of the locker room. Florescent lights flickered. Benches faced narrow metal lockers that lined the walls. Caleb was in the center of it all. A huge smile curled his lips. Fellow employees patted him on the back, gave him high fives. The sadness that lurked in his eyes and on his face that first day she'd met him was gone. New confidence made him look taller. Her stomach knotted.

A hush fell over the room when his coworkers saw them. Now the admiration was silent, with nudges to the shoulder, nods of encouragement.

He looked over, saw them, and slammed his locker closed before they got closer. There was something in there he didn't want them to see.

"Caleb," Williams said. "We wanted to ask you a few more questions about the convenience store murder."

Nostrils flared, eyes cold, he cracked his knuckles and avoided Williams's gaze. "How many times I gotta tell you I don't know anything?"

Thanks to her recent power boost she saw that his soul, once bright when she first saw he had one, was now dim. Either he'd sold his soul to the Devil or done something to tarnish its purity. With the apocalypse approaching, the Devil had too much to do to mingle with mortals this early. Even his demons wouldn't be around to interfere. At least not yet. Conquest was the only explanation.

"You might not know that you know something. Any detail, no matter how small, could help us catch the person who murdered Mrs. Newman." She hated the desperation in her voice, but she was desperate.

He pulled out his phone and hit the button to bring the screen to life. Notifications zoomed by as he scrolled. He pocketed the device and looked at her, defiance in his eyes. "I can't tell you anything I don't know."

"She was pregnant. Did you know that?" She'd read the note from Dr. Malani this morning.

He shrugged. "Nah, man. How the fuck would I know that?" He checked his phone again, then shoved it back in his pocket.

"Do you have to be somewhere?" Williams asked.

"Matter of fact, yes. My father gets angry when I'm late."

"Haven't been late in a while, I take it." Rachel pointed to his face. The bruises on his face were almost healed and there were no new ones. "Not late or not living there anymore?"

"Whatever. I have to go."

"Fine," Williams said. "We'll be in touch again later."

He made it halfway to the door when Rachel said, "No coat? It's cold out there."

Caleb huffed and hurried back to his locker. He yanked the door open and pulled out a ball of leather that he tucked under his arm. No matter how much he tried to disguise the leather jacket, Rachel spotted the telltale stripes of the Grange.

When he dashed out of the locker room, Rachel nudged Williams. "Let's follow him. Did you see that stripe on his jacket?"

Outside, they spotted Caleb climbing into a white SUV. The same vehicle Rachel saw the night Darla had been thrown from the car to make a statement. They walked closer, blending into the crowd so the driver wouldn't see them approach. When they were close enough for her to see the man behind the wheel, her stomach knotted. Conquest grinned at Caleb as the young man settled into the passenger seat, then threw the car into drive. The vehicle sped off. The horseman had a hold of Caleb, and he had a habit of not letting go.

Without a word, Williams and Rachel raced to their car and followed them. Twenty minutes later, they pulled up in front of the Grange HQ. The two men got out and strode to the door, nodding at the two sentries posted outside the main entryway. She'd failed Caleb. How could she convince him that being a part of a gang was the last thing he wanted?

Chapter Eighteen

Victor regarded Caleb while the young man pondered what to do next. On the other side of the gym, there was silence from the gang members on the wooden benches lining the back wall as they watched him put Caleb through his paces. They barely breathed, waiting for the next punch to be thrown, the next kick to land. With none of the usual distractions of a normal gym, they had nothing to do but watch or fight.

Caleb bounced from foot to foot, moving his head from side to side, working out kinks in his neck. The young man's fists clenched.

Victor sidestepped Caleb's attack, dodging a punch before it got close to his face. The young man was getting better at fighting, carrying himself with more confidence, landing more blows than when they'd first started training. But he was still green. There was a part of him that didn't belong to the gang yet. Something was holding him back. Victor took a deep breath as he dodged another punch. The man's soul hadn't turned completely.

If he gave the members free rein, no consequences for

severely hurting Caleb, would that make him learn faster? Probably, but he wanted the guy to feel safe, trust him. Allow his soul to be corrupted thoroughly. To do that, he had to be better than the guy's father. Maybe, as a reward, he'd take care of the asshole for Caleb.

Despite years of practice, whenever the apocalypse drew close due to worldwide happenings, it was harder to convert the souled than he remembered. During times of war, it was easier. Drawing on fear and people's inherent greed had the souls flip faster than the subway turnstiles during morning rush hour.

A few of the gang members had souls. He glanced around the room. Headphones on, Manny absently lifted weights while keeping an eye on him and Caleb. Though everyone had to kill someone to get into the gang, Manny hadn't done much in the way of criminal activity since. For a gang member, he lacked the drive to be anything but a minion.

Victor threw a punch. Caleb blocked, bounced, and retaliated, landing the blow on Victor's cheek. Pain exploded in his head. He shook it off. Taking human form had its drawbacks, but it also had pluses.

"When am I going to get to train with the guns?" Caleb asked, moving his feet one way and his torso another.

"Not until I say you're ready. Do you think people fear you yet?" Victor nodded at the audience they had. "Do you think any of them fear you yet?"

Doubt cast a shadow on the man's face. "I guess not."

Caleb stood straighter, hands up, prepared to block. Victor came at him fast, throwing punch after punch to see how fast Caleb's hands could move. When he blocked his face, Victor swung low to hit his ribs. Caleb blocked again, so Victor went high to punch him in the jaw.

Sweat beaded on Caleb's forehead. His breathing came in short gasps. But he kept his gaze focused, his arms up, his legs moving, prepared for another assault.

"That's it for today," Victor said.

"I can go longer." Caleb dropped his shoulders but stayed alert.

"I know, but we have business we must get to first. We'll train again tomorrow."

Victor walked over to the bench by the window and threw one of the towels sitting there to Caleb.

"Men, finish up here, get everyone from the game room, and meet in the conference room. Ten minutes."

Gang members scrambled to obey, immediately dropping what they were doing. They rushed out of the room. Victor's lips curled into a smile. He loved the fear. He wanted the city to tremble with it. To do that, he had to move up his timetable. Father Ianetti wouldn't object. The priest was even more eager than he was to bring about the apocalypse.

The conference room was located across from his office. Two nights ago, he'd blocked off the area, putting up tarps, and told everyone there was construction going on. In reality, he'd zapped in a state-of-the-art conference room, complete with video conferencing and HDMI connections for his laptop. For too long, the gang fumbled about, making more than decent money, but not living up to its potential. They could do so much more with a city the size of Toronto.

He pushed through the double-glass doors. Floor-to-ceiling windows opposite the door let in the sunshine. At the back of the room, a small credenza against the wall provided coffee, tea, and water. Everyone currently present at HQ sat around large, dark wood tables, positioned so they formed a U shape. He stood in the well of the U and regarded each member. The ones who weren't here would be briefed later. He couldn't have everyone at HQ. There was still work that needed to be done on the streets.

He connected his laptop to the HDMI cable. The screen behind him flared to life. Splashed across his screen, a graph of activity showed the shortcomings of the group.

"See these numbers? This is not acceptable. Recruitment is down. Esskays' recruitment is up." He paused, scrutinizing the members. Would they fail him? "I need someone for a special project."

Every member shot their hand in the air, except Manny. Caleb waved his around like it was on fire.

Victor pointed at Chris. "You. You're going to 'defect' to the Esskays."

The man's mouth fell open, eyes wide. He hesitated a second before nodding. "Whatever you say, boss."

Victor walked over to a cabinet by the screen. He waved his hand in front of it, then opened the door. He took out a newly conjured bomb, complete with cell phone activation. "I need you to place this somewhere where it can do the most damage."

All eyes widened. A few of the members leaned away from the device. Chris moved closer to it, examining the bomb. "I attach the wire here?" He pointed to an unattached wire. "And then dial in the number?"

"Exactly. You can attach the wire now if you want. It's not connected for safety reasons, but I'm sure you'll be careful with it until it arrives at its proper destination."

"Consider it done."

"Good. War is coming, men." He smiled at his inside joke. A gang war was just the start. Once War actually arrived, all hell would break loose. "We have to be prepared. We have to be the strongest left standing."

Cheers went up. Caleb sat up straighter, chiming in

with the shouts. Relief crossed his face as he watched Chris take the bomb back to his seat.

"Is there anything you want us to do?" Caleb asked.

"For now, no. After the bomb goes off, we will be the largest gang. We'll control the most territory once we grab what little territory they have. With fewer numbers, they won't be able to handle it all."

He dismissed them. They hurried out, everyone rushing to be the first out of the conference room. No one wanted to be left in the room with a bomb. Chris took off his jacket and wrapped it around the device, careful not to nudge anything that might set it off.

As the members left, Victor smiled to himself. He couldn't wait to see how Detective Malak handled what was coming next.

Tuesday evening, Rachel sat on the sofa with the TV tuned to Becky's newscast, waiting for Leah and Sarah to get home. Instead of enjoying the rarity of having the loft to herself, she listened to Becky's coverage on the gang violence in the city. It was like her sister was still in the room with her.

When Becky switched stories and introduced the peace talks in Prague to take place in a week, Rachel pushed herself off the soft cushions and went to the kitchen. Though it was customary to wait for all of them to be home before having the evening meal, she still wanted something to eat. She pulled out the ice cream from the freezer. The thought of eating it out of the tub crossed her mind, but she grabbed a bowl and scooped out half of the ice cream.

Plodding back to the living room, she arrived in time to

catch Becky still talking about the peace talks to be held in Prague. All indications pointed to the talks going well once they started, but that caused the ever-present knot in Rachel's stomach to worsen. Once countries got to a point that peace talks were necessary, it was already too late. Another sign of the apocalypse to check off the list.

Voices from the hallway pulled her off the sofa again. She finished her ice cream, cringing at the spike of pain in her head. She put the bowl in the dishwasher, then took a seat at the kitchen island.

Sarah and Leah walked into the loft together, laughing at something one of them had said or seen. They looked like they'd grown up together. Real sisters. The power of magic never ceased to amaze her.

"According to Becky's report, things are not looking good," Rachel said. She focused her attention on Leah. "Do we have all the ingredients to send Conquest back to limbo?"

Leah lifted a shoulder to grab the strap of her laptop bag. She put the computer on the table and took a seat beside Rachel, back straight, hands folded in front of her. She grinned. "I have everything we need to summon him. For sending him back, the limestone from Mount Hermon still isn't in. And then, of course, we require the opportunity."

"Working on that. Based on intel from Detective Littman, a raid of the headquarters will be any day now. His confidential informant told him things are a lot more dangerous. Something's brewing."

"You think Conquest knows?" Sarah asked.

Rachel shrugged. "I don't want to risk it." Her stomach grumbled.

Sarah smiled. She proceeded to pull out ingredients from the fridge, placing them on the counter. Once everything was assembled, she took out pots, pans, knives, measuring spoons.

"I'll start making dinner. Becky should be home soon."

An hour later, Sarah plated dinner. Becky breezed into the loft, hair still picture-perfect, gently lowered her laptop bag to the floor, and plopped down on her stool. "I'm famished."

Sarah got drinks and filled glasses. They sat around the counter, enjoying their meal in silence for a few minutes while everyone savored the dish.

After a few bites, Becky paused with her fork halfway to her mouth. "We got a tip today on the secret the government is hiding."

"Another tip? What did this one say?" Rachel asked.

"They told us to follow the history."

"Follow the history? That's a new one. Usually it's follow the money," Rachel said.

"They didn't say what history to follow. Cryptic tips are frustrating."

When they finished eating, Sarah put her hands on the counter to push herself up.

Becky held up a hand. "I'll do it. You've been on your feet all day."

They all gave her a surprised look. "Are you feeling okay?" Leah asked.

Relieved that she hadn't been the one to ask the question, Rachel waited for an answer. She had been thinking the exact same thing.

Where Becky would glare at Rachel for such a question, the reporter smiled at Leah. The youngest always got a pass, it seemed. "You're so funny. I sit all day behind a desk. I need to stretch out, move a little more."

She gathered the plates, wiped off any leftovers into the

compost bin, then loaded them into the dishwasher. She did a little shiver on the way back to the counter.

Rachel steamed as she bolted off her stool to inspect Becky's limbs. "You have a huge patch of white near your spine. Way more than I remember the last time I looked."

Becky shrugged. "I don't tell you every time I get that tingly feeling."

"How about everyone else?" Rachel asked.

Sarah and Leah showed their wings. Leah hadn't been here as long as the rest of them, but already, she had a patch of white larger than Rachel's.

Sarah looked at Rachel's wings. "You do have some still, but it is small."

Before she could go on a tirade, her cell phone buzzed. She pulled it out of her pocket and swiped to answer when she saw Williams's name flash on the screen.

"Malak. What's up?"

"Can you come to the station? Things are about to be afoot."

"Be there in ten."

She pocketed her phone again and rankled at the disappointment on Leah's face.

"I thought we were going to work on the return spell tonight."

"You said you have everything except the limestone. This call into work might help with the opportunity part."

Before the others could protest, Rachel grabbed her badge and gun, threw on her coat, and left.

At the station, Littman sat on the edge of Williams's desk. The two men were deep in conversation, Williams's face a mask of concern. When she approached, they looked up. Littman barely mustered a smile.

She plopped into her seat. "This isn't good, is it?"

Littman shook his head. He filled her in on his CI learning about a defection.

"You think it's a ruse to take them out from the inside?" she asked. There was no way in hell she believed a member of the Grange defected to a rival gang. They were up to something.

"My source says a gang war is coming."

The phone on Williams's desk rang. He held up a finger to stop the conversation until he could participate again. He yanked the receiver off the hook. As the person on the other end spoke, the look of dismay on Williams's face got worse.

Standing as he hung up, he said, "There's been an explosion at the Esskays' hangout."

The bad feeling in her stomach kicked up a hundred notches.

Chapter Nineteen

B y the time they arrived on scene, first responders had cordoned off a large area around the building that held back onlookers. Neighbors clutched coats closed at the neck; slippered feet moved from side to side to keep warm. They stood outside the tape, pointing, crying, coughing. Red and orange flames brightened the night sky. Three fire trucks attempted to put out the flames. Firefighters dashed out, carrying the living and the dead. The scent of burning wood mingled with chemicals tainted the crisp air.

Dark plumes of smoke rose from the windows. The building, once a rickety two-story home, now mostly rubble, creaked and groaned under the consuming flames.

The timing of the explosion nagged at Rachel. While they didn't have anything concrete to nail Conquest and the gang, they were getting closer. Caleb might turn to their side if she spoke with him again. The whole thing had distraction written all over it.

Williams put the car in park, and they got out, Detective Littman pulling in behind them. They walked over to one of the police constables guarding the area. Covered in soot, his haggard face spoke of the loss of life. Rarely venturing out of her division, she didn't recognize him. If he was a rookie, this was a hell of a way to get experience.

Flashing their badges, Rachel said, "How are you doing, Constable?"

"Okay. They have the flames under control. Not many coming out alive."

He looked over at a grouping of tarps on the grass in front of the building. Five so far and probably more based on how many members they knew to be in the Esskays.

"Thanks."

Littman jogged ahead, a constable lifting the tape for him as he approached. He spoke with another plainclothes detective, the frown on his face growing. The look in his eyes told her something else had happened.

He jogged back over, shaking his head. "You two need to head over to Dundas Street West and Spadina Avenue."

"What's happened?" Williams asked.

"Gang shooting."

Sometimes, she hated being right. "We'll head over and let you know what we find out."

"Thanks. I need to stay here for the time being. Then regroup." Littman shook his head and rubbed his hand over his face.

Back in the car, Williams threw it into gear and stomped on the gas. Almost mid-week, traffic wasn't too bad since there was no game going on downtown. It was rare that none of the city's professional sports teams were playing that night, but she was thankful for their rest. With lights and sirens, it allowed them to get to the shooting in under fifteen minutes.

Chinatown bustled, tourists and locals eager to take in the sights, sounds, and tastes of the community. More crime scene tape blocked off an area of the sidewalk and part of the street in front of a pharmacy. Cruisers blocked off the road, redirecting traffic around the incident. From a distance, she spotted three tarps. Gang members? Civilians? Any death at the hands of another human being was bad, but she prayed there were no more civilians dead.

A quick check-in with the responding constable alleviated some of her fears. Three dead gang members were still a loss of life. One from the Esskays. The other two were from the Grange. All had numerous guns on them.

After a thorough briefing, a check of the scene, and interviews with bystanders, it was clear they wouldn't learn anything until they had ballistics reports back on the guns. Once the bodies had been taken away, she would request a rush on that report.

Out of the corner of her eye, she spotted Caleb hovering at the far side of the street. Yellow light from the streetlights showered him in a golden glow. He stared ahead, not focusing on anything that was going on. Arms crossed over his chest, his hands in his armpits, told her a story. If he'd been with the gang members when the Esskays member opened fire, maybe she could convince Caleb to help them. Playing gang member might have been fun until the shooting started, but how close had he come to getting hit by one of the bullets? Would it be enough to get him to switch sides? Brushes with death had made people do stranger things.

When they walked in his direction, Caleb spotted them right away. He glared at the scene in front of him, shook his head sadly, and turned the corner. Rachel scanned the crowd, looking for other gang members, but she didn't see anyone. Conquest, usually by Caleb's side, was nowhere to be seen. That might make convincing Caleb to talk a little easier.

She and Williams rounded the corner and stopped short when they almost bumped into Caleb. Sweat beaded on his forehead. He wiped a shaking hand across his face.

"Caleb, can you tell us what happened?" Rachel asked, her voice low, sympathetic. She'd been asking him that a lot lately. If she'd pushed harder, convinced him she could be trusted, maybe he would have avoided almost getting shot in the cross fire.

Caleb stared at the brick wall in front of him for a moment. "They started shooting as soon as we hit the intersection."

"Who did?" Williams asked.

She had an idea, but she needed confirmation. The gang war they'd been warned about was here, and it was going to be bloody for all sides if they didn't do something to stop it. She glanced back around the corner to make sure no one was coming. Most of the bystanders were still behind the tape, some talking to police, others chatting amongst themselves. A lot were taking pictures.

Social media would be a firestorm of activity. One of humanity's greatest and worst inventions. No more letting the families grieve in peace. The entire city would know almost as much as the police.

"Esskays. I don't know his name. He pulled out his gun when he saw us." He took a deep breath. "There were two other members with him. They took off when Frank got off a round."

"This isn't the kind of life you want, is it?" Rachel asked. "Always looking over your shoulder in fear of more retaliation."

Williams nodded. "You know Victor will do something to get back at them. Then, they'll do the same. It will never end."

Rachel looked into Caleb's eyes. His soul hadn't

dimmed any more than the last time she'd seen him. At least that was a small comfort. "We can help you. Protect you."

He opened his mouth, hesitated, then snapped it shut again. He glanced over his shoulder, nodded. "What do you want to know? I can't tell you here. Come by my work tomorrow."

Rachel eyed him suspiciously. She wanted him to come to the station, but she knew he couldn't be seen with law enforcement. Not if he wanted to live once he left the station.

"Fine, but no funny business. We can't help you unless you're honest with us. Go over and give your official statement of you saw nothing to the constable taking witness accounts."

He nodded, then ran around the corner.

With everything well in hand, they strode back to the car. Once the witness statements were in, they could go over those. Her cell phone pinged as an email came through. She swiped to read it.

"Good news. The ballistics are back on the gun that shot Felicia Newman."

"Great. Now we need to match it to one of the thousands in the city," Williams said as he climbed into the car.

"I have a suspicion, but we'll see once they get to the guns on the Grange members." She pointed to the crime scene.

Father Ianetti finished the sermon by closing his Bible and placing it on the pulpit. As with most of his sermons since he'd started talking about the apocalypse, his congregation gave him a loud round of applause. Give the people what they want, and they'll reward you. It was human nature to speculate on the end. Movies, television shows, books, even songs dealt with the subject matter, each of them with a different perspective.

He looked out over his flock, and sadness filled him at the realization most of them wouldn't survive the Rapture. Even though they attended his services regularly, he knew their secrets. Knew the darkness in their souls. No amount of Hail Marys was going to absolve some of them, though he offered comfort that they would be absolved.

He hurried to the exit of the church to shake hands with people as they left. If the staff had listened to him, they were gone by now. He'd told them he could clean up. Said it was a reward for their hard work in the last few weeks.

When the last parishioner left, he poked his head outside to look at the sky. Storm clouds swirled, obscuring the moon. At this time of year, it could end up as rain, snow, hail, sleet. None of that mattered, though. The storm brewing meant it was time for him to summon the next horseman.

Though Conquest said everything was under control, Father Ianetti didn't feel that it was. Ideally, he would wait to summon War until he'd prepared more. Summoning dark magic took a toll, and he was barely recovered from the first time. But God's will couldn't wait. The Earth needed to be cleansed. Purified. A new dawn needed to begin.

He ducked back inside and locked the door. As he walked down through the nave, he picked up tissues, put prayer books back in the slot in the pews. He veered to the left, checking the confessionals. All he needed was a straggler to interrupt him. How would he explain what he was doing? Both the chambers were empty.

Next, he checked the church's office. Everything was neat and tidy. The coffee pot had been emptied. A pile of messages in the center of his desk could wait until morning.

Satisfied he was alone, he hurried into his chamber, bathed quickly, put on a robe, then gathered the items he needed.

Outside, a tall brick fence encircled the back of the church. Protected from prying eyes, he walked to the center of the yard and laid out the candles in the shape of a pentagram. With a flick of his wrist, the lighter he retrieved from his pockets roared to life. He lit each candle, flicked the lighter closed, and took a deep breath.

His calculations would be proven true. That detective, Malak, suspected what he was up to, but it didn't matter. There was no way she and her sisters could stop what was coming. It surprised him that she believed in that sort of thing.

He dug into his robe's pockets again, careful to avoid the athame, and pulled out the pewter bowl. He didn't want to bleed unnecessarily or too early.

He assembled the rest of the ingredients for the summoning ritual and took a step back to survey his work. Everything had to be perfect. If his alignment was off by even a millimeter, the spell might fail. He only had so many pure black pillar candles to use. Now that the cop was nosing around shops, he didn't know if he'd be able to get any more.

Once everything was perfect, he shed the robe and started reciting the spell from memory, changing the parts that needed to be altered to summon War instead of Conquest. He swayed from side to side, trance like, as he spoke the words in Latin.

A crunch of dead leaves behind him startled him out

of his trance. He spun around to see who intruded on the sacred ritual.

One of his parishioners, a man with almost perfect attendance, stood, gaze transfixed on the candles. He shook his head and focused on the priest, confused eyes locking with his. "Sorry, Father. I thought I heard something back here and wanted to make sure everything was okay."

Father Ianetti bent to pick up the robe, quickly donning the garment, lashing the belt tightly around his waist. Cursing under his breath, he smiled. "Quite all right. It must have sounded odd."

In a flash, he reached into his robe, pulled out the athame, and jammed it into the man's heart. Too bad the ritual called for holy blood.

The man keeled over, hitting the ground in a flurry of dead leaves, gasping for breath, his hands grasping for the knife.

"If you're impaled by an object, you shouldn't pull it out," Father Ianetti said. "It could do more damage. It could be causing a seal that is preventing blood from draining out of you."

The man's face paled.

Father Ianetti yanked the knife out of the man's chest and wiped the blood on his robe.

Angry at having to start over, he marched back to the candles. Squaring his shoulders, rocking his head from side to side, he took a deep breath. This time, he whispered the ritual so it was barely audible. At the appropriate time, he sliced the tip of his finger, bleeding into the pewter bowl. He set the sigil for War on fire and dropped it into the bowl. The flash ignited the contents.

Clouds swirled overhead. The ground shook. Hoofbeats filled the night air. The scent of a lathered horse wafted in the breeze. The hair on his arms rose. Wisps of red smoke formed the shape of a horse. War popped into existence, glaring at him with malice. Like Conquest before him, War was naked. A sword tattooed on his arm bunched as War flexed his muscles. His light blue eyes surveyed the area.

"When is this?"

"First quarter of the twenty-first century."

Dark jeans formed over the man's legs. A cable knit sweater and heavy coat formed over the man's body.

Remembering how quickly Conquest rushed off, Father Ianetti held up a hand to stay the horseman. "Before you find your brother, could you do something with that?" He pointed to the dead man.

A grin spread across War's face. In a cloud of dust and leaves, War and the dead parishioner vanished from the church's courtyard.

Chapter Twenty

The next morning, Rachel and Williams sat in their unmarked police car in front of the warehouse where Caleb worked. She didn't want to get her hopes up, but she knew the shooting had shaken Caleb. Maybe enough for him to turn on his fellow gang members. He'd only been associated with the Grange for a short time, hopefully not long enough to create lasting ties to anyone.

Her thoughts went to Victor. Conquest had an influence over the entire city, not just Caleb. Skyrocketing incidents of citizens being dicks in general to each other plagued not only the city, but the entire province. Maybe the whole country.

"You think he'll give us anything useful?" Williams asked as he opened his door.

Rachel shrugged. "Only one way to find out."

They entered the warehouse through the back door, the same door all the workers used. The parking lot in the back was half full. Night shift workers still had an hour to go. Day shift workers hadn't shown up yet.

After a quick chat with the night manager, they made their way to the back of the floor. Inside the break room, Caleb waited for them, sitting on the far side of the table. Though he sat straighter, eyes focused on them as they entered, he fidgeted in his seat.

"You're here early," Rachel said, taking a seat opposite him.

Williams eased into the chair beside her. They both pulled out their notebooks. She didn't want to chance missing anything Caleb might tell them.

"I wanted to get this over with. Get back to my life."

He never broke eye contact. The fidgeting stopped. He took a deep breath and waited for their questions.

"I guess I can believe that," Rachel said.

Anger flashed in the young man's eyes, but he took a deep breath. "Ask me anything."

"What will we find when we examine the guns from the shooting?" Williams asked.

Rachel wanted to go deeper, back to the beginning when Conquest first arrived, but the shooting was freshest in everyone's minds.

"Every gang member has his own gun. No one else uses it."

"So, if we search the hangout and find guns, we'll find the one that was used to kill Felicia Newman?" Rachel asked.

A flash of pain crossed Caleb's face, but it was gone just as quickly. "I don't know who killed her, but I know the bullets will match one of the Grange members' guns."

"And was it an initiation?" Williams asked.

Caleb nodded.

Rachel leaned back in her chair and took a deep breath. "What about Bruno De Luca?"

Caleb shrugged. "That was before my time. To become leader, though, you have to kill the leader. Pretty sure Victor did just that."

Her brain raced, putting things together. With Caleb's information and the raid that was going to happen tomorrow, they could close a lot of cases. The paperwork would be a bitch, but the satisfaction of giving people closure was worth a month of paperwork.

"And the gas stations?" Rachel asked.

"That was all Victor's idea. He didn't do any of the beatings. It was a test. To see who was worthy. He talked about creating an army, waiting for war."

A shiver went through Caleb, and Rachel narrowed her eyes.

"I was afraid for my life. That's why I hung out with the gang. I wasn't supposed to be at the gas station that morning."

Rachel stood and walked over to the vending machines that were pushed against the back wall. Fishing change out of her pockets, she gazed over the selections. Chips, chocolate bars, hard candy in one machine. A variety of pop in the other. She shoved the change back in her pocket and took a seat again.

She leaned closer to Caleb. Hunches never let her down before, and she hoped they didn't this time. "What about the homeless man, the street prophet?"

Williams shot her a quizzical look.

Caleb's brows drew together, and he shrugged. "Bad for business, I guess. I heard Victor talk about taking care of the trash, but I didn't see him do anything."

Williams pinned Caleb with a stare. "Let's get back to why you were in the gang."

"I wasn't really. Victor decided to mentor me."

"So, you didn't kill anyone to get into the gang?" Rachel asked.

Caleb's eyes widened. "No, man. I couldn't do that."

Everyone could kill if they had to. Did Caleb have to in order to stay in the gang? She didn't believe his story for a second that Victor wanted to mentor him. Conquest wouldn't let dead weight hang around. The horseman saw something in Caleb and that worried her.

"Everyone else had to kill to get into the gang," Williams said.

"I was different. Victor felt sorry for me because my father beat me."

Rachel let out a short burst of laughter. Caleb glared at her.

"Sorry. Is there anything else you can tell us?"

Caleb produced a piece of paper from under the table. He shoved it across the table at Williams. It had numbers on it, file names, room names.

"What's this?" Williams asked.

"Combinations to safes, passwords for computers, and the rooms where they file all of their ledgers and paperwork."

Rachel regarded him with suspicion. "How did you get this?"

Caleb smiled. "Victor trusts me."

The information on the paper would save them days of work. Eventually, they would have found all the files and paperwork. The combinations and passwords would have taken more time. With this, they could find answers a lot sooner and start building the case against Victor and most of the gang members. She couldn't help feeling like they were being set up somehow.

After two hours of questions, reconfirming his answers

and grilling him on the information he had on the paper, Rachel and Williams stood.

"Thank you for your time, Caleb. It's been a big help." Rachel forced sincerity into her voice.

"Stay in town, but steer clear of the gang's headquarters," Williams said.

"Why? Won't that make me look like I snitched?"

Rachel tilted her head to the side. "Maybe, maybe not. You're not a full-blown member, are you?"

Caleb shook his head.

She didn't believe him. Why would he have a jacket with stripes if he wasn't a full member? Whatever his reasons for wanting to get out, she was more than happy to help him.

"What about your gun?" Rachel asked.

Caleb's eyes widened. "Gun?"

"You said every member has their own. Where's yours? We'll need it for testing."

Would he refuse to hand it over? What crimes would they be able to tie to it?

Caleb hunched his shoulders and he let out a loud sigh. "It's in my locker."

He gave them his combination and Williams went to retrieve the weapon. A few minutes later, he returned to the break room, the gun in an evidence bag clutched in his left hand.

"Steer clear as much as you can. We'll be in touch," Williams said.

The door to the break room swished open as they left. Chatter on the warehouse floor, louder than when they'd first arrived, fell silent as they walked through and left the building.

Back in the car, Rachel flipped through the pages of notes she'd taken. "We'll have to get this information to

Detective Littman and send Caleb's gun to ballistics. We have a raid to gear up for."

The next morning, Rachel sat in the passenger side of the car in front of the Grange HQ, waiting for the rest of the units to get into place. They were taking the HQs of all the gangs simultaneously across the city. Well, the ones they had enough intel on, anyway. With Caleb's help and a ton of evidence from the raids, they would have enough to put away every gang member for several life sentences, if they all went to trial. It bothered her that there was nothing overly criminal for Caleb, though. He'd only been in the gang less than two weeks, but her gut told her he'd committed crimes to prove his loyalty. She didn't buy his story about Victor taking pity on him.

"When will they be in place?" she asked, checking her messages.

"You need some patience," Williams said. He smiled to take the edge off his words.

He was right, of course, but how could she be patient when they were about to take Conquest into custody? Fear skittered up her spine at the thought he wouldn't be there. They'd been watching the place nonstop for twenty-four hours and knew all the key members were there. Caleb was conspicuously absent, as she'd requested, not caring if it made him look like a snitch. She hoped he continued to stay away, go to a new city. Protective custody only went so far. Before Conquest took over, he might have been safe, but now that the gang was more organized, Victor would find a way to exact revenge.

He still had his power. With the place under surveillance, there had been no way to put any magical lockdowns on the warehouse. At least she had the special handcuffs, specifically designed to hold demons. But as soon as the raid started, he could disappear. She wouldn't know until the moment of truth. There was no way to fast forward this one to see what the outcome was first.

She opened an email from the lab. "Ballistics are back on the gun from Frank, from the shooting two days ago. Same gun was used to kill Felicia Newman."

"At least we solved that murder."

"Yeah." She pocketed her phone, unconvinced. Searching through her memories of the convenience store crime scene, she didn't recall seeing him there at all. Of course, if he'd just murdered someone, the natural instinct would be to get the hell out of there. Far away from the scene.

"You don't sound convinced."

"If ballistics says it's him, it's him."

No point airing her concerns right now. They couldn't do much to follow up until the raid was complete. And maybe that would give them more evidence.

"Caleb said all the members have their own guns. They don't share."

"I know. The lab rushed the tests on Caleb's gun, and it doesn't match any recent murders."

She pushed the thoughts of the murder out of her head, focusing her attention on the raid at hand. The car radio squawked, announcing the arrival of other units across the city. Three unmarked cars pulled up in strategic spots near the Grange HQ.

Adrenaline raced through her body. Her heart beat faster. She sucked in breaths in an attempt to calm herself. Everything moved slowly compared to how she felt at that moment. She wanted to burst through the doors, round up all the members, and bring them into the station. She had never been good at waiting.

Finally, the call came over the radio that they were ready to go.

All police present surrounded the building. Four officers used a battering ram to burst through the door, and everyone stormed inside. Shouts rang out from all directions. Police informed the occupants of the warrant and told people to stay where they were. Gang members shouted angry insults at the cops.

A shot rang out, then another one.

With all exits covered, the gang members didn't have anywhere to go. But they tried. Three of them were stopped as soon as they exited the building. One of them carried a gun, his arm dripping blood from a gunshot wound in his shoulder. Gang members in the gym were easily rounded up and handcuffed.

Rachel stepped into the building in time to see Detective Littman standing behind Conquest, reaching into his back pocket for his handcuffs. Praying no one would notice, she zapped Littman's cuffs away and left hers in their place. Without missing a beat or noticing the difference, Littman positioned the handcuffs at Conquest's wrists. Conquest grinned at her. A grin that sent a shiver down her spine.

Before Littman could snap them around Conquest's wrists, the horseman turned, quick as a flash, and punched Littman in the face. Smoke rose up all around the horseman, then a loud cracking sound filled the room. Littman flew out of the smoke, hitting a wall. He slumped to the floor with a groan, the handcuffs clinking to the floor.

Everyone drew their weapons, but it was too late. When the smoke cleared, Conquest was gone.

Littman shook off the blow and stood. "Find him!"

Two of the constables, there to help process and tag evidence, dashed off after Victor.

Rachel gritted her teeth. She should have known it wouldn't be that easy to restrain a horseman. Now she and her sisters would have to summon him. That had been the plan all along, once they'd found the summoning spells, but having him in custody would have been easier.

From inside the office, a constable yelled, "Jackpot! Paperwork and DVDs."

Farther away, from another room in the building, another voice chimed in, "Guns and drugs here."

The constables who had run off after Victor returned shaking their heads.

"Anything?" Rachel asked.

The taller of the two answered, "He's nowhere to be found on the premises."

"How did he move so fast?" the shorter one asked.

Littman walked over, rubbing the back of his head. "We'll get him. With his warehouse and most of his members in custody, he can't do much."

Rachel nodded, wishing that were true. One horseman out there alone could do a Hell of a lot of damage.

Once they cleared out the members and did a thorough search of the property, she was sure they would find a lot more. How much of it was Conquest and how much the gang leader before him, she'd probably never know. But all of it would be bad. The city, for a while at least, would be a little safer with the gang out of commission. Conquest wouldn't be on the loose for long. She and her sisters would see to that.

Hours later, back at the station, Rachel stood with Williams in the audio-visual lab going through the DVDs that had been collected. So far, most of them were homemade porn videos. According to the ledgers they'd recovered, porn was a new development for the gang. All the other ways of making money weren't getting them to their financial goals, so they'd branched out. At least porn wasn't illegal, unless the actors were minors, or they filmed in public places. The porn angle was the least of their worries at the moment.

They had a mountain of evidence to sort through, and she wanted to find the smoking gun for the convenience store murder. Well, technically they had that, but she wanted visual proof that Frank pulled the trigger. She still wasn't convinced.

Abby, the lab tech, ejected the video after a minute and popped in a different one. There was no label on this one, so hope sprang that it was something else.

On the screen, an image of the convenience store showed everyone who had been present the day of the murder. It wasn't anything she hadn't seen before about a hundred times since the woman had been killed. When the video feed usually blurred, this one stayed in focus. At the bottom of the screen, Frank came into view. He marched to the back where Felicia Newman was picking out a carton of milk. Then he shot her three times. Milk sprayed everywhere.

Ballistics and the video confirmed he killed Felicia. Despite seeing the evidence with her own eyes, she didn't believe he did it. After the shooting, Caleb's soul had dimmed. That didn't mean he did it, either; he could have done something else to get into the gang. Or maybe he was a probationary member until he committed a murder and that was why he turned against them. Because he couldn't bring himself to kill anyone. Right now, it didn't matter. Based on the official evidence, Frank killed Felicia. Mr. Newman would have closure.

"You want to go through the rest of them?" Abby asked.

Rachel shook her head. "Could you write up the report and send it to both of us?"

Abby nodded. "It will take a few days. There were dozens of DVDs."

"Thanks."

Rachel and Williams strode back down the hall to their desks. It would take a while to go through everything. Gang members were looking at multiple charges for a variety of crimes. She would be at the station late every day for weeks to stay on top of everything. That was okay with her; they'd gotten the Grange off the street for now.

Detective Sergeant Reyes approached with a smile on his face. "Great work!"

"Rachel did a lot, convincing Caleb to give us the information we needed to execute the raids," Williams said.

Rachel shook her head. "It was a team effort. We couldn't have done it without everyone's help. Detective Littman was a huge help with tying up some of the loose ends."

"Still, three murders solved with one raid. I'd call that a win."

"Three?" Rachel asked. She was sure they'd be able to flip some of the gang members to confirm Conquest had killed Bruno, but who was the third?

"Didn't you get the report? They found the murder weapon in the homeless man's killing. Fingerprints on the knife match Frank. A new recruit. Also, one of the attackers in the gas station incident."

"Victor is still out there, though."

Reyes clapped her on the back. "Not for long. He'll trip up, get caught. Take the win."

The welcome feeling of power rushing back to her wings washed over her. She would need all the power she could get for her next stop. Confronting Conquest. She messaged her sisters and told them to meet her at the loft.

Chapter Twenty-One

S arah and Becky were already home, sitting at the island watching the door by the time Rachel got there. She'd stopped off at a grocery store first and then a church near her office to get ordinary water blessed as holy and to pick up holy oil. Leah was picking up the limestone on the way home.

Nestled in a large reusable fabric bag, the water and oil sloshed when she plunked them on the island. "Where did Leah put the rest of the stuff?"

Sarah pointed to a cupboard above the sink. "Everything we need for summoning and sending back except the large items that won't fit. She's divided it by horseman. Bottom left is for Conquest."

Rachel yanked open the cupboard door and pulled all the ingredients out along with the sigil and printouts of both incantations. She divided the items into two piles. Summon and vanquish. The vanquish pile was one item light, but that would be rectified as soon as Leah got home.

"Where's the bowl?"

Becky slid off her stool and opened the door beside the

one Rachel already had open. "For things used in all spells, she put them in here."

Becky grabbed the pewter bowl, matches, and holy basil and put them on the counter.

"I'll get the bow and arrow. We need to use one of the bottles of holy water to cleanse the weapon. Keep the other bottles on hand in case we need them."

Becky peeked into the bag. "How many did you get him to create?"

"Twelve bottles. And I got as much holy oil as they could spare. We should have enough of that for at least three tries at vanquishing them. The priest raised an eyebrow at my request but didn't ask questions."

Rachel dashed into her bedroom to get the bow and arrow set. She handed it to Sarah, who ripped off the packaging, then placed the weapon in the sink. While Sarah used the holy water to purify the weapon, Rachel turned her attention to the incantations. She should have been going over them as soon as Leah found them, but she hadn't had time. In the back of her mind, maybe she thought this day wouldn't come, even though they'd been working at it for weeks.

She read over the summoning incantation repeatedly, making sure she memorized every line. Leah would have no trouble when it came to summoning a horseman or sending them back. Everything that went into her head stayed there.

Antsy, anxious to get started, Rachel paced between the living room and the kitchen, willing Leah to come through the door. She wanted to get this done. The longer Conquest was out there, the more damage he could do. Taking his members away wouldn't hold him back for long. The horseman would find another way to cause chaos in the city, perhaps start up another gang, a larger one that covered the entire GTA. No more rival gangs to stand in his way.

Finally, the loft door slid open and Leah tromped into the room carrying a large paper bag. She placed it on the island beside the remaining bottles of holy water.

"Limestone from Mount Hermon! I took what they could give me, but we'll need more if Father Ianetti manages to summon Famine and Death."

"Great! You three will stay as close to the rooftop door as possible. Give me a signal when you're going to start the incantation to vanquish him. I'll be in the circle of holy oil with Conquest to distract him."

Everyone nodded. Now that it was time, Rachel's stomach flipped. Failure wasn't an option. She didn't know how long it would take to send the horseman back to limbo, or if the incantation even worked. No one had had to use it until now.

Though she didn't think the purification bath applied to angels, she grabbed the sea salt from the kitchen and marched to the bathroom. Since they hadn't known when they would be able to summon the horseman, they hadn't been able to get the water ready beforehand. Only one of them could be responsible for summoning Conquest and since she'd already dealt with him as gang leader, it was up to her. She ran a bath of cool water, dumped in the salt, stripped, then settled into the tub. After what she considered a sufficient amount of time, she pulled the plug and stood, letting the water sluice off her. A plush towel soaked up the moisture.

With the towel wrapped around her, she trudged into her room beside the bathroom. Reaching into the closet, she shoved blazer jackets aside until she found her angelic robe. Despite the summoning calling for nudity, she would wear the angelic garments instead. Dressed again as she'd been upon arriving on Earth, she headed back to the kitchen.

"All pure now?" Sarah asked.

Rachel nodded. "Let's do this."

They gathered everything they needed and headed for the roof.

Becky stuck a brick in the door so they wouldn't be locked up there. Becky, Leah, and Sarah pulled a wrought iron table over, away from the door, and placed on it the items they needed to vanquish Conquest. Rachel grabbed the bow and arrow. She would be too close to him to fire the thing, but the pointy end could still be used as a stabbing tool if she got within reach. It would also come in handy for the pricking her finger part of the summoning spell.

As far away from the door as possible, Rachel set up the altar and pentagram, placing all the arrows in front of the bowl. It was closer to the edge than she wanted, but she needed to keep her sisters away from Conquest. And it had a wood outcropping from the rooftop shed that kept that side dry when it rained and free of snow in the winter.

She poured a circle of holy oil around the pentagram. They had to get the timing right and keep Conquest distracted while Becky ignited the oil. If they failed this time, another attempt would have to wait until they regained whatever strength this drained from them.

Becky stood outside the ring of holy oil, lighter in hand, ready to flick it open.

"Ready?" Becky asked.

Hummingbirds buzzed in her stomach, but Rachel nodded. She took a step forward.

Inside both circles now, Rachel lit the candles, then called the four corners of the Earth. She dropped everything except the sigil into the bowl. Her heart raced. She picked up an arrow, pierced the tip of her finger, and squeezed drops of blood into the bowl. She took a deep breath, then lit the sigil on fire and dropped it in to mix with the rest of the items. She recited the incantation over and over again, willing Conquest to join them on the roof.

Rachel twirled around in the circle. Had they missed something? Was an ingredient missing from their summoning concoction? She continued to recite the incantation, shrugging when Becky asked what went wrong.

A few minutes after starting, a puff of white smoke appeared. The air around her heated, weighed down on her, until she could barely suck in a breath. Her head pounded and she gasped for air. Becky's foot moved forward. If the circle was broken, the spell wouldn't work.

Rachel raised a hand to stop her.

The sound of hooves filled the rooftop.

The air cooled again, oxygen pouring into her lungs when she drew a deep breath. The pounding in her head that matched the beat of her heart disappeared.

Conquest materialized a few feet away from her.

"Now!"

Becky lunged forward, flicked a lighter open, and touched the ring of holy oil with the fire. Flames encircled Rachel and Conquest. The first time an angel had touched holy fire, he'd burnt to ashes in seconds. Once God had seen the consequence of such a powerful weapon, he'd made all celestial beings immune to the fire's effects. All other creatures, mystical, demonic, human, animal, would succumb to the flames. Some faster than others. One touch wouldn't kill them anymore, but for higher demons and horsemen, it would trap them as long as the fire burned.

He sneered. "You won't stop what's happening. War is already here."

Able to breathe properly, Rachel pulled in a fortifying breath and stood with her legs hip width apart. "We'll see."

He raised a hand, flicked his wrist. Rachel lifted off the ground and flew through the air, the flames of the holy fire warming her wings as she passed through it. She bounced on the hard roof, fifteen meters away from the circle, scraping her hands to slow herself down. Her wings and her body were still intact.

Conquest raised an eyebrow. "Interesting."

Rachel marched back to the circle of fire and stepped through.

"Hurry!" she yelled over her shoulder.

Becky had already run back to Sarah and Leah. They were tossing things into the second pewter bowl, mixing them together in the correct order.

Rachel charged at Conquest, fist raised, hoping to take him off guard. He stood his ground and blocked her punch. With a powerful roundhouse kick, he sent her flying again, through the flames. She landed farther away than the last time.

Shaking herself off, she stood. No matter what happened, she had to keep him busy long enough for her sisters to start the incantation. Until then, he'd have all of his power, while she had whatever she'd managed to earn back. It had to be enough. Teamwork was the only way they would win.

A shiver skittered up her spine. Strength coursed through her. The wounds on her hands stopped stinging. She glanced down and saw them disappear.

She marched back to the circle of fire and stepped inside. With a wave of her hand, the flames flickered faster, brighter, then returned to normal. Tired of being flown across the rooftop, that little bit of magic would stop her from passing through the flames.

"What did you do?"

Rachel shrugged. "Why don't you come at me again and find out?"

He charged her. She bent her knees, ready for him. Leading with her shoulder, she rained punches down on him the moment he was within reach. They landed with satisfying groans coming from Conquest.

After a few good shots, he blocked her, then punched her faster than she could protect herself. Pain exploded in her face.

She jumped back before he could strike her again. With a kick to his chest, he hit the wall of flames and fell to the ground. A sizzling sound resonated for a few seconds, then stopped when he lost contact with the fire.

He pushed himself off the ground and scowled at her. Though she was ready for the roundhouse kick, it still surprised her with its force. She flew through the air again but bounced off the flames and landed in the circle with him.

"Almost ready!" Leah yelled.

A growl of anger from Conquest sent fear snaking through her. He picked her up and dropped her on the ground again as if she weighed nothing. Air whooshed out of her body. She gasped but couldn't pull in enough to take a deep breath. Her ribs hurt. Blood dripped down from her face, stinging her eyes. She wiped the blood away.

With a shaking hand, she grabbed an arrow that still sat near the very edge of the circle. She raised her hand to stab him with it, but he yanked it out of her hand.

His palm sizzled.

He flicked it out of the circle. It traveled at high speed, right for Becky.

"Becky, look out!"

Too late, her sister looked up. The arrow sank into her

shoulder. She crumbled to the ground but pushed herself up. Sarah pushed the arrow through Becky's shoulder, then the light of Sarah's healing hand illuminated the area around the door.

Rachel breathed a sigh of relief that Becky wasn't hurt any worse.

She stood and circled Conquest. They were like two fighters in a ring and only one of them would get out alive.

"Ready!" Sarah yelled.

After a count of three, Rachel began the incantation, hoping she was in time with the others. She repeated it three times. With her magic, she flung the remaining arrows in Conquest's direction. As they circled each other, the arrows hit him in the back, in the chest, in the thighs. He howled in pain and fell to his knees, reaching behind himself to get to the arrow in his back. He couldn't grasp it.

When her sisters were ten meters away, another flick of her wrist released the barrier that kept her inside the circle. They recited the incantation as they walked, Becky carrying the pewter bowl.

Inside the circle with her, Becky handed Rachel the bowl. Rachel dumped the contents of the bowl onto the horseman. Sparks erupted. He yowled this time, loud enough to make the tables and chairs on the rooftop shake. Flames began consuming him.

Rachel rolled out of the ring of holy fire, and her sisters followed her out. It was the only thing that contained the detonation when Conquest exploded out of Earth's plane.

Rachel collapsed, her head lolling forward, too heavy to keep up any longer. Becky's shoulder was almost healed. It looked like Sarah had started the process along but didn't finish. Whether that was because she didn't want to use too much power or because they needed to fight Conquest, Rachel didn't know. But at least Becky wasn't mortally wounded.

If Conquest was telling the truth and War was already here, they would need time to recuperate before attempting to send him back to limbo.

<hr>

After a short rest and much-needed ice cream, Rachel sat at the kitchen island in the loft, thinking about their next step. Vanquishing Conquest was one thing, but Victor needed to go to jail. The leader of the gang needed to be caught so Detective Littman wouldn't have a gaping hole in his case. Or the frustration of having one that got away.

Becky groaned from the sofa in the living room. "I need to sleep for a week."

Rachel forced herself to get off the stool. "We can do that later. We have one more thing to take care of."

"Victor." Sarah held a bag containing a golem, more ingredients for a magic spell, and the printout of the spell.

"We should get it over with so we can relax for a little while," Leah said.

"Get your coats. We need to go to the station."

Fifteen minutes later, they stood outside the station, Becky using her magic to keep the cameras on a loop of the street.

Rachel placed the golem on the ground. She sprinkled it with holy basil, pricked the tip of her finger with an iron blade, and squeezed three drops of blood on it. The four angels murmured in Latin together, waving their hands over the golem. Arms formed, legs grew. The head took on the appearance of Conquest. After a minute, it sprang to life. The golem grinned at Rachel the way the real Conquest had earlier.

"You'll be going for a bail hearing tomorrow," Rachel said. "Play the part right."

The golem nodded.

Rachel pulled out her handcuffs, pointed her finger toward the sky, and moved it in a circular motion. The fake Victor drew his eyebrows together, then his eyes widened. He turned around. Rachel slapped the cuffs on him. To keep it as authentic as possible, she informed him of his rights.

"Show time."

Becky pointed at the video cameras to take them off the loop, replacing them with them showing up with Victor already handcuffed.

Rachel took the golem's arm and guided him to the doors of the station, her sisters close behind her. She breezed past the desk clerk and stopped at lockup.

She smiled at the constable at the desk.

"Civilians can't go in there, Detective," he said.

"I know. They're going to wait here for me while I process him."

Impressed, the constable nodded to the golem. "That the gang leader? How did you catch him?"

Rachel shrugged. "Right place, right time. Gave me a run for my money." She pointed at her face. Wanting to conserve as much magic as possible, she'd declined magical assistance with healing and didn't tap into her own power for it, either.

The constable pressed a button and the door to lockup buzzed. She yanked it open.

"I shouldn't be too long."

She marched him through the doors and to the processing area. Mug shots were taken, fingerprints collected. She did the paperwork, checking everything three times before signing it. She didn't want anything to bite them in the ass later.

When she closed the cell door on him, a wave of relief washed over her. "Do good while you're in there."

The golem nodded.

Rachel rushed back down the hall to the main desk. Her sisters were chatting with the constable, probably regaling him with the made-up tale of how Rachel had caught Victor. It was the best way for news to spread through the department of Victor's capture.

"Ready?"

They hurried out of the building. Outside, she took a deep breath of the night air. A chill in the air soothed her.

"We can check the damage to our power later. Who wants a drink? I'm buying."

They all raised their hands. Rachel smiled. For the first time since all of them had arrived on Earth, they'd truly worked as a team. Maybe the world wasn't doomed after all.

They defeated Conquest. Only three horsemen to go.

Thank you for reading Rachel's story. I hope you liked spending time with her and her sisters. Want to see how Becky deals with War? Her book is up on all major retailers.

Dear Reader,

Thank you for reading my book!

The original plan for the angels was to have one book with four angels all dealing with the four horsemen. I was struggling to figure out points of view and knew the story would end up being a huge tome if I tried to fit everything in one book. That's when I decided to give each angel her own book, dealing with her own horseman, and trying to figure out why she was exiled.

I really hope you loved the book as much as I did. Black Feathers was fun to write and research and I have to give credit to my husband for coming up with the titles of all the books. I was stumped with what to call them and I had to come up with something fast. The cover artist I wanted had an opening and she agreed to do the series, but she needed a title. Without missing a beat he rattled off all four titles.

There are four books in the series, but I suspect there will be more series in the angels' world. Stay tuned for that. You can sign up for my mailing list to be notified when new stories come out, plus get a copy of Fallen, the prequel short story. Sign up at https://www.cindycarroll.com/angelslist/

Happy Reading,

Cindy

About the Author

Cindy is a member of Sisters in Crime and a graduate of Hal Croasmun's screenwriting ProSeries. She writes screenplays, thrillers, horror, urban fantasy, science fiction and paranormals, occasionally exploring an erotic twist. A background in banking and IT doesn't allow much in the way of excitement so she turns to writing stories that are a little dark and usually have a dead body. She lives in Ontario, Canada with her husband and two cats. When she's not writing you can usually find her painting landscapes in oil, playing video games (Sims 3 and Sims 4 are favourites), or watching her favourite television shows marathon style.

Check out Cindy's website:
https://www.cindycarroll.com
Check out Cindy's other books:
https://books2read.com/cindycarroll

facebook.com/AuthorCindyCarroll

twitter.com/CindyPCarroll

instagram.com/CindyPCarroll

goodreads.com/writesbooks

bookbub.com/authors/cindy-carroll

www.ingramcontent.com/pod-product-compliance
Lightning Source LLC
Chambersburg PA
CBHW051142190726
48290CB00006B/1952